Illinois Central College
Learning Resources Center

The Lost Boy

THOMAS WOLFE

The Lost Boy

With a Note on Thomas Wolfe
by Edward C. Aswell

PERENNIAL LIBRARY

Harper & Row, Publishers

NEW YORK AND EVANSTON

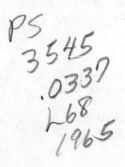

All of the short stories now included in *The Lost Boy* were
part of a collection entitled *The Hills Beyond*, which was
originally published by Harper & Brothers in 1941.

THE LOST BOY. Copyright 1935, 1937, 1939, 1941 by Maxwell
Perkins as Executor.

First PERENNIAL LIBRARY edition published 1965 by Harper &
Row, Publishers, Incorporated, New York and Evanston.

C-P

Library of Congress catalog card number: 65-19111

Contents

The Lost Boy

The Lost Boy

❦

Light came and went and came again, the booming
strokes of three o'clock beat out across the town in
thronging bronze from the courthouse bell, light
winds of April blew the fountain out in rainbow
sheets, until the plume returned and pulsed, as Grover
turned into the Square. He was a child, dark-eyed and
grave, birthmarked upon his neck—a berry of warm
brown—and with a gentle face, too quiet and too listening for his years. The scuffed boy's shoes, the
thick-ribbed stockings gartered at the knees, the short
knee pants cut straight with three small useless buttons at the side, the sailor blouse, the old cap battered
out of shape, perched sideways up on top of the raven
head, the old soiled canvas bag slung from the shoulder, empty now, but waiting for the crisp sheets of the
afternoon—these friendly, shabby garments, shaped
by Grover, uttered him. He turned and passed along
the north side of the Square and in that moment saw
the union of Forever and of Now.

Light came and went and came again, the great
plume of the fountain pulsed and winds of April
sheeted it across the Square in a rainbow gossamer of
spray. The fire department horses drummed on the
floors with wooden stomp, most casually, and with
dry whiskings of their clean, coarse tails. The street
cars ground into the Square from every portion of the
compass and halted briefly like wound toys in their
familiar quarter-hourly formula. A dray, hauled by a

3

boneyard nag, rattled across the cobbles on the other side before his father's shop. The courthouse bell boomed out its solemn warning of immediate three, and everything was just the same as it had always been.

He saw that haggis of vexed shapes with quiet eyes —that hodgepodge of ill-sorted architectures that made up the Square, and he did not feel lost. For "Here," thought Grover, "here is the Square as it has always been—and papa's shop, the fire department and the City Hall, the fountain pulsing with its plume, the street cars coming in and halting at the quarter hour, the hardware store on the corner there, the row of old brick buildings on this side of the street, the people passing and the light that comes and changes and that always will come back again, and everything that comes and goes and changes in the Square, and yet will be the same again. And here," the boy thought, "is Grover with his paper bag. Here is old Grover, almost twelve years old. Here is the month of April, 1904. Here is the courthouse bell and three o'clock. Here is Grover on the Square that never changes. Here is Grover, caught upon this point of time."

It seemed to him that the Square, itself the accidental masonry of many years, the chance agglomeration of time and of disrupted strivings, was the center of the universe. It was for him, in his soul's picture, the earth's pivot, the granite core of changelessness, the eternal place where all things came and passed, and yet abode forever and would never change.

He passed the old shack on the corner—the wooden fire-trap where S. Goldberg ran his wiener stand. Then he passed the Singer place next door, with its gleaming display of new machines. He saw them and admired them, but he felt no joy. They brought back to him the busy hum of housework and of women sewing, the intricacy of stitch and weave, the mystery of style and pattern, the memory of women bending over flashing needles, the pedaled thread, the busy whir. It was women's work: it filled him with unknown associations of dullness and of vague depression. And always, also, with a moment's twinge of horror, for his dark eye would always travel toward that needle stitching up and down so fast the eye could never follow it. And then he would remember how his mother once had told him she had driven the needle through her finger, and always, when he passed this place, he would remember it and for a moment crane his neck and turn his head away.

He passed on then, but had to stop again next door before the music store. He always had to stop by places that had shining perfect things in them. He loved hardware stores and windows full of accurate geometric tools. He loved windows full of hammers, saws, and planing boards. He liked windows full of strong new rakes and hoes, with unworn handles, of white perfect wood, stamped hard and vivid with the maker's seal. He loved to see such things as these in the windows of hardware stores. And he would fairly gloat upon them and think that some day he would own a set himself.

Also, he always stopped before the music and piano store. It was a splendid store. And in the window was a small white dog upon his haunches, with head cocked gravely to one side, a small white dog that never moved, that never barked, that listened attentively at the flaring funnel of a horn to hear "His Master's Voice"—a horn forever silent, and a voice that never spoke. And within were many rich and shining shapes of great pianos, an air of splendor and of wealth.

And now, indeed, he *was* caught, held suspended. A waft of air, warm, chocolate-laden, filled his nostrils. He tried to pass the white front of the little eight-foot shop; he paused, struggling with conscience; he could not go on. It was the little candy shop run by old Crocker and his wife. And Grover could not pass.

"Old stingy Crockers!" he thought scornfully. "I'll not go there any more. But—" as the maddening fragrance of rich cooking chocolate touched him once again—"I'll just look in the window and see what they've got." He paused a moment, looking with his dark and quiet eyes into the window of the little candy shop. The window, spotlessly clean, was filled with trays of fresh-made candy. His eyes rested on a tray of chocolate drops. Unconsciously he licked his lips. Put one of them upon your tongue and it just melted there, like honeydew. And then the trays full of rich homemade fudge. He gazed longingly at the deep body of the chocolate fudge, reflectively at maple walnut, more critically, yet with longing, at the mints, the nougatines, and all the other dainties.

"Old stingy Crockers!" Grover muttered once again, and turned to go. "I wouldn't go in *there* again."

And yet he did not go away. "Old stingy Crockers" they might be; still, they did make the best candy in town, the best, in fact, that he had ever tasted.

He looked through the window back into the little shop and saw Mrs. Crocker there. A customer had gone in and had made a purchase, and as Grover looked he saw Mrs. Crocker, with her little wrenny face, her pinched features, lean over and peer primly at the scales. She had a piece of fudge in her clean, bony, little fingers, and as Grover looked, she broke it, primly, in her little bony hands. She dropped a morsel down into the scales. They weighted down alarmingly, and her thin lips tightened. She snatched the piece of fudge out of the scales and broke it carefully once again. This time the scales wavered, went down very slowly, and came back again. Mrs. Crocker carefully put the reclaimed piece of fudge back in the tray, dumped the remainder in a paper bag, folded it and gave it to the customer, counted the money carefully and doled it out into the till, the pennies in one place, the nickels in another.

Grover stood there, looking scornfully. "Old stingy Crocker—afraid that she might give a crumb away!"

He grunted scornfully and again he turned to go. But now Mr. Crocker came out from the little partitioned place where they made all their candy, bearing a tray of fresh-made fudge in his skinny hands. Old Man Crocker rocked along the counter to the front and put it down. He really rocked along. He was a cripple. And like his wife, he was a wrenny, wizened little creature, with bony hands, thin lips, a pinched and meager face. One leg was inches shorter than the other, and on this leg there was an enormous thick-soled boot, with a kind of wooden, rocker-like arrangement, six inches high at least, to make up for the deficiency. On this wooden cradle Mr. Crocker rocked along, with a prim and apprehensive little smile, as if he were afraid he was going to lose something.

"Old stingy Crocker!" muttered Grover. "Humph! He wouldn't give you anything!"

And yet—he did not go away. He hung there curiously, peering through the window, with his dark and gentle face now focused and intent, alert and curious, flattening his nose against the glass. Unconsciously he scratched the thick-ribbed fabric of one stockinged leg with the scuffed and worn toe of his old shoe. The fresh, warm odor of the new-made fudge was delicious. It was a little maddening. Half consciously he began to fumble in one trouser pocket, and pulled out his purse, a shabby worn old black one with a twisted clasp. He opened it and prowled about inside.

What he found was not inspiring—a nickel and two pennies and—he had forgotten them—the stamps. He took the stamps out and unfolded them. There were five twos, eight ones, all that remained of the dollar-sixty-cents' worth which Reed, the pharmacist, had given him for running errands a week or two before.

"Old Crocker," Grover thought, and looked somberly at the grotesque little form as it rocked back into the shop again, around the counter, and up the other side. "Well—" again he looked indefinitely at the stamps in his hand—"he's had all the rest of them. He might as well take these."

So, soothing conscience with this sop of scorn, he went into the shop and stood looking at the trays in the glass case and finally decided. Pointing with a slightly grimy finger at the fresh-made tray of chocolate fudge, he said, "I'll take fifteen cents' worth of this, Mr. Crocker." He paused a moment, fighting with embarrassment, then he lifted his dark face and said quietly, "And please, I'll have to give you stamps again."

Mr. Crocker made no answer. He did not look at Grover. He pressed his lips together primly. He went rocking away and got the candy scoop, came back, slid open the door of the glass case, put fudge into the scoop, and, rocking to the scales, began to weigh the candy out. Grover watched him as he peered and squinted, he watched him purse and press his lips together, he saw him take a piece of fudge and break it in two parts. And then old Crocker broke two parts in two again. He weighed, he squinted, and he hovered, until it seemed to Grover that by calling *Mrs.* Crocker stingy he had been guilty of a rank injustice.

But finally, to his vast relief, the job was over, the scales hung there, quivering apprehensively, upon the very hair-line of nervous balance, as if even the scales were afraid that one more move from Old Man Crocker and they would be undone.

Mr. Crocker took the candy then and dumped it in a paper bag and, rocking back along the counter toward the boy, he dryly said: "Where are the stamps?" Grover gave them to him. Mr. Crocker relinquished his clawlike hold upon the bag and set it down upon the counter. Grover took the bag and dropped it in his canvas sack, and then remembered. "Mr. Crocker—" again he felt the old embarrassment that was almost like strong pain— "I gave you too much," Grover said. "There were eighteen cents in stamps. You—you can just give me three ones back."

Mr. Crocker did not answer. He was busy with his bony little hands, unfolding the stamps and flattening them out on top of the glass counter. When he had done so, he peered at them sharply for a moment, thrusting his scrawny neck forward and running his eye up and down, like a bookkeeper who totes up rows of figures.

When he had finished, he said tartly: "I don't like this kind of business. If you want candy, you should have the money for it. I'm not a post office. The next time you come in here and want anything, you'll have to pay me money for it."

Hot anger rose in Grover's throat. His olive face suffused with angry color. His tarry eyes got black and bright. He was on the verge of saying: "Then why did you take my other stamps? Why do you tell me now, when you have taken all the stamps I had, that you don't want them?"

But he was a boy, a boy of eleven years, a quiet, gentle, gravely thoughtful boy, and he had been taught how to respect his elders. So he just stood there looking with his tar-black eyes. Old Man Crocker, pursing at the mouth a little, without meeting Grover's gaze, took the stamps up in his thin, parched fingers and, turning, rocked away with them down to the till.

He took the twos and folded them and laid them in one rounded scallop, then took the ones and folded them and put them in the one next to it. Then he closed the till and started to rock off, down toward the other end. Grover, his face now quiet and grave, kept looking at him, but Mr. Crocker did not look at Grover. Instead he began to take some stamped cardboard shapes and fold them into boxes.

In a moment Grover said, "Mr. Crocker, will you give me the three ones, please?"

Mr. Crocker did not answer. He kept folding boxes, and he compressed his thin lips quickly as he did so. But Mrs. Crocker, back turned to her spouse, also folding boxes with her birdlike hands, muttered tartly: "Hm! *I'd* give him nothing!"

Mr. Crocker looked up, looked at Grover, said, "What are you waiting for?"

"Will you give me the three ones, please?" Grover said.

"I'll give you nothing," Mr. Crocker said.

He left his work and came rocking forward along the counter. "Now you get out of here! Don't you come in here with any more of those stamps," said Mr. Crocker.

"I should like to know where he gets them—that's what *I* should like to know," said Mrs. Crocker.

She did not look up as she said these words. She inclined her head a little to the side, in Mr. Crocker's direction, and continued to fold the boxes with her bony fingers.

"You get out of here!" said Mr. Crocker. "And don't

you come back here with any stamps. . . . Where did you get those stamps?" he said.

"That's just what *I've* been thinking," Mrs. Crocker said. "*I've* been thinking all along."

"You've been coming in here for the last two weeks with those stamps," said Mr. Crocker. "I don't like the look of it. Where did you get those stamps?" he said.

"That's what *I've* been thinking," said Mrs. Crocker, for a second time.

Grover had got white underneath his olive skin. His eyes had lost their luster. They looked like dull, stunned balls of tar. "From Mr. Reed," he said. "I got the stamps from Mr. Reed." Then he burst out desperately: "Mr. Crocker—Mr. Reed will tell you how I got the stamps. I did some work for Mr. Reed, he gave me those stamps two weeks ago."

"Mr. Reed," said Mrs. Crocker acidly. She did not turn her head. "I call it mighty funny."

"Mr. Crocker," Grover said, "if you'll just let me have three ones——"

"You get out of here!" cried Mr. Crocker, and he began rocking forward toward Grover. "Now don't you come in here again, boy! There's something funny about this whole business! I don't like the look of it," said Mr. Crocker. "If you can't pay as other people do, then I don't want your trade."

"Mr. Crocker," Grover said again, and underneath the olive skin his face was gray, "if you'll just let me have those three——"

"You get out of here!" Mr. Crocker cried, rocking down toward the counter's end. "If you don't get out, boy——"

"I'd call a policeman, that's what I'd do," Mrs. Crocker said.

Mr. Crocker rocked around the lower end of the counter. He came rocking up to Grover. "You get out," he said.

He took the boy and pushed him with his bony little hands, and Grover was sick and gray down to the hollow pit of his stomach.

"You've got to give me those three ones," he said.

"You get out of here!" shrilled Mr. Crocker. He seized the screen door, pulled it open, and pushed Grover out. "Don't you come back in here," he said, pausing for a moment, and working thinly at the lips. He turned and rocked back in the shop again. The screen door slammed behind him. Grover stood there on the pavement. And light came and went and came again into the Square.

The boy stood there, and a wagon rattled past. There were some people passing by, but Grover did not notice them. He stood there blindly, in the watches of the sun, feeling this was Time, this was the center of the universe, the granite core of changelessness, and feeling, this is Grover, this the Square, this is Now.

But something had gone out of day. He felt the overwhelming, soul-sickening guilt that all the children, all the good men of the earth, have felt since Time began. And even anger had died down, had been drowned out, in this swelling tide of guilt, and "This is the Square"—thought Grover as before— "This is Now. There is my father's shop. And all of it is as it has always been—save I."

And the Square reeled drunkenly around him, light went in blind gray motes before his eyes, the fountain sheeted out to rainbow iridescence and returned to its proud, pulsing plume again. But all the brightness had gone out of day, and "Here is the Square, and here is permanence, and here is Time—and all of it the same as it has always been, save I."

The scuffed boots of the lost boy moved and stumbled blindly. The numb feet crossed the pavement— reached the cobbled street, reached the plotted central square—the grass plots, and the flower beds, so soon to be packed with red geraniums.

"I want to be alone," thought Grover, "where I cannot go near him. . . . Oh God, I hope he never hears, that no one ever tells him——"

The plume blew out, the iridescent sheet of spray blew over him. He passed through, found the other side and crossed the street, and—"Oh God, if papa ever hears!" thought Grover, as his numb feet started up the steps into his father's shop.

He found and felt the steps—the width and thickness of old lumber twenty feet in length. He saw it all—the iron columns on his father's porch, painted with the dull anomalous black-green that all such columns in this land and weather come to; two angels, fly-specked, and the waiting stones. Beyond and all around, in the stonecutter's shop, cold shapes of white and marble, rounded stone, the languid angel with strong marble hands of love.

He went on down the aisle, the white shapes stood around him. He went on to the back of the workroom. This he knew—the little cast-iron stove in left-hand corner, caked, brown, heat-blistered, and the elbow of the long stack running out across the shop; the high and dirty window looking down across the Market Square toward Niggertown; the rude old shelves, plank-boarded, thick, the wood not smooth but pulpy, like the strong hair of an animal; upon the shelves the chisels of all sizes and a layer of stone dust; an emery wheel with pump tread; and a door that let out on the alleyway, yet the alleyway twelve feet below. Here in the room, two trestles of this coarse spiked wood upon which rested gravestones, and at one, his father at work.

The boy looked, saw the name was Creasman: saw the carved analysis of John, the symmetry of the s, the fine sentiment that was being polished off beneath the name and date: "John Creasman, November 7, 1903."

Gant looked up. He was a man of fifty-three, gaunt-visaged, mustache cropped, immensely long and tall and gaunt. He wore good dark clothes—heavy, massive—save he had no coat. He worked in shirt-sleeves with his vest on, a strong watch chain stretching across his vest, wing collar and black tie, Adam's apple, bony forehead, bony nose, light eyes, gray-green, undeep and cold, and, somehow, lonely-looking, a striped apron going up around his shoulders, and starched cuffs. And in one hand a tremendous rounded wooden mallet like a butcher's bole; and in his other hand, a strong cold chisel.

"How are you, son?"

He did not look up as he spoke. He spoke quietly, absently. He worked upon the chisel and the wooden mallet, as a jeweler might work on a watch, except that in the man and in the wooden mallet there was power too.

"What is it, son?" he said.

He moved around the table from the head, started up on "J" once again.

"Papa, I never stole the stamps," said Grover.

Gant put down the mallet, laid the chisel down. He came around the trestle.

"What?" he said.

As Grover winked his tar-black eyes, they brightened, the hot tears shot out. "I never stole the stamps," he said.

"Hey? What is this?" his father said. "What stamps?"

"That Mr. Reed gave me, when the other boy was sick and I worked there for three days. . . . And Old Man Crocker," Grover said, "he took all the stamps. And I told him Mr. Reed had given them to me. And now he owes me three ones—and Old Man Crocker says he don't believe that they were mine. He says—he says—that I must have taken them somewhere," Grover blurted out.

"The stamps that Reed gave you—hey?" the stone-cutter said. "The stamps you had—" He wet his thumb upon his lips, threw back his head and slowly swung his gaze around the ceiling, then turned and strode quickly from his workshop out into the store-room.

Almost at once he came back again, and as he passed the old gray painted-board partition of his office he cleared his throat and wet his thumb and said, "Now, I tell you——"

Then he turned and strode up toward the front again and cleared his throat and said, "I tell you now —" He wheeled about and started back, and as he came along the aisle between the marshaled rows of gravestones he said beneath his breath, "By God, now——"

He took Grover by the hand and they went out flying. Down the aisle they went by all the grave-stones, past the fly-specked angels waiting there, and down the wooden steps and across the Square. The fountain pulsed, the plume blew out in sheeted irides-cence, and it swept across them; an old gray horse, with a peaceful look about his torn lips, swucked up the cool mountain water from the trough as Grover and his father went across the Square, but they did not notice it.

They crossed swiftly to the other side in a direct line to the candy shop. Gant was still dressed in his long striped apron, and he was still holding Grover by the hand. He opened the screen door and stepped inside.

"Give him the stamps," Gant said.

Mr. Crocker came rocking forward behind the counter, with the prim and careful look that now was somewhat like a smile. "It was just—" he said.

"Give him the stamps," Gant said, and threw some coins down on the counter.

Mr. Crocker rocked away and got the stamps. He came rocking back. "I just didn't know—" he said.

The stonecutter took the stamps and gave them to the boy. And Mr. Crocker took the coins.

"It was just that—" Mr. Crocker began again, and smiled.

Gant cleared his throat: "You never were a father," he said. "You never knew the feelings of a father, or understood the feelings of a child; and that is why you acted as you did. But a judgment is upon you. God has cursed you. He has afflicted you. He has made you lame and childless as you are—and lame and childless, miserable as you are, you will go to your grave and be forgotten!"

And Crocker's wife kept kneading her bony little hands and said, imploringly, "Oh, no—oh don't say that, please don't say that."

The stonecutter, the breath still hoarse in him, left the store, still holding the boy tightly by the hand. Light came again into the day.

"Well, son," he said, and laid his hand on the boy's back. "Well, son," he said, "now don't you mind."

They walked across the Square, the sheeted spray of iridescent light swept out on them, the horse swizzled at the water-trough, and "Well, son," the stonecutter said.

And the old horse sloped down, ringing with his hoofs upon the cobblestones.

"Well, son," said the stonecutter once again, "be a good boy."

And he trod his own steps then with his great stride and went back again into his shop.

The lost boy stood upon the Square, hard by the porch of his father's shop.

"This is Time," thought Grover. "Here is the Square, here is my father's shop, and here am I."

And light came and went and came again—but now not quite the same as it had done before. The boy saw the pattern of familiar shapes and knew that they were just the same as they had always been. But something had gone out of day, and something had come in again. Out of the vision of those quiet eyes some brightness had gone, and into their vision had come some deeper color. He could not say, he did not know through what transforming shadows life had passed within that quarter hour. He only knew that something had been lost—something forever gained.

Just then a buggy curved out through the Square, and fastened to the rear end was a poster, and it said "St. Louis" and "Excursion" and "The Fair."

2. The Mother

As we went down through Indiana—you were too young, child, to remember it—but I always think of all of you the way you looked that morning, when we went down through Indiana, going to the Fair. All of the apple trees were coming out, and it was April; it was the beginning of spring in southern Indiana and everything was getting green. Of course we don't have farms at home like those in Indiana. The childern had never seen such farms as those, and I reckon, kidlike, they had to take it in.

So all of them kept running up and down the aisle —well, no, except for you and Grover. *You* were too young, Eugene. You were just three, I kept you with me. As for Grover—well, I'm going to tell you about that.

But the rest of them kept running up and down the aisle and from one window to another. They kept calling out and hollering to each other every time they saw something new. They kept trying to look out on all sides, in every way at once, as if they wished they had eyes at the back of their heads. It was the first time any of them had ever been in Indiana, and I reckon that it all seemed strange and new.

And so it seemed they couldn't get enough. It seemed they never could be still. They kept running up and down and back and forth, hollering and shouting to each other, until—"I'll vow! You childern! I never saw the beat of you!" I said. "The way that you keep running up and down and back and forth and never can be quiet for a minute beats all I ever saw," I said.

You see, they were excited about going to St. Louis, and so curious over everything they saw. They couldn't help it, and they wanted to see everything. But—"I'll vow!" I said. "If you childern don't sit down and rest you'll be worn to a frazzle before we ever get to see St. Louis and the Fair!"

Except for Grover! He—no, sir! not him. Now, boy, I want to tell you—I've raised the lot of you—and if I do say so, there wasn't a numbskull in the lot. But *Grover!* Well, you've all grown up now, all of you have gone away, and none of you are childern any more. . . . And of course, I hope that, as the fellow says, you have reached the dignity of man's estate. I suppose you have the judgment of grown men. . . . But *Grover! Grover* had it even then!

Oh, even as a child, you know—at a time when I was almost afraid to trust the rest of you out of my sight—I could depend on Grover. He could go anywhere, I could send him anywhere, and I'd always know he'd get back safe, and do exactly what I told him to!

Why, I didn't even have to tell him. You could send that child to market and tell him what you wanted, and he'd come home with *twice* as much as you could get yourself for the same money!

Now you know, I've always been considered a good trader. But *Grover!*—why, it got so finally that I wouldn't even tell him. Your papa said to me: "You'd be better off if you'd just tell him what you want and leave the rest to him. For," your papa says, "damned if I don't believe he's a better trader than you are. He gets more for the money than anyone I ever saw."

Well, I had to admit it, you know. I had to own up then. Grover, even as a child, was a far better trader than I was. . . . Why, yes, they told it on him all over town, you know. They said all of the market men, all of the farmers, knew him. They'd begin to laugh when they saw him coming—they'd say: "Look out! Here's Grover! Here's one trader you're not going to fool!"

And they were right! *That* child! I'd say, "Grover, suppose you run uptown and see if they've got anything good to *eat* today"—and I'd just wink at him, you know, but he'd know what I meant. I wouldn't let on that I *wanted* anything exactly, but I'd say, "Now it just occurs to me that some good fresh stuff may be coming in from the country, so suppose you take this dollar and just see what you can do with it."

Well, sir, that was all that was needed. The minute you told that child that you depended on his judgment, he'd have gone to the ends of the earth for you —and, let me tell you something, he wouldn't *miss*, either!

His eyes would get as black as coals—oh! the way that child would look at you, the intelligence and sense in his expression. He'd say: "Yes, *ma'am!* Now don't you worry, mama. You leave it all to me—and I'll do *good!*" said Grover.

And he'd be off like a streak of lightning and—oh Lord! As your father said to me, "I've been living in this town for almost thirty years," he said—"I've seen it grow up from a crossroads village, and I thought I knew everything there was to know about it—but that child—" your papa says—"he knows places that I never heard of!" . . . Oh, he'd go right down there to that place below your papa's shop where the draymen and the country people used to park their wagons—or he'd go down there to those old lots on Concord Street where the farmers used to keep their wagons. And, child that he was, he'd go right in among them, sir—*Grover* would!—go right in and barter with them like a grown man!

And he'd come home with things he'd bought that would make your eyes stick out. . . . Here he comes one time with another boy, dragging a great bushel basket full of ripe termaters between them. "Why, Grover!" I says. "How on earth are we ever going to use them? Why they'll go bad on us before we're half way through with them." "Well, mama," he says, "I know—" oh, just as solemn as a judge—"but they were the last the man had," he says, "and he wanted to go home, and so I got them for ten cents," he says. "They were so cheap," said Grover, "I thought it was a shame to let 'em go, and I figgered that what we couldn't eat—why," says Grover, "you could *put up!*" Well, the way he said it—so earnest and so serious—I had to laugh. "But I'll vow!" I said. "If you don't beat all!" . . . But that was *Grover!*—the way he was in *those* days! As everyone said, boy that he was, he had the sense and judgment of a grown man. . . . Child, child, I've seen you all grow up, and all of you were bright enough. There were no half-wits in *my* family. But for all-round intelligence, judgment, and general ability, Grover surpassed the whole crowd. I've never seen his equal, and everyone who knew him as a child will say the same.

So that's what I tell them now when they ask me about all of you. I have to tell the truth. I always said that *you* were smart enough, Eugene—but when they come around and brag to me about you, and about how you have got on and have a kind of name—I don't let on, you know. I just sit there and let them talk. I don't brag on you—if *they* want to brag on you, that's *their* business. I never bragged on one of my own childern in my life. When father raised us up, we were all brought up to believe that it was not good breeding to brag about your kin. "If the others want to do it," father said, "well, let *them* do it. Don't ever let on by a word or sign that you know what they are talking about. Just let *them* do the talking, and say nothing."

So when they come around and tell me all about the things *you've* done—I don't let on to them, I never say a word. Why yes!—why, here, you know—oh, along about a month or so ago, this feller comes—a well-dressed man, you know—he looked intelligent, a good substantial sort of person. He said he came from New Jersey, or somewhere up in that part of the country, and he began to ask me all sorts of questions— what you were like when you were a boy, and all such stuff as that.

I just pretended to study it all over and then I said, "Well, yes"—real serious-like, you know—"well, yes —I reckon I ought to know a little something about him. Eugene was my child, just the same as all the others were. I brought him up just the way I brought up all the others. And," I says—oh, just as solemn as you please—"he wasn't a *bad* sort of a boy. Why," I says, "up to the time that he was twelve years old he was just about the same as any other boy—a good, average, normal sort of fellow."

"Oh," he says. "But didn't you notice something? Wasn't there something kind of strange?" he says— "something different from what you noticed in the other childern?"

I didn't let on, you know—I just took it all in and looked as solemn as an owl—I just pretended to study it all over, just as serious as you please.

"Why no," I says, real slow-like, after I'd studied it all over. "As I remember it, he was a good, ordinary, normal sort of boy, just like all the others."

"Yes," he says—oh, all excited-like, you know— "But didn't you notice how brilliant he was? Eugene must have been more brilliant than the rest!"

"Well, now," I says, and pretended to study that all over too. "Now let me see. . . . Yes," I says—I just looked him in the eye, as solemn as you please—"he did pretty well. . . . Well, yes," I says, "I guess he was a fairly bright sort of a boy. I never had no complaints to make of him on that score. He was bright enough," I says. "The only trouble with him was that he was lazy."

"Lazy!" he says—oh, you should have seen the look upon his face, you know—he jumped like someone had stuck a pin in him. "Lazy!" he says. "Why, you don't mean to tell me——"

"Yes," I says—oh, I never cracked a smile—"I was telling him the same thing myself the last time that I saw him. I told him it was a mighty lucky thing for him that he had the gift of gab. Of course, he went off to college and read a lot of books, and I reckon that's where he got this flow of language they say he has. But as I said to him the last time that I saw him: 'Now look a-here,' I said. 'If you can earn your living doing a light, easy class of work like this you do,' I says, 'you're mighty lucky, because none of the rest of your people,' I says, 'had any such luck as that. They had to work hard for a living.'"

Oh, I told him, you know. I came right out with it. I made no bones about it. And I tell you what—I wish you could have seen his face. It was a study.

"Well," he says, at last, "you've got to admit this,

haven't you—he was the brightest boy you had, now wasn't he?"

I just looked at him a moment. I had to tell the truth. I couldn't fool him any longer. "No," I says. "He was a good, bright boy—I got no complaint to make about him on that score—but the brightest boy I had, the one that surpassed all the rest of them in sense, and understanding, and in judgment—the best boy I had —the smartest boy I ever saw—was—well, it wasn't Eugene," I said. "It was another one."

He looked at me a moment, then he said, "Which boy was that?"

Well, I just looked at him, and smiled. I shook my head, you know. I wouldn't tell him. "I never brag about my own," I said. "You'll have to find out for yourself."

But—I'll have to tell *you*—and you know yourself, I brought the whole crowd up, I knew you all. And you can take my word for it—the best one of the lot was— *Grover!*

And when I think of Grover as he was along about that time, I always see him sitting there, so grave and earnest-like, with his nose pressed to the window, as we went down through Indiana in the morning, to the Fair.

All through that morning we were going down along beside the Wabash River—the Wabash River flows through Indiana, it is the river that they wrote the song about—so all that morning we were going down along the river. And I sat with all you childern gathered about me as we went down through Indiana, going to St. Louis, to the Fair.

And Grover sat there, so still and earnest-like, looking out the window, and he didn't move. He sat there like a man. He was just eleven and a half years old, but he had more sense, more judgment, and more understanding than any child I ever saw.

So here he sat beside this gentleman and looked out the window. I never knew the man—I never asked his name—but I tell you what! He was certainly a fine-looking, well-dressed, good, substantial sort of man, and I could see that he had taken a great liking to Grover. And Grover sat there looking out, and then turned to this gentleman, as grave and earnest as a grown-up man, and says, "What kind of crops grow here, sir?" Well, this gentleman threw his head back and just hah-hahed. "Well, I'll see if I can tell you," says this gentleman, and then, you know, he talked to him, they talked together, and Grover took it all in, as solemn as you please, and asked this gentleman every sort of question—what the trees were, what was growing there, how big the farms were—all sorts of questions, which this gentleman would answer, until I said: "Why, I'll vow, Grover! You shouldn't ask so many questions. You'll bother the very life out of this gentleman."

The gentleman threw his head back and laughed right out. "Now you leave that boy alone. He's all right," he said. "He doesn't bother me a bit, and if I know the answers to his questions I will answer him. And if I don't know, why, then, I'll tell him so. But he's *all right*," he said, and put his arm round Grover's shoulders. "You leave him alone. He doesn't bother me a bit."

And I can still remember how he looked that morning, with his black eyes, his black hair, and with the birthmark on his neck—so grave, so serious, so earnest-like—as he sat by the train window and watched the apple trees, the farms, the barns, the houses, and the orchards, taking it all in, I reckon, because it was strange and new to him.

It was so long ago, but when I think of it, it all comes back, as if it happened yesterday. Now all of you have either died or grown up and gone away, and nothing is the same as it was then. But all of you were there with me that morning and I guess I should remember how the others looked, but somehow I don't. Yet I can still see Grover just the way he was, the way he looked that morning when we went down through Indiana, by the river, to the Fair.

3. *The Sister*

Can you remember, Eugene, how Grover used to look? I mean the birthmark, the black eyes, the olive skin. The birthmark always showed because of those open sailor blouses kids used to wear. But I guess you must have been too young when Grover died. . . . I was looking at that old photograph the other day. You know the one I mean—that picture showing mama and papa and all of us children before the house on Woodson Street. *You* weren't there, Eugene. *You* didn't get in. *You* hadn't arrived when that was taken. . . . You remember how mad you used to get when we'd tell you that you were only a dishrag hanging out in Heaven when something happened?

You were the baby. That's what you get for being the baby. You don't get in the picture, do you? . . . I was looking at that old picture just the other day. There we were. And, my God, what is it all about? I mean, when you see the way we were—Daisy and Ben and Grover, Steve and all of us—and then how everyone either dies or grows up and goes away—and then—look at us now! Do you ever get to feeling funny? You know what I mean—do you ever get to feeling *queer*—when you try to figure these things out? You've been to college and you ought to know the answer—and I wish you'd tell me if you know.

My Lord, when I think sometimes of the way I used to be—the dreams I used to have. Playing the piano, practicing seven hours a day, thinking that some day I would be a great pianist. Taking singing lessons from Aunt Nell because I felt that some day I was going to have a great career in opera. . . . Can you beat it now? Can you imagine it? *Me!* In grand opera! . . . Now I want to ask you. I'd like to know.

My Lord! When I go uptown and walk down the street and see all these funny-looking little boys and girls hanging around the drug store—do you suppose any of them have ambitions the way we did? Do you suppose any of these funny-looking little girls are thinking about a big career in opera? . . . Didn't you ever see that picture of us? I was looking at it just the other day. It was made before the old house down on Woodson Street, with papa standing there in his swallow-tail, and mama there beside him—and Grover, and Ben, and Steve, and Daisy, and myself, with our feet upon our bicycles. Luke, poor kid, was only four or five. *He* didn't have a bicycle like us. But there he was. And there were all of us together.

Well, there I was, and my poor old skinny legs and long white dress, and two pigtails hanging down my back. And all the funny-looking clothes we wore, with the doo-lolley business on them. . . . But I guess you can't remember. You weren't born.

But, well, we were a right nice-looking set of people, if I do say so. And there was "86" the way it used to be, with the front porch, the grape vines, and the flower beds before the house—and "Miss Eliza" standing there by papa, with a watch charm pinned upon her waist. . . . I shouldn't laugh, but "Miss Eliza"—well, mama was a pretty woman then. Do you know what I mean? "Miss Eliza" was a right good-looking woman, and papa in his swallow-tail was a good-looking man. Do you remember how he used to get dressed up on Sunday? And how grand we thought he was? And how he let me take his money out and count it? And how rich we all thought he was? And how wonderful that dinkey little shop on

the Square looked to us? . . . Can you beat it, now?
Why we thought that papa was the biggest man in
town and—oh, you can't tell me! You can't tell me! He
had his faults, but papa was a wonderful man. You
know he was!

And there was Steve and Ben and Grover, Daisy,
Luke, and me lined up there before the house with
one foot on our bicycles. And I got to thinking back
about it all. It all came back.

Do you remember anything about St. Louis? You
were only three or four years old then, but you must
remember something. . . . Do you remember how
you used to bawl when I would scrub you? How
you'd bawl for Grover? Poor kid, you used to yell for
Grover every time I'd get you in the tub. . . . He was
a sweet kid and he was crazy about you—he almost
brought you up.

That year Grover was working at the Inside Inn out
on the Fair Grounds. Do you remember the old Inside
Inn? That big old wooden thing inside the Fair? And
how I used to take you there to wait for Grover when
he got through working? And old fat Billy Pelham at
the newsstand—how he always used to give you a
stick of chewing gum?

They were all crazy about Grover. Everybody liked
him. . . . And how proud Grover was of you! Don't
you remember how he used to show you off? How he
used to take you around and make you talk to Billy
Pelham? And Mr. Curtis at the desk? And how Grover would try to make you talk and get you to say
"Grover"? And you couldn't say it—you couldn't pro-
nounce the "r." You'd say "Gova." Have you forgotten
that? You shouldn't forget *that*, because—you were a
cute kid, then—Ho-ho-ho-ho-ho—I don't know
where it's gone to, but you were a big hit in those
days. . . . I tell you, boy, you were Somebody back
in those days.

And I was thinking of it all the other day when I was looking at that photograph. How we used to go and meet Grover there, and how he'd take us to the Midway. Do you remember the Midway? The Snake-Eater and the Living Skeleton, the Fat Woman and the Chute-the-chute, the Scenic Railway and the Ferris Wheel? How you bawled the night we took you up on the Ferris Wheel? You yelled your head off—I tried to laugh it off, but I tell you, I was scared myself. Back in those days, that was Something. And how Grover laughed at us and told us there was no danger. . . . My lord! poor little Grover. He wasn't quite twelve years old at the time, but he seemed so grown up to us. I was two years older, but I thought he knew it all.

It was always that way with him. Looking back now, it sometimes seems that it was Grover who brought us up. He was always looking after us, telling us what to do, bringing us something—some ice cream or some candy, something he had bought out of the poor little money he'd gotten at the Inn.

Then I got to thinking of the afternoon we sneaked away from home. Mama had gone out somewhere. And Grover and I got on the street car and went downtown. And my Lord, we thought that we were going Somewhere. In those days, that was what we called a *trip*. A ride in the street car was something to write home about in those days. . . . I hear that it's all built up around there now.

So we got on the car and rode the whole way down into the business section of St. Louis. We got out on Washington Street and walked up and down. And I tell you, boy, we thought that that was Something. Grover took me into a drug store and set me up to soda water. Then we came out and walked around some more, down to the Union Station and clear over to the river. And both of us half scared to death at

what we'd done and wondering what mama would
say if she found out.

We stayed down there till it was getting dark, and
we passed by a lunchroom—an old one-armed joint
with one-armed chairs and people sitting on stools
and eating at the counter. We read all the signs to see
what they had to eat and how much it cost, and I
guess nothing on the menu was more than fifteen
cents, but it couldn't have looked grander to us if it
had been Delmonico's. So we stood there with our
noses pressed against the window, looking in. Two
skinny little kids, both of us scared half to death, getting the thrill of a lifetime out of it. You know what I
mean? And smelling everything with all our might
and thinking how good it all smelled. . . . Then Grover turned to me and whispered: "Come on, Helen.
Let's go in. It says fifteen cents for pork and beans.
And I've got the money," Grover said. "I've got sixty
cents."

I was so scared I couldn't speak. I'd never been in a
place like that before. But I kept thinking, "Oh Lord,
if mama should find out!" I felt as if we were commit-
ting some big crime. . . . Don't you know how it is
when you're a kid? It was the thrill of a lifetime.
. . . I couldn't resist. So we both went in and sat
down on those high stools before the counter and ordered pork and beans and a cup of coffee. I suppose
we were too frightened at what we'd done really to
enjoy anything. We just gobbled it all up in a hurry,
and gulped our coffee down. And I don't know
whether it was the excitement—I guess the poor kid
was already sick when we came in there and didn't
know it. But I turned and looked at him, and he was
white as death. . . . And when I asked him what
was the matter, he wouldn't tell me. He was too
proud. He said he was all right, but I could see that
he was sick as a dog. . . . So he paid the bill. It came

to forty cents—I'll never forget *that* as long as I live.
. . . And sure enough, we no more than got out the
door—he hardly had time to reach the curb—before it
all came up.

And the poor kid was so scared and so ashamed.
And what scared him so was not that he had gotten
sick, but that he had spent all that money and it had
come to nothing. And mama would find out. . . .
Poor kid, he just stood there looking at me and he
whispered: "Oh Helen, don't tell mama. She'll be mad
if she finds out." Then we hurried home, and he was
still white as a sheet when we got there.

Mama was waiting for us. She looked at us—you
know how "Miss Eliza" looks at you when she thinks
you've been doing something that you shouldn't.
Mama said, "Why, where on earth have you two childern been?" I guess she was all set to lay us out. Then
she took one look at Grover's face. That was enough
for her. She said, "Why, child, what in the world!" She
was white as a sheet herself. . . . And all that Grover
said was—"Mama, I feel sick."

He was sick as a dog. He fell over on the bed, and
we undressed him and mama put her hand upon his
forehead and came out in the hall—she was so white
you could have made a black mark on her face with
chalk—and whispered to me, "Go get the doctor
quick, he's burning up."

And I went chasing up the street, my pigtails flying,
to Dr. Packer's house. I brought him back with me.
When he came out of Grover's room he told mama
what to do but I don't know if she even heard him.

Her face was white as a sheet. She looked at me
and looked right through me. She never saw me. And
oh, my Lord, I'll never forget the way she looked, the
way my heart stopped and came up in my throat. I
was only a skinny little kid of fourteen. But she

looked as if she was dying right before my eyes. And I knew that if anything happened to him, she'd never get over it if she lived to be a hundred.

Poor old mama. You know, he always was her eyeballs—you know that, don't you?—not the rest of us! —no, sir! I know what I'm talking about. It always has been Grover—she always thought more of him than she did of any of the others. And—poor kid!—he was a sweet kid. I can still see him lying there, and remember how sick he was, and how scared I was! I don't know why I was so scared. All we'd done had been to sneak away from home and go into a lunchroom—but I felt guilty about the whole thing, as if it was my fault.

It all came back to me the other day when I was looking at that picture, and I thought, my God, we were two kids together, and I was only two years older than Grover was, and now I'm forty-six. . . . Can you believe it? Can you figure it out—the way we grow up and change and go away? . . . And my Lord, Grover seemed so grown-up to me. He was such a quiet kid—I guess that's why he seemed older than the rest of us.

I wonder what Grover would say now if he could see that picture. All my hopes and dreams and big ambitions have come to nothing, and it's all so long ago, as if it happened in another world. Then it comes back, as if it happened yesterday. . . . Sometimes I lie awake at night and think of all the people who have come and gone, and how everything is different from the way we thought that it would be. Then I go out on the street next day and see the faces of the people that I pass. . . . Don't they look strange to you? Don't you see something funny in people's eyes, as if all of them were puzzled about something? As if they were wondering what had happened to them since they were kids? Wondering what it is that they have lost? . . . Now am I crazy, or do you know what I mean? You've been to college, Gene, and I want you to tell me if you know the answer. Now do they look that way to you? I never noticed that look in people's eyes when I was a kid—did you?

My God, I wish I knew the answer to these things. I'd like to find out what is wrong—what has changed since then—and if we have the same queer look in our eyes, too. Does it happen to us all, to everyone? . . . Grover and Ben, Steve, Daisy, Luke, and me—all standing there before that house on Woodson Street in Altamont—there we are, and you see the way we were—and how it all gets lost. What is it, anyway, that people lose?

How is it that nothing turns out the way we thought it would be? It all gets lost until it seems that it has never happened—that it is something we dreamed somewhere. . . . You see what I mean? . . . It seems that it must be something we heard somewhere—that it happened to someone else. And then it all comes back again.

And suddenly you remember just how it was, and see again those two funny, frightened, skinny little kids with their noses pressed against the dirty window of that lunchroom thirty years ago. You remember the way it felt, the way it smelled, even the strange smell in the old pantry in that house we lived in then. And the steps before the house, the way the rooms looked. And those two little boys in sailor suits who used to ride up and down before the house on tricycles. . . . And the birthmark on Grover's neck. . . . The Inside Inn. . . . St. Louis, and the Fair.

It all comes back as if it happened yesterday. And then it goes away again, and seems farther off and stranger than if it happened in a dream.

4. *The Brother*

"*This* is King's Highway," the man said.

And then Eugene looked and saw that it was just a street. There were some big new buildings, a large hotel, some restaurants and "bar-grill" places of the modern kind, the livid monotone of neon lights, the ceaseless traffic of motor cars—all this was new, but it was just a street. And he knew that it had always been just a street, and nothing more—but somehow— well, he stood there looking at it, wondering what else he had expected to find.

The man kept looking at him with inquiry in his eyes, and Eugene asked him if the Fair had not been out this way.

"Sure, the Fair was out beyond here," the man said. "Out where the park is now. But this street you're looking for—don't you remember the name of it or nothing?" the man said.

Eugene said he thought the name of the street was Edgemont, but that he wasn't sure. Anyhow it was something like that. And he said the house was on the corner of that street and of another street.

Then the man said: "What was that other street?"

Eugene said he did not know, but that King's Highway was a block or so away, and that an interurban line ran past about half a block from where he once had lived.

"What line was this?" the man said, and stared at him.

"The interurban line," Eugene said.

Then the man stared at him again, and finally, "I don't know no interurban line," he said.

Eugene said it was a line that ran behind some houses, and that there were board fences there and grass beside the tracks. But somehow he could not say that it was summer in those days and that you could smell the ties, a wooden, tarry smell, and feel a kind of absence in the afternoon after the car had gone. He only said the interurban line was back behind some-where between the backyards of some houses and some old board fences, and that King's Highway was a block or two away.

He did not say that King's Highway had not been a street in those days but a kind of road that wound from magic out of some dim and haunted land, and that along the way it had got mixed in with Tom the Piper's son, with hot cross buns, with all the light that came and went, and with coming down through Indiana in the morning, and the smell of engine smoke, the Union Station, and most of all with voices lost and far and long ago that said "King's Highway."

He did not say these things about King's Highway because he looked about him and he saw what King's Highway was. All he could say was that the street was near King's Highway, and was on the corner, and that the interurban trolley line was close to there. He said it was a stone house, and that there were stone steps before it, and a strip of grass. He said he thought the house had had a turret at one corner, he could not be sure.

The man looked at him again, and said, "This is King's Highway, but I never heard of any street like that."

Eugene left him then, and went on till he found the place. And so at last he turned into the street, finding the place where the two corners met, the huddled block, the turret, and the steps, and paused a moment, looking back, as if the street were Time.

For a moment he stood there, waiting—for a word, and for a door to open, for the child to come. He waited, but no words were spoken; no one came.

Yet all of it was just as it had always been, except that the steps were lower, the porch less high, the strip of grass less wide than he had thought. All the rest of it was as he had known it would be. A gray-stone front, three-storied, with a slant slate roof, the side red brick and windowed, still with the old arched entrance in the center for the doctor's use.

There was a tree in front, and a lamp post; and behind and to the side, more trees than he had known there would be. And all the slatey turret gables, all the slatey window gables, going into points, and the two arched windows, in strong stone, in the front room.

It was all so strong, so solid, and so ugly—and all so enduring and so good, the way he had remembered it, except he did not smell the tar, the hot and caulky dryness of the old cracked ties, the boards of back-yard fences and the coarse and sultry grass, and ab-sence in the afternoon when the street car had gone, and the twins, sharp-visaged in their sailor suits, pumping with furious shrillness on tricycles up and down before the house, and the feel of the hot after-noon, and the sense that everyone was absent at the Fair.

Except for this, it all was just the same; except for this and for King's Highway, which was now a street; except for this, and for the child that did not come.

It was a hot day. Darkness had come. The heat rose up and hung and sweltered like a sodden blanket in St. Louis. It was wet heat, and one knew that there would be no relief or coolness in the night. And when one tried to think of the time when the heat would go away, one said: "It cannot last. It's bound to go away," as we always say it in America. But one did not believe it when he said it. The heat soaked down and men sweltered in it; the faces of the people were pale and greasy with the heat. And in their faces was a patient wretchedness, and one felt the kind of des-olation that one feels at the end of a hot day in a great city in America—when one's home is far away, across the continent, and he thinks of all that distance, all that heat, and feels, "Oh God! but it's a big country!"

And he feels nothing but absence, absence, and the desolation of America, the loneliness and sadness of the high, hot skies, and evening coming on across the Middle West, across the sweltering and heat-sunken land, across all the lonely little towns, the farms, the fields, the oven swelter of Ohio, Kansas, Iowa, and Indiana at the close of day, and voices, casual in the heat, voices at the little stations, quiet, casual, somehow faded into that enormous vacancy and weariness of heat, of space, and of the immense, the sorrowful, the most high and awful skies.

Then he hears the engine and the wheel again, the wailing whistle and the bell, the sound of shifting in the sweltering yard, and walks the street, and walks the street, beneath the clusters of hard lights, and by the people with sagged faces, and is drowned in desolation and in no belief.

He feels the way one feels when one comes back, and knows that he should not have come, and when he sees that, after all, King's Highway is—a street; and St. Louis—the enchanted name—a big, hot, common town upon the river, sweltering in wet, dreary heat, and not quite South, and nothing else enough to make it better.

It had not been like this before. He could remember how it would get hot, and how good the heat was, and how he would lie out in the backyard on an airing mattress, and how the mattress would get hot and dry and smell like a hot mattress full of sun, and how the sun would make him want to sleep, and how, sometimes, he would go down into the basement to feel coolness, and how the cellar smelled as cellars always smell—a cool, stale smell, the smell of cobwebs and of grimy bottles. And he could remember, when you opened the door upstairs, the smell of the cellar would come up to you—cool, musty, stale and dank and dark—and how the thought of the dark cellar always filled him with a kind of numb excitement, a kind of visceral expectancy.

He could remember how it got hot in the afternoons, and how he would feel a sense of absence and vague sadness in the afternoons, when everyone had gone away. The house would seem so lonely, and sometimes he would sit inside, on the second step of the hall stairs, and listen to the sound of silence and of absence in the afternoon. He could smell the oil upon the floor and on the stairs, and see the sliding doors with their brown varnish and the beady chains across the door, and thrust his hands among the beady chains, and gather them together in his arms, and let them clash, and swish with light beady swishings all around him. He could feel darkness, absence, varnished darkness, and stained light within the house, through the stained glass of the window on the stairs, through the small stained glasses by the door, stained light and absence, silence and the smell of floor oil and vague sadness in the house on a hot mid-afternoon. And all these things themselves would have a kind of life: would seem to wait attentively, to be most living and most still.

He would sit there and listen. He could hear the girl next door practice her piano lessons in the afternoon, and hear the street car coming by between the backyard fences, half a block away, and smell the dry and sultry smell of backyard fences, the smell of coarse hot grasses by the car tracks in the afternoon, the smell of tar, of dry caulked ties, the smell of bright worn flanges, and feel the loneliness of backyards in the afternoon and the sense of absence when the car was gone.

Then he would long for evening and return, the slant of light, and feet along the street, the sharp-faced twins in sailor suits upon their tricycles, the smell of supper and the sound of voices in the house again, and Grover coming from the Fair.

That is how it was when he came into the street, and found the place where the two corners met, and turned at last to see if Time was there. He passed the house: some lights were burning, the door was open, and a woman sat upon the porch. And presently he turned, came back, and stopped before the house again. The corner light fell blank upon the house. He stood looking at it, and put his foot upon the step.

Then he said to the woman who was sitting on the porch: "This house—excuse me—but could you tell me, please, who lives here in this house?"

He knew his words were strange and hollow, and he had not said what he wished to say. She stared at him a moment, puzzled.

Then she said: "I live here. Who are you looking for?"

He said, "Why, I am looking for——"

And then he stopped, because he knew he could not tell her what it was that he was looking for.

"There used to be a house—" he said.

The woman was now staring at him hard.

He said, "I think I used to live here."

She said nothing.

In a moment he continued, "I used to live here in this house," he said, "when I was a little boy."

She was silent, looking at him, then she said: "Oh. Are you sure this was the house? Do you remember the address?"

"I have forgotten the address," he said, "but it was Edgemont Street, and it was on the corner. And I know this is the house."

"This isn't Edgemont Street," the woman said. "The name is Bates."

"Well, then, they changed the name of the street," he said, "but this is the same house. It hasn't changed."

She was silent a moment, then she nodded: "Yes. They did change the name of the street. I remember when I was a child they called it something else," she said. "But that was a long time ago. When was it that you lived here?"

"In 1904."

Again she was silent, looking at him. Then presently: "Oh. That was the year of the Fair. You were here then?"

"Yes." He now spoke rapidly, with more confidence. "My mother had the house, and we were here for seven months. And the house belonged to Dr. Packer," he went on. "We rented it from him."

"Yes," the woman said, and nodded, "this was Dr. Packer's house. He's dead now, he's been dead for many years. But this was the Packer house, all right."

"That entrance on the side," he said, "where the steps go up, that was for Dr. Packer's patients. That was the entrance to his office."

"Oh," the woman said, "I didn't know that. I've often wondered what it was. I didn't know what it was for."

"And this big room in front here," he continued, "that was the office. And there were sliding doors, and next to it, a kind of alcove for his patients——"

"Yes, the alcove is still there, only all of it has been made into one room now—and I never knew just what the alcove was for."

"And there were sliding doors on this side, too, that opened on the hall—and a stairway going up upon this side. And halfway up the stairway, at the landing, a little window of colored glass—and across the sliding doors here in the hall, a kind of curtain made of strings of beads."

She nodded, smiling. "Yes, it's just the same—we still have the sliding doors and the stained glass window on the stairs. There's no bead curtain any more," she said, "but I remember when people had them. I know what you mean."

"When we were here," he said, "we used the doctor's office for a parlor—except later on—the last month or two—and then we used it for—a bedroom."

"It is a bedroom now," she said. "I run the house—I rent rooms—all of the rooms upstairs are rented—but I have two brothers and they sleep in this front room."

Both of them were silent for a moment, then Eugene said, "My brother stayed there too."

"In the front room?" the woman said.

He answered, "Yes."

She paused, then said: "Won't you come in? I don't believe it's changed much. Would you like to see?"

He thanked her and said he would, and he went up the steps. She opened the screen door to let him in.

Inside it was just the same—the stairs, the hallway, the sliding doors, the window of stained glass upon the stairs. And all of it was just the same, except for absence, the stained light of absence in the afternoon, and the child who once had sat there, waiting on the stairs.

It was all the same except that as a child he had sat there feeling things were *Somewhere*—and now he *knew*. He had sat there feeling that a vast and sultry river was somewhere—and now he knew! He had sat there wondering what King's Highway was, where it began, and where it ended—now he knew! He had sat there haunted by the magic word "downtown"—now he knew!—and by the street car, after it had gone—and by all things that came and went and came again, like the cloud shadows passing in a wood, that never could be captured.

And he felt that if he could only sit there on the stairs once more, in solitude and absence in the afternoon, he would be able to get it back again. Then would he be able to remember all that he had seen and been—the brief sum of himself, the universe of his four years, with all the light of Time upon it—that universe which was so short to measure, and yet so far, so endless, to remember. Then would he be able to see his own small face again, pooled in the dark mirror of the hall, and peer once more into the grave eyes of the child that he had been, and discover there in his quiet three-years' self the lone integrity of "I," knowing: "Here is the House, and here House listening; here is Absence, Absence in the afternoon; and here in this House, this Absence, is my core, my kernel—here am I!"

But as he thought it, he knew that even if he could sit here alone and get it back again, it would be gone as soon as seized, just as it had been then—first coming like the vast and drowsy rumors of the distant and enchanted Fair, then fading like cloud shadows on a hill, going like faces in a dream—coming, going, coming, possessed and held but never captured, like lost voices in the mountains long ago—and like the dark eyes and quiet face of the dark, lost boy, his brother, who, in the mysterious rhythms of his life and work, used to come into this house, then go, and then return again.

The woman took Eugene back into the house and through the hall. He told her of the pantry, told her where it was and pointed to the place, but now it was no longer there. And he told her of the backyard, and of the old board fence around the yard. But the old board fence was gone. And he told her of the carriage house, and told her it was painted red. But now there was a small garage. And the backyard was still there, but smaller than he thought, and now there was a tree.

"I did not know there was a tree," he said. "I do not remember any tree."

"Perhaps it was not there," she said. "A tree could grow in thirty years." And then they came back through the house again and paused at the sliding doors.

"And could I see this room?" he said.

She slid the doors back. They slid open smoothly, with a rolling heaviness, as they used to do. And then he saw the room again. It was the same. There was a window at the side, the two arched windows at the front, the alcove and the sliding doors, the fireplace with the tiles of mottled green, the mantle of dark mission wood, the mantel posts, a dresser and a bed, just where the dresser and the bed had been so long ago.

"Is this the room?" the woman said. "It hasn't changed?"

He told her that it was the same.

"And your brother slept here where my brothers sleep?"

"This is his room," he said.

They were silent. He turned to go, and said, "Well, thank you. I appreciate your showing me."

She said that she was glad and that it was no trouble. "And when you see your family, you can tell them that you saw the house," she said. "My name is Mrs. Bell. You can tell your mother that a Mrs. Bell has the house now. And when you see your brother, you can tell him that you saw the room he slept in, and that you found it just the same."

He told her then that his brother was dead.

The woman was silent for a moment. Then she looked at him and said: "He died here, didn't he? In this room?"

He told her that it was so.

"Well, then," she said, "I knew it. I don't know how. But when you told me he was here, I knew it."

He said nothing. In a moment the woman said, "What did he die of?"

"Typhoid."

She looked shocked and troubled, and said involuntarily, "My two brothers——"

"That was a long time ago," he said. "I don't think you need to worry now."

"Oh, I wasn't thinking about that," she said. "It was just hearing that a little boy—your brother—was—was in this room that my two brothers sleep in now——"

"Well, maybe I shouldn't have told you then. But he was a good boy—and if you'd known him you wouldn't mind."

She said nothing, and he added quickly: "Besides, he didn't stay here long. This wasn't really his room—but the night he came back with my sister he was so sick—they didn't move him."

"Oh," the woman said, "I see." And then: "Are you going to tell your mother you were here?"

"I don't think so."

"I—I wonder how she feels about this room."

"I don't know. She never speaks of it."

"Oh. . . . How old was he?"

"He was twelve."

"You must have been pretty young yourself."

"I was not quite four."

"And—you just wanted to see the room, didn't you? That's why you came back."

"Yes."

"Well—" indefinitely—"I guess you've seen it now."

"Yes, thank you."

"I guess you don't remember much about him, do you? I shouldn't think you would."

"No, not much."

The years dropped off like fallen leaves: the face came back again—the soft dark oval, the dark eyes, the soft brown berry on the neck, the raven hair, all bending down, approaching—the whole appearing to him ghost-wise, intent and instant.

"Now say it—*Grover!*"

"Gova."

"No—not Gova—*Grover!* . . . Say it!"

"Gova."

"Ah-h—you didn't say it. You said Gova. *Grover*—now say it!"

"Gova."

"Look, I tell you what I'll do if you say it right. Would you like to go down to King's Highway? Would you like Grover to set you up? All right, then. If you say Grover and say it right, I'll take you to King's Highway and set you up to ice cream. Now say it right—*Grover!*"

"Gova."

"Ah-h, you-u. You're the craziest little old boy I ever did see. Can't you even say Grover?"

"Gova."

"Ah-h, you-u. Old Tongue-Tie, that's what you are. . . . Well, come on, then, I'll set you up anyway."

It all came back, and faded, and was lost again. Eugene turned to go, and thanked the woman and said good-bye.

"Well, then, good-bye," the woman said, and they shook hands. "I'm glad if I could show you. I'm glad if —" She did not finish, and at length she said: "Well, then, that was a long time ago. You'll find everything changed now, I guess. It's all built up around here now—and way out beyond here, out beyond where the Fair Grounds used to be. I guess you'll find it changed."

They had nothing more to say. They just stood there for a moment on the steps, and then shook hands once more.

"Well, good-bye."

And again he was in the street, and found the place where the corners met, and for the last time turned to see where Time had gone.

And he knew that he would never come again, and that lost magic would not come again. Lost now was all of it—the street, the heat, King's Highway, and Tom the Piper's son, all mixed in with the vast and drowsy murmur of the Fair, and with the sense of absence in the afternoon, and the house that waited, and the child that dreamed. And out of the enchanted wood, that thicket of man's memory, Eugene knew that the dark eye and the quiet face of his friend and brother—poor child, life's stranger, and life's exile, lost like all of us, a cipher in blind mazes, long ago—the lost boy was gone forever, and would not return.

No Cure for It

~~~~~~

"Son! Son! Where are you, boy?"

He heard her call again, and listened plainly to her now, and knew she would break in upon his life, his spell of time, and wondered what it was she wanted of him. He could hear her moving in the front of the house.

Suddenly he heard her open the front door and call out sharply: "Oh, Doctor McGuire! . . . Will you stop in here a minute? . . . There's something I want to ask you."

He heard the iron gate slam, and the doctor's slow, burly tread, the gruff rumble of his voice, as he came up the steps. Then he heard them talking in low voices at the front hall door. He could not distinguish their words until, after a minute or two, she raised her voice somewhat and he heard her say reflectively, "Why-y, no-o!"—and knew that she was pursing her lips in a startled, yet thoughtful manner, as she said it. Then she went on in her curiously fragmentary, desperate, and all-inclusive fashion: "I don't think so. At least, he's always seemed all right. Never complained of anything. . . . It's only the last year or so. . . . I got to thinkin' about it—it worried me, you know. . . . He seems strong an' healthy enough. . . . But the way he's growin'! I was speakin' to his father about it the other day—an' he agreed with me, you know. Says, 'Yes, you'd better ask McGuire the next time you see him.'"

46

"Where is he?" McGuire said gruffly. "I'll take a look at him."

"Why, yes!" she said quickly. "That's the very thing! . . . Son! . . . Where are you, boy?"

Then they came back along the hall, and into the sitting room. The gangling boy was still stretched out on the smooth, worn leather of his father's couch, listening to the time-strange tocking of the clock, and regarding his bare brown legs and sun-browned toes with a look of dreamy satisfaction as they entered.

"Why, boy!" his mother cried in a vexed tone. "What on earth do you mean? I've been callin' for you everywhere!"

He scrambled up sheepishly, unable to deny that he had heard her, yet knowing, somehow, that he had not willfully disobeyed her.

Doctor McGuire came over, looking like a large, tousled bear, smelling a little like his horse and buggy, and with a strong stench of cigar and corn whisky on his breath. He sat his burly figure down heavily on Gant's couch, took hold of the boy's arm in one large, meaty hand, and for a moment peered at him comically through his bleared, kindly, dark-yellow eyes.

"How old are you?" he grunted.

Eugene told him he was seven, going on eight, and McGuire grunted indecipherably again.

He opened the boy's shirt and skinned it up his back, and then felt carefully up and down his spinal column with thick, probing fingers. He wriggled the boy's neck back and forth a few times, held the skinny arm out and inspected it solemnly, and then peered with grave, owlish humor at the boy's enormous hands and feet. After that he commanded the boy to stoop over without bending his knees and touch the floor.

Eugene did so; and when the doctor asked him if he could bend no farther, the boy put his hands down flat upon the floor, and remained bent over, holding them that way, until the doctor told him to stand up and let his arms hang naturally. When he stood up and let his arms fall, his hands hung level with his knees, and for a moment McGuire peered at him very carefully. Then he turned and squinted comically at Eliza with his look of owlish gravity, and said nothing. She stood there, her hands clasped in their loose, powerful gesture at her apron strings, and when he looked at her she shook her puckered face rapidly in a movement of strong concern and apprehension.

"Hm! Hm! Hm! Hm! Hm!" she said. "I don't like it! It don't seem natural to me!"

McGuire made no comment, and did not answer her. After staring at her owlishly a moment longer, he turned to the boy again and told him to lie down upon the couch. Eugene did so. McGuire then told him to raise his legs and bend them back as far as they would go, and kept grunting, "Farther! Farther!" until the boy was bent double. Then McGuire grunted sarcastically:

"Go on! Is that the best you can do? I know a boy who can wrap his legs all the way around his neck."

When he said this, the boy stuck his right leg around his neck without any trouble at all, and remained in that posture for some time, happily wriggling his toes under his left ear. McGuire looked at him solemnly, and at last turned and squinted at his mother, saying nothing.

"Whew-w!" she shrieked with a puckered face of disapproval. "Get out of here! I don't like to look at anything like that! . . . Hm! Hm! Hm! Hm! Hm!" she muttered, shaking her head rapidly with an expression of strong concern, as the boy unwound his legs and straightened out again.

Eugene stood up. For a moment McGuire held him by the arm and squinted comically at him through his bleared eyes, without saying a word. Then his burly, bearlike shoulders began to heave slowly, a low, hoarse chuckle rose in his throat, and he said, poking the boy in the ribs with one fat thumb:

"Why, you little monkey!"

"Hah! What say? What is it?" cried his mother in a sharp, startled tone.

The doctor's huge shoulders heaved mountainously again, the hoarse sound rumbled in his throat, and, shaking his head slowly, he said:

"I've seen them when they were knock-kneed, bow-legged, cross-eyed, pigeon-toed and rickety—but that's the damndest thing I ever saw! I never saw the beat of it!" he said—and the boy grinned back at him proudly.

"Hah! What say? What's wrong with him?" Eliza said sharply.

The burly shoulders heaved again:

"Nothing," McGuire said. "Nothing at all! He's all right! He's just a little monkey!"—and the rumbling noises came from his inner depths again.

He was silent for a moment, during which he squinted at Eliza as she stood there pursing her lips at him, then he went on:

"I've seen them when they shot up like weeds, and I've seen them when you couldn't make them grow at all," he said, "but I never saw one before who grew like a weed in one place while he was standing still in another! . . . Look at those arms and legs!" he cried. "And good God! Will you look at his hands and feet! Did you ever in your life see such hands and feet on a child his age?"

"Why, it's awful!" his mother agreed, nodding. "I know it is! We can't find anything in the stores to fit him now! What's it goin' to be like when he gets older? It's an awful thing!" she cried.

"Oh, he'll be all right," McGuire said, as he heaved

slowly. "He'll get all of his parts together some day and grow out of it! . . . But God knows what he'll grow into!" he said, rumbling inside again and shaking his head as he peered at the boy. "A mountain or an elephant—I don't know which!" He paused, then added: "But at the present time he's just a little monkey. . . . That's what you are—a monkey!" and the tremendous shoulders heaved again.

Just then the iron gate slammed, and the boy heard his father lunge across the walk, take the front porch steps in bounds of three, and come striding around the porch into the sitting room. He was muttering madly to himself, but stopped short as he came upon the little group, and, with a startled look in his uneasy cold-gray eyes, he cried out—"Hey?" although no one had spoken to him.

Then, wetting his great thumb briefly on his lips, and slamming down the package he was carrying, he howled:

"Woman, this is your work! Unnatural female that you are, you have given birth to a monster who will not rest until he has ruined us all, eaten us out of house and home, and sent me to the poorhouse to perish in a pauper's grave! Nor man nor beast hath fallen so far! . . . Well, what's your opinion, hey?" he barked abruptly at McGuire, half bending toward him in a frenzied manner.

"He's all right," McGuire said, slowly heaving. "He's just a monkey."

For a moment Gant looked at his son with his restless, cold-gray eyes.

"Merciful God!" he said. "If he had hair on him, they couldn't tell him from a monkey now!" Then, wetting his great thumb, he grinned thinly and turned away. He strode rapidly about the room, his head thrown back, his eyes swinging in an arc about the ceiling; then he paused, grinned again, and came over to the boy. "Well, son," he said kindly, putting his great hand gently upon the boy's head, "I'm glad to know that it's all right. I guess it was the same with me. Now don't you worry. You'll grow up to be a big man some day."

They all stood looking at the boy—his mother with pursed, tremulous, bantering, proudly smiling lips, his father with a faint, thin grin, and McGuire with his owlish, bleared, half-drunken, kindly stare. The boy looked back at them, grinning proudly, worried about nothing. He thought his father was the grandest, finest person in the world, and as the three of them looked at him he could hear, in the hush of brooding noon, the time-strange tocking of his father's clock.

Gentlemen of the Press

Time: A hot night in June, 1916.

Scene: The city room of a small-town newspaper.

The room has three or four flat-topped desks, type-writers, green-shaded lights hanging from the ceiling by long cords, some filing cabinets. Upon the wall, a large map of the United States. Upon the desks, news-paper clippings, sheets of yellow flimsy, paste pots, pencils, etc. Over all, a warm smell of ink, a not un-pleasant air of use and weariness.

To the right, a door opening to a small room which houses the A.P. man, his typewriter, and his instruments. To the left, a glass partition and a door into the compositors' room. This door stands open and compositors may be seen at work before the linotype machines, which make a quiet slotting sound. The A.P. man's door is also open and he can be seen within, typing rapidly, to the accompaniment of the clattering telegraph instrument on the table beside him.

In the outer room, Theodore Willis, a reporter, sits at his desk, banging away at a typewriter. He is about twenty-eight years old, consumptive, very dark of feature, with oval-shaped brown eyes, jet black hair, thin hands, and a face full of dark intelligence, quick-ness, humor, sensitivity. At another desk, his back to-ward Willis, sits another reporter—young, red-headed, red-necked, stocky—also typing. All the men wear green eyeshades. Theodore Willis is smoking a ciga-rette, which hangs from the corner of his mouth and which he inhales from time to time, narrowing his eyes to keep the smoke out.

THE A.P. WIRE (*clattering rapidly*): . . . Wash June 18 Walter Johnson was invincible today held Athletics to four scattered hits Senators winning three to nothing batteries Washington Johnson and Ainsmith Philadelphia Bender Plank and Schang.

(*The telegraph instrument stops suddenly. The A.P. man gets up, pulls a sheet from the machine, comes out in the city room, and tosses it on Theodore Willis's desk.*)

THE A.P. MAN: Well, the big Swede was burning 'em in today.

WILLIS (*typing, without looking up*): Washington win?

THE A.P. MAN: Three-nothing.

WILLIS: How many did he fan?

A.P. MAN: Fourteen. (*He lights a cigarette and inhales.*) Christ! If he had a decent team behind him he'd never lose a game.

(*Far off across the town, the screeching noise of Pretty Polly is heard, coming from the roof of the Appalachicola Hotel. She is a local character who for years has earned her living by singing in public places, and nobody ever calls her anything but Pretty Polly.*)

PRETTY POLLY (*singing away in the distance, and plainly audible to the last syllable*): . . . threels—mee-uh—and stuh-heels—mee-uh—and luh-hulls—mee-uh—to r-r-r-rest . . .

(*Benjamin Gant passes through city room on way to compositors' room. Pauses a moment with lean fingers arched upon his hips, head cocked slightly in direction of the sound.*)

PRETTY POLLY (*as before, but fading away now*): . . . threels—mee-uh—and stuh-heels—mee-uh—and luh-hulls—mee-uh—to r-r-r-rest.

BEN GANT (*jerking his head up scornfully and speak-*

ing to some unknown auditor): Oh for God's sake! Listen to that, won't you? (*He goes out into the compositors' room.*)

A.P. MAN: Christ, what a voice!

WILLIS: Voice! That's not a voice! It's a distress signal! They ought to take her out to sea and anchor her off Sandy Hook as a warning to in-coming liners.

(*Harry Tugman, the chief pressman, enters at this moment with a bundle tied in a newspaper under his arm. He is a powerful man, brutally built, with the neck, shoulders, and buttered features of a prize fighter. His strong, pitted face is colorless, and pocked heavily with ink marks.*)

TUGMAN (*yelling as he enters*): Wow! Wouldn't that old battle-ax be somethin' in a fog! She's hot tonight! Boy, she's goin' good! (*These remarks are addressed to no one in particular, but now he pauses beside the little group of reporters and speaks to them with abusive good nature.*) Hello, you lousy reporters. Is that lousy rag of yours ready to be run off yet?

WILLIS (*quietly, and without looking up*): Hello, you gin-swizzling sot. Yes, the lousy rag is ready to be run off, and so are you if the Old Man ever gets a whiff of that breath of yours. You'd better beat it downstairs now and get your press to rolling before he comes in and takes you for a brewery.

TUGMAN (*with riotous good nature*): Whew! That's it, Ted—give 'em hell! (*Boisterously*) Boys, I've been in a crap game and I took 'em for a hundred and fifty bucks.

WILLIS: Which means you're a dollar and a quarter to the good, I suppose. (*Quietly, viciously*) A hundred and fifty bucks—why, God-damn your drunken soul, you never saw that much at one time in your whole life.

A.P. MAN: How much of it you got left, Tug?

TUGMAN: Not a lousy cent. They took me to the

cleaners afterwards. Tell you how it was, boys. We was down at Chakales Pig. When I picked up the loot I looked around and counted up the house and decided it was safe to buy a round of drinks, seein' as there was only five guys there. (*His manner grows more riotously extravagant as with coarse but eloquent improvisation he builds up the farce.*) Well, I goes up to the bar, thinkin' I'm safe, and says: 'Step right up, gentlemen. This one's on me.' And you know what happens? (*He pauses a moment for dramatic effect.*) Well, boys, I ain't hardly got the words out of my mouth when there is a terrific crash of splintered glass and eighteen booze hounds bust in from the sidewalk, six more spring through the back windows, and the trap doors of the cellar come flyin' open and thirty-seven more swarm up like rats out of the lower depths. By that time the place is jammed. Then I hear the sirens goin' in the street, and before I know it the village fire department comes plungin' in, followed by two-thirds of the local constabulary. I tries to crawl out between the legs of One-eye McGloon and Silk McCarthy, but they have me cornered before I gets as far as the nearest spittoon. Well, to make a long story short, they rolled me for every nickel I had. Somebody got my socks and B.V.D.'s, and when I finally crawled to safety Chakales had my shirt and told me he was holdin' it as security until I came through with the six bits I still owed him for the drinks.

(*Ben Gant returns from the compositors' room, and, as he passes, Harry Tugman slaps him violently on his bony back.*)

TUGMAN (*yelling boisterously*): How's that, Ben? Is that gettin' 'em told, or not?

BEN (*arching his hands upon his hips, sniffing scornfully, and jerking his head toward his unknown auditor*): Oh for God's sake! Listen to this, won't you?

TUGMAN (*still boisterously*): Did I ever tell you boys about the time I came back from Scandinavia, where I'd been managin' Jack Johnson on a barn-stormin' tour?

WILLIS (*starting up suddenly, laughing, and seizing a paper weight*): Get out of here, you son-of-a-bitch. Scandinavia! You've never been north of Lynchburg. The last time you told that story it was South America.

TUGMAN (*laughing heartily*): That was another time. (*Loudly, immensely pleased with himself*) Whew! God-*damn!* Give 'em hell, boys!

WILLIS: On your way, bum. It's time to roll.

TUGMAN (*going out in high spirits, singing loudly a bawdy parody of Pretty Polly's song*): . . . sla-hays —mee-uh—and la-hays—me-uh—and luh-hulls—mee-uh—to r-r-r-rest.

WILLIS (*now standing at his desk and reading a sheet of yellow flimsy with an air of growing stupefaction*): Well I'll be—in the name of God, who wrote this anyway? (*Reads*) 'By this time the police had arrived and thrown a cordon around the blazing tenement in an effort to keep the milling throngs at a safe distance.' (*With an air of frank amazement*) Well, I'll be God-damned! (*Suddenly, irritably, in a rasping voice*) Who wrote this crap? 'Blazing tenement'—'milling throngs'—now ain't that nice? (*Reading again, slowly, deliberately*) 'By—this—time—the—police— had—arrived—and—thrown—a—cordon . . . a—*cordon*—'

RED (*the young reporter, whose neck and face during this recital had become redder than ever*): We always said 'cordon' on the *Atlanta Constitution.*

WILLIS (*looking at him with an air of stunned disbelief*): Did you write this? Is this your story?

RED (*sulkily*): Who the hell do you think wrote it? The Angel Gabriel?

WILLIS (*with an air of frank defeat*): Well I'll be

damned! If that's not the damndest description I ever read of a fire in Niggertown, I'll kiss a duck. (*With wicked insistence*) 'Blazing tenement.' What blazing tenement are you talking about—a two-roomed nigger shack in Valley Street? For Christ's sake, you'd think the whole East Side of New York was afire. And 'milling throngs.' Well, I'm a monkey's uncle if that ain't perfectly God-damned delightful! What do you mean by milling throngs—forty-two niggers and a couple of one-eyed mules? And 'cordon.' (*A trifle more emphatically*) Cordon! (*He holds the paper at arm's length and surveys it daintily, with a show of mincing reflection.*)

RED (*sulkily*): We always said 'cordon' on the *Constitution*.

WILLIS: *Constitution*, my—! If old man Matthews, John Ledbetter, and Captain Crane constitute a cordon then I'm a whole God-damn regiment of the United States Marines!

RED (*angrily*): All right, then. If you don't like the way the story's written, why the hell don't you write it yourself?

WILLIS: Why the hell should I? That's your job, not mine. Christ Almighty, man! I've got enough to do on my own hook without having to rewrite your whole damned story every time I send you out to cover a lousy little fire in Niggertown.

RED: That story would have gone on the *Constitution*. (*Sarcastically*) But apparently it's not good enough for a one-horse paper in a hick town. (*He pulls off his eyeshade and tosses it down upon the desk; puts on his vest and coat and begins to button himself up viciously.*) To hell with it anyway! To hell with this whole damn outfit! I'm through with it! The trouble with you guys is that you're all a bunch of illiterate half-wits who don't know anything about style and don't appreciate a piece of writing when you see one!

WILLIS: Style, hell! What I'd appreciate from you is a simple declarative sentence in the English language. If you've got to get all that fancy palaver out of your system, write it in your memory book. But for God's sake, don't expect to get it published in a newspaper.

RED (*savagely, tugging at his vest*): I'll get it published all right, and it won't be in your lousy paper either!

WILLIS (*ironically, sitting down and adjusting his eyeshade*): No? Where are you going to get it published—in the *Woman's Home Companion?*

RED (*contemptuously*): You guys give me a pain. Wait till my book comes out. Wait till you read what the critics have to say about it.

WILLIS (*beginning to work on the unhappy story with a blue pencil*): Go on, go on. The suspense is awful. What are we going to do when we read it? Turn green with envy, I suppose?

RED (*wagging his head*): All right, all right. Have it your own way. Only you'll be laughing out of the other corner of your mouth some day. You wait and see.

WILLIS (*working rapidly with the blue pencil and still speaking ironically, but in a more kindly tone than before*): Don't make us wait too long, Red. I've got only one lung left, you know. (*He coughs suddenly into a wadded handkerchief, stares intently for an instant at the small stain of spreading red, then thrusts the crumpled handkerchief back into his pocket.*)

RED (*flushing uncomfortably, suddenly moved*): Oh, well—(*eagerly*) Jesus, Ted, I've got a whale of an idea! If I can come through on this one, it'll knock 'em loose!

WILLIS (*a trifle absently, still working busily on the story*): What is it this time, Red—something hot? The love affairs of a police court reporter, or something like that?

RED: Nah, nah. Nothing like that! It's a historical novel. It's about Lincoln.

WILLIS: Lincoln! You mean Abe?

RED (*nodding vigorously*): Sure! It's a romance—an adventure story. I've been working on the idea for years, and boy, it's a lulu if I can put it over! (*Looks around craftily toward the door to see if he is being overheard, lowers his voice carefully, with an insinuating tone*) Listen, Ted——

WILLIS (*absently*): Well?

RED (*in a tone of cunning secrecy*): If I let you in on the idea (*he peers around apprehensively again*), you won't tell anyone, will you?

WILLIS: You know me, Red. Did you ever hear of a newspaper reporter giving away a secret? All right, kid, spill it.

RED (*lowering his voice still more, to a confidential whisper*): The big idea is this. Lincoln—you know Lincoln——

WILLIS: Sure. You mean the guy that got shot.

RED: Sure. (*Then, cunningly, secretively*) Well, Ted, all the history books—all the big authorities and the wise guys—*they* tell you he was born out in Kentucky——

WILLIS: And you mean to tell me he wasn't?

RED (*scornfully*): You're God-damn right he wasn't! Nah! (*Coming closer and whispering earnestly*) Why, Ted, that guy was no more born in Kentucky than you and I were. (*Nodding vigorously*) Sure. I'm telling you. I've got the dope—and I know. (*Whispering impressively*) Why, Ted, that guy grew up right out here in Yancey County, not more than fifty miles from town.

WILLIS (*in a tone of mock astonishment*): Go on! You're kidding me!

RED (*very earnestly*): No I'm not. It's the truth, Ted!
I know what I'm talking about. I've got all the dope
now—I've been working on the thing for years. (*He
looks around cautiously again, then whispers*) And
say, Ted, you know what else I've got? I've got a little
dress that Lincoln wore when he was a baby. And say
(*his voice sinking now to an awed whisper*), do you
know what I found?

WILLIS (*working, absently*): What was it, Red?

RED (*whispering*): They say, you know, that Lincoln's parents were poor—but that little baby dress is
made of the finest lace! And Ted, it's all embroidered,
too. It's got initials on it! (*His voice sinks to an almost
inaudible whisper*) Ted, it's embroidered with the
letter N. (*He pauses significantly to let this sink in,
then repeats in a meaningful tone*) N, Ted. . . . N.
. . . Do you get it?

WILLIS: Do I get what? N what?

RED (*impatiently*): N nothing. Just N, Ted. (*He
pauses anxiously for this to sink in, but gets no response.*)

WILLIS (*after waiting a moment*): Well? What
about it?

RED (*disappointedly, whispering*): Why, don't you
see, Ted? Lincoln's name begins with L, and this little
dress I got is embroidered with the letter N. (*Again
he waits hopefully for a satisfactory response and gets
none.*) N, Ted. . . . N. . . . Don't you see?

WILLIS (*looking up a trifle impatiently and slapping
his blue pencil down on the desk*): What are you driv-
ing at, Red? Spill it, for Christ's sake!

RED: Why, Ted, Lincoln's name begins with L, and
this little dress I got is embroidered with the letter——

WILLIS (*nodding wearily*): The letter N. Sure, I get
you, Red. (*Picks up his pencil and resumes work
again*) Well, maybe the laundry got the tags mixed.

RED (*in a disgusted tone*): Nah, Ted. (*Slowly, sig-

nificantly) N . . . N . . . (*Slyly*) Can't you think of anyone, Ted, whose name begins with N?

WILLIS (*casually*): Napoleon Bonaparte.

RED (*patiently*): Not exactly, Ted. (*Looking around craftily again, then whispering cunningly*) But you're coming close. You're getting warm.

WILLIS (*throwing down his pencil, pushing up his eyeshade, and settling back in his chair with an air of weary resignation*): Look here, what the hell are you trying to give me? Are you trying to hint that Lincoln was related to Napoleon?

RED: You're on the scent, Ted. (*Looking around craftily, then whispering*) You're getting warm, all right. (*A look of triumphant satisfaction expands across his countenance, and he nods his head in affirmation*) Sure! I'm telling you!

WILLIS (*staring at him with frank amazement*): You mean to stand there and say that Abraham Lincoln was Napoleon's nephew or something?

RED: No, Ted. Not his nephew. (*Craftily, in a hoarse whisper*) His son.

WILLIS (*staring helplessly*): Well, I'll be ——!

RED (*nodding vigorously*): Sure, sure, I'm telling you! You see, Ted, Napoleon's son didn't die in Austria. That's what the history books say, but it's the bunk. What really happened was this. (*He looks slyly around the room before continuing in a hoarse whisper.*) After the battle of Waterloo the Bourbons captured Napoleon's son, who was just a child then, and were going to send him back with his mother to the Hapsburgs in Vienna. But the Bonapartists got wind of the plan, and with Maria Louisa's help they put another child of the same age in the young prince's place. This imposter was the one that was sent back to Austria, and he died there. Meanwhile a trusted officer of Napoleon's took the young prince and escaped with him. They got away all right, but the curious thing is that they were never heard of again. No one ever knew what became of them. No one, that is (*lowering his voice confidingly*) —except me. But I found out. I got the dope. I've been working on the thing for years, and I got it all nailed down now. The officer and the young prince escaped to this country—in a sailing ship.

WILLIS (*in a tone of ironic mockery*): Aw, go on, Red! You know people like that never would have taken a common sailing ship. They'd at least have come over on the *Berengaria*.

RED (*disregarding the sarcasm and whispering earnestly*): Nah, Ted. It was a sailing ship. I've got all the dope—the name of the ship, the captain, everything. And the officer took an assumed name—he called himself Thomas Lincoln, and pretended that the young prince was his son.

WILLIS (*as before*): Go on, I don't believe you!

RED (*earnestly*): It's the truth, Ted. They landed at Baltimore, and then came south. They settled over here in Yancey County—and the officer lived to be an old, old man. (*Looking around again, and cautiously whispering*) Why hell, Ted! He only died about thirty years ago! He was way over a hundred when he died. And there are people out there in Yancey County who knew him! They talked to him. They remember stories about the child, and how he grew up and was sent to Illinois when he was a young man. And they say it was Napoleon's son, all right. Oh, I got all the dope. And what's more, this young man—this royal prince— (*pausing for effect and whispering dramatically*)— was also Abraham Lincoln.

WILLIS (*lying sprawled in his chair as though he had collapsed, with his thin hands upon the desk, his mouth slightly ajar, staring at his companion with paralyzed astonishment, and speaking very slowly*): Well—I'll— be—God—damned!

RED (*taking the words as tribute, beaming trium-*

phantly): Ain't it a lulu, boy? Ain't it a wham? Won't it knock 'em for a goal?

WILLIS (*waving his thin hand groggily before his face*): You win, kid. Pick up the marbles. You've got me licked.

RED (*exuberantly*): Boy, I've got the hit of the century here—the greatest story since *The Count of Monte Cristo!*

WILLIS (*feebly*): Don't stop at *Monte Cristo*, kid. You can go the whole way back to the Holy Bible as far as I'm concerned.

RED (*delighted, yet a trifle anxiously*): You won't say anything about it, Ted? You won't let it out?

WILLIS (*exhausted*): Not for the world and a cage of pet monkeys. (*He holds out a thin, limp hand.*) Put it there.

(*Red, his face crimson with happiness, seizes Theodore Willis's thin hand and wrings it heartily. And then, with a jubilant "Good night," he goes out. For a moment Willis sits quietly, in an exhausted attitude, then he opens his mouth and lets out a long sigh.*)

WILLIS: Whew-w!

THE A.P. MAN (*coming to his door and peering out*): What is it?

WILLIS (*slowly shaking his head*): That wins the gold-enameled mustache cup. That guy!

A.P. MAN: What is it now—a new idea for a book he's going to write?

WILLIS: Yep—and he's got the whole idea nailed down, trussed up, and hog-tied. It's going to paralyze the public, upset history, and make the faculty at Harvard look like a set of boobs.

A.P. MAN: What is it? What's the idea?

WILLIS (*shaking his head solemnly*): That, sir, I can nevermore divulge. He has my promise, my word of honor. And the word of a Willis is as good as his bond—in fact, a damn sight better. Wild horses could not drag his secret from me. But I'll tell you this, my friend. If you should suddenly read absolute historic proof that Shakespeare had come over on the *Mayflower* and was the grandfather of George Washington, you'd get some faint notion of what this book is going to do to us. (*He coughs suddenly, rackingly, spits carefully into his wadded handkerchief, looks intently at the small red stain, then, with an expression of weariness and disgust, thrusts the wadded rag back in his pocket.*) Christ! Maybe some day I'll write a book myself—about all the poor hams I've known in this game who were going to write a book—and never did. What a life!

(*The A.P. man shrugs and goes back into his little room. The telephone rings. With an expression of weariness Theodore Willis takes the receiver from the hook.*)

WILLIS: Hello. . . . Yes, this is the *Courier*. . . . (*In an agreeable tone that is belied by the expression of extreme boredom on his face*) Yes, Mrs. Purtle. Yes, of course. . . . Oh, yes, there's still time. . . . No, she's not here, but I'll see that it gets in. . . . Certainly, Mrs. Purtle. Oh, absolutely. . . . (*He rolls his dark eyes aloft with an expression of anguished entreaty to his Maker.*) Yes, indeed, I promise you. It will be in the morning edition. . . . Yes, I can well understand how important it is. (*He indicates his understanding of its importance by scratching himself languidly on the hind quarter.*) . . . Oh, absolutely without fail. You can depend on it. . . . Yes, Mrs. Purtle. . . . (*He sprawls forward on one elbow, takes the moist fag end of a cigarette from his mouth and puts it in a tray, picks up a pencil, and wearily begins to take notes.*) Mr. and Mrs. S. Frederick Purtle. . . . No, I won't forget the S. . . . Yes, I know we had it Fred last time. We had a new man on the job. . . . No, we'll get it right this time. Mr. and Mr. S. Frederick Purtle . . . dinner and bridge . . . tomorrow night at eight . . . at their residence, 'Oaknook,' 169 Woodbine Drive . . . in honor of—Now just a moment, Mrs. Purtle. I want to be sure to get this straight. (*Then, very slowly, with an expression of fine concern*) In honor of their house guest . . . Mrs. J. Skidmore Pratt, of Paterson, New Jersey . . . the former Miss Annie Lou Bass of this city. (*Writing casually as he continues*) Those invited include Mr. and Mrs. Leroy Dingley . . . Mr. and Mrs. E. Seth Hooton . . . Mr. and Mrs. Claude Belcher . . . Mr. Nemo McMurdie . . . all of this city . . . and Miss May Belle Buckmaster of Florence, South Carolina. . . . Now, just a moment, Mrs. Purtle, to see if I've got it all straight. (*He reads it over to her. The lady is apparently satisfied, for at length he says*) Oh absolutely. No, I won't forget. . . . Not at all, Mrs. Purtle. (*He laughs falsely.*) Delighted, of course. . . . Good-bye.

(*He hangs up the receiver, lights a cigarette, inserts a fresh sheet in the typewriter, and begins to type it out. The A.P. man comes out chuckling with a piece of paper in his hand.*)

A.P. MAN: Here's a hot one. Fellow out in Kansas has made himself a pair of wings and sent word around to all the neighbors that tomorrow's going to be the last day of the world and he's going to take off for the Promised Land at four o'clock. Everyone's invited to be present. And what's more, all of them are coming.

WILLIS (*typing*): Not a bad idea at that. (*Pulls the paper from the machine viciously and looks at it*) Christ! If I could only be sure tomorrow was going to be the last day of the world, what a paper I'd get out! That's my idea of heaven—to have, just for once in my life, the chance to tell these bastards what they are.

A.P. MAN (*grinning*): Boy, you could sure go to

town on that, couldn't you? Only, you couldn't get it in an ordinary edition. You'd need an extra-extra-extra feature edition with fourteen supplements.

WILLIS (*clutching the sheet he has just typed and shaking it viciously*): Listen to this, will you. (*Reads*) 'Mr. and Mrs. Fred Purtle' (*he coughs in an affected tone*)—I beg your pardon, 'Mr. and Mrs. S. Frederick Purtle'—and be sure to get in the Frederick, and don't leave out the S . . . 'Mr. and Mrs. Leroy Dingley' . . . 'Mr. and Mrs. E. Seth Hooton'—and don't leave out the E . . . 'in honor of Mrs. J. Skidmore Pratt'—now there's a good one! (*Throws down the paper savagely*) Why, God-damn that bunch of mountaineers—half of 'em never owned an extra pair of pants until they were twenty-one. As for Fred Purtle, he was brought up out in Yancey County on hawg and hominy. His father used to go over him with a curry comb and horse clippers every Christmas, whether he needed it or not. Why, hell yes. They had to throw him down to hold him while they put shoes on him. And now, for Christ's sake, it's Mr. S. Frederick Purtle—and don't leave out the S. My God! What a world! And what a job I could do on all the bastards in this town if I only had the chance! To be able, just for once, to tell the truth, to spill the beans, to print the facts about every son-of-a-bitch of them. To tell where they came from, who they were, how they stole their money, who they cheated, who they robbed, whose wives they slept with, who they murdered and betrayed, how they got here, who they really are. My God, it would be like taking a trip down the sewer in a glass-bottomed boat! But it would be wonderful—if tomorrow were the last day of the world. Only it's not (*he coughs suddenly, chokingly, and spits carefully into his handkerchief*)—not for most of us.

(*In the little office the telegraph instrument begins to clatter and the A.P. man goes back, types rapidly for a moment, and returns with another paper in his hand.*)

A.P. MAN: Here's something, Ted. It might be a story for you. Did you know this guy?

WILLIS (*taking the paper and reading it*): 'In an official communiqué the French Air Ministry today confirmed the report that Flight Lieutenant Clifford McKinley Brownlow of the Lafayette Escadrille was killed in action Tuesday morning over the lines near Soissons. Lieut. Brownlow, who in point of service was one of the oldest pilots in the Escadrille, had previously brought down fourteen German planes and had been decorated with the Croix de Guerre. He was twenty-four years old, and a native of Altamont, Old Catawba.'

(*When he has finished reading, Theodore Willis is silent for a moment and stares straight ahead of him. Then:*)

WILLIS (*speaking very slowly, as if to himself*): Did I know him? . . . Clifford Brownlow . . . Mrs. Brownlow's darling boy . . . the one we used to call 'Miss Susie' . . . and chase home from school every day, calling (*changing his voice to a parody of throaty refinement*): 'Oh Clifford! Are you the-ah?' . . . His mother used to call him like that, and we all took it up. Poor little devil! He must have had a wretched life. Clifford seemed a perfect name for him—for his ice cream pants, his effeminate way of walking and of talking, and all the rest of him. And now? Lieutenant Clifford Brownlow . . . Lafayette Escadrille . . . killed in action. . . . Somehow that seems perfect, too. And not funny either. There'll be speeches now, and ceremonies for 'Miss Susie.' There'll be a statue, too, a park named after him, a Clifford Brownlow school, a Brownlow auditorium. And why? What makes a hero, anyway? . . . Was it because we used to call him 'Miss Susie' and run him home, calling after him: 'Oh

Clifford! Are you the-ah?' Was it because we tormented
the poor little bastard until we almost drove him mad?
Was it because his mother wouldn't let him play with
us, wouldn't let him mingle with the rough, rude boys?
Is that the way a hero's made? . . . Poor kid, he used
to have a game he had invented that he played all by
himself. It was a sort of one-man football game. He had
a dummy rigged up in the yard, something he had
made himself, stuffed with straw and hung on a pulley
and a wire. He had a football uniform, too, complete
with jersey, shoulder pads, and cleated shoes—his
mother always bought him the best of everything. And
we used to go by in the afternoon and see him playing
at his one-man game, running with his brand-new ball,
tackling his home-made dummy, sprinting for a touch-
down through an imaginary broken field. And we—
may God have mercy on our souls—we used to stand
by the fence and jeer at him! . . . Well, he's a hero
now—about the only hero we have. And there'll be
ceremonies, honors, letters to his mother from the
President of the French Republic. He's a hero, and he's
dead. And we? (*He coughs suddenly, chokingly, spits
into his wadded handkerchief, and stares intently at
the spreading blot.*) Well, Joe, (*huskily*) tomorrow
may be the last day of the world. Is there any other
war news?

A.P. MAN: Just the usual run. The French claim
they've broken through and gained another hundred
yards upon a half-mile front. The Germans say they
killed six hundred Frenchmen.

WILLIS (*looking at his watch*): Twelve-two. Two
minutes after five o'clock in France . . . and some
bastard's getting his right at this moment. . . . Another day. . . . For how many will it be the last day
of the world? God, if I only knew that it would be for
me! (*Coughs, goes through the ritual with the handkerchief, then rises, takes off his eyeshade, throws it on*

the desk, and stretches slowly with an air of great weariness and disgust.) Ah-h, Christ!

(The scene fades out. Far off, in darkness, is heard the baying of a hound.)

A Kinsman of His Blood

From time to time, during his Sunday visits to his
Uncle Bascom's house, Eugene would meet his cousin,
Arnold Pentland. Arnold was the only one of Bascom's
children who ever visited his father's house: the rest
were studiously absent, saw their father only at
Christmas or Thanksgiving, and then like soldiers who
will make a kind of truce upon the morning of the
Lord's nativity. And certainly the only reason that
poor, tormented Arnold ever came to Bascom's house
was not for any love he bore him—for their relation to
each other was savage and hostile, as it had been
since Arnold's childhood—but rather, he came
through loneliness and terror, as a child comes home,
to see his mother, to try to find some comfort with her
if he could.

Even in the frequency of these visits, the dissonant
quality of his life was evident. After months of absence he would appear suddenly, morosely, without a
word of explanation, and then he would come back
every Sunday for several weeks. Then he would disap-
pear again, as suddenly as he came: for several
months, sometimes for a year or more, none of them
would see him. The dense and ancient web of Boston
would repossess him—he would be engulfed in oblivion as completely as if the earth had swallowed him.
Then after months of silence, he would again be
heard from: his family would begin to receive postal
cards from him, of which the meaning was often so
confused that nothing was plain save that the furious

resentment that sweltered in him against them was again at work.

Thus, in the same day, Bascom, his daughters, and his other son might all receive cards bearing a few splintered words that read somewhat as follows:

Have changed my name to Arthur Penn. *Do not try to find me, it is useless!* You have made an outcast out of me —now I want only to forget that I ever knew you, have the same blood in my veins. *You have brought this on yourselves—I hope I shall never see your faces again!*
Arthur Penn.

After this explosion they would hear nothing from him for months. Then one day he would reappear without a word of explanation, and for several weeks would put in a morose appearance every Sunday.

Eugene had met him first one Sunday afternoon in February at his uncle's house. Arnold was sprawled out on a sofa as he entered, and his mother, approaching him, spoke to him in the tender, almost pleading tone of a woman who is conscious of some past negligence in her treatment of her child and who is now, pitiably too late, trying to remedy it.

"Arnold," she said coaxingly, "Arnold—will you get up now, please, dear—this is your cousin—won't you say hello to him?"

The great fat obscenity of belly on the sofa stirred, the man got up abruptly and, blurting out something desperate and incoherent, thrust out a soft, grimy hand and turned away.

Arnold Pentland was a man of thirty-six. He could have been rather small of limb and figure had it not been for his great shapeless fatness—a fatness pale and grimy that suggested animal surfeits of unwholesome food. He had lank, greasy hair of black, carelessly parted in the middle, his face, like all the rest of him, was pale and soft, the features blurred by fatness and further disfigured by a greasy smudge of beard. And from this fat, pale face his eyes, brown and weak, looked out on the world with a hysterical shyness of retreat, his mouth trembled uncertainly with a movement that seemed always on the verge of laughter or hysteria, and his voice gagged, worked, stuttered incoherently, or wrenched out desperate, shocking phrases with an effort that was almost as painful as the speech of a paralytic.

His clothing was indescribably dirty. He wore a suit of old blue serge, completely shapeless, shiny with the use of years, and spotted with the droppings of a thousand meals. Half the buttons were burst off the vest, and between vest and trousers there was a six-inch hiatus of dirty shirt and mountainous fat belly. His shoes were so worn that his naked toes showed through, and his socks were barely more than rags, exposing his dirty heels every time he took a step. The whole creature was as grievously broken, dissonant, and exploded as it is possible for a human life to be, and all the time his soft brown eyes looked out with the startled, pleading look of a stricken animal.

It was impossible to remain with him without a painful feeling of embarrassment—a desire to turn away from this pitiable exposure of disintegration. Everyone felt this but his father; as for Bascom, he just dismissed the conduct of his son impatiently, snorting down his nose derisively, or turning away as one would turn away from the gibberings of an idiot.

Dinner that day—the Sunday of Eugene's first meeting with his cousin—was an agonizing experience for everyone save Bascom. Arnold's conduct of his food was a bestial performance; he fell upon it ravenously, tearing at it, drawing it in with a slobbering suction, panting, grunting over it like an animal until layers of perspiration stood out on his pale wide forehead. Meanwhile, his mother was making a pitiable effort to

distract attention from this painful performance; with
a mask of attempted gayety she tried to talk to her
nephew about a dozen things—the news of the day,
the latest researches in "psychology," the base conduct
of the Senate "unreconcilables," or the researches of
Professor Einstein, the wonder-working miracle of the
human mind. At which Arnold, looking up and glaring
defiantly at both of them, would suddenly explode
into a jargon of startling noises that was even more
shocking than his bestial ruminations over food:

"M-m-man at Harvard . . . fourteen languages.
. . . A guh-guh-guh-guh-" he paused and glared at
his mother with a look of desperate defiance while she
smiled pitiable encouragement at him—"a gorilla," he
marched it out at last triumphantly, "can't speak one!"
and he paused again, his mouth trembling, his throat
working convulsively, and then burst out again—"Put
gorilla in cage with man . . . all over! . . . done for!
. . . half a minute!" He snapped his fingers. "Gorilla make mince meat of him. . . . Homer . . .
Dante . . . Milton . . . Newton . . . Laws of Gravity . . . Muh-muh-muh-muh-" again he gagged,
craned his fat neck desperately along the edges of his
dirty collar and burst out—"Mind of man! . . . Yet
when dead—nothing! . . . No good! . . . Seven ten-
penny nails worth more!" He paused, glaring, his
throat working desperately again, and at length
barked forth with triumphant concision: "Brisbane!"
and was still.

"Ah-h!" Bascom muttered at this point, and, his features contorted in an expression of disgust, he pushed
his chair back, and turned half away. "What is he
talking about, anyway? . . . Gorillas—Harvard—
fourteen languages!" Here he laughed sneeringly
down his nose. "Phuh! Phuh! Phuh! Phuh! Phuh!
. . . Homer—Dante—Newton—seven ten-penny nails
—Brisbane! . . . Phuh! Phuh! Phuh! Phuh! Phuh! . . .

Did anyone ever hear such stuff since time began!"
And, contorting his powerful features, he laughed
sneeringly down his nose again.

"Yes!" cried Arnold angrily, throwing down his napkin and glaring at his father with wild, resentful eyes,
shot suddenly with tears—"And you, too! . . . No
match for guh-guh-guh-guh-*gorilla!*" he yelled. "Think
you are! . . . Egotist! . . . Muh-muh-muh-" he paused,
gagging, worked his neck along his greasy collar and
burst out—"Megalomaniac! . . . Always were! . . .
But no match for gorilla. . . . Get you!"

"Ah-h!" Bascom muttered, confiding his eloquent
features into vacancy with an expression of powerful
disgust—"You don't know what you're talking about!
. . . He has no conception—oh, not the slightest!—
not the faintest!—none whatever!" he howled, waving
his great hand through the air with a gesture of scornful dismissal.

The next Sunday, when Eugene went again to Bascom's house, he was surprised when the old man himself came to the door and opened it. In response to
the boy's quick inquiry about his aunt, Bascom,
puckering his face in a gesture of disgust, and jerking
his head toward the kitchen, muttered:

"Ah-h! She's in there talking to that—fool! . . . But
come in, my boy!" he howled, with an instant change
to cordiality. "Come in, come in!" he yelled enthusiasti-
cally. "We've been expecting you."

From the kitchen came the sound of voices—a
woman's and a man's, at first low, urgent, blurred,
then growing louder; and suddenly Eugene could
hear Arnold's voice, the wrenched-out, desperate
speech now passionately excited:

"Got to! . . . I tell you, mother, I've got to! . . .
She needs me . . . and I've got to go!"

"But, Arnold, Arnold!" his mother's voice was tenderly persuasive and entreating. "Now quiet, dear, quiet! Can't you quiet yourself a moment while we talk about it?"

"Nothing to talk about!" his voice wrenched the words out desperately. "You've seen the letters, mother. . . . You see what she says, don't you?" His voice rose to a hysterical scream.

"Yes, dear, but——"

"Then what is there to talk about?" he cried frantically. "Don't you see she wants me? . . . Don't you see she's in some terrible trouble with that—that brute . . . that she's begging me to come and take her away from him?"

"Oh, Arnold, Arnold!" his mother's voice was filled with pitiable entreaty, hushed with an infinite regret. "My poor boy, can't you see that all she says is that if you ever go out there she would be glad to see you." He made some blurted-out reply that was indecipherable, and then, speaking gently but incisively, she continued: "Arnold—listen to me, my dear. This woman is a married woman, twenty years older than yourself, with grown children of her own. Don't you understand, my dear, that those letters are just the friendly letters that a woman would write to a boy she once taught in school? Don't you see how much these letters you have written her have frightened her—how she is trying in a kind way to let you know——"

"It's a lie!" he said in a choking tone—"a dirty lie! You're against me like all the rest of them! I'll not listen to you any longer! I'll go and get her. . . . I'll bring her back with me, no matter what you say . . . and to hell with you!" he yelled. "To hell with all of you!"

There was a sound of scrambling confusion, and then he came flying through the swinging door that led from the kitchen, jamming his battered hat down on his head, his eyes wild with grief and anger, his lips trembling and convulsed, murmuring soundless imprecations as he fled. And his mother followed him, a small wrenlike figure of a woman, her face haggard, stamped with grief and pity, calling: "Arnold! Arnold!" desperately to that fat, untidy figure that went past like a creature whipped with furies, never pausing to look or speak or say good-bye to anyone, as he ran across the room, and left the house, slamming the door behind him.

The story, with its wretched delusion, was pitiable enough. Since his second year at high school, Arnold had cherished a deep affection for a woman who had taught him at that time. She was one of the few women who had ever shown a scrap of understanding for him, and her interest had been just the kindly interest that a warm-hearted and intelligent woman might feel for a wretched little boy. To her, as to everyone else, he had been an ugly duckling, but this had wakened her protective instinct, and actually made him dearer to her than the more attractive children. And because of this she had taught him more —done more for him—than any other person he had ever known, and he had never forgotten her.

When Arnold had left school, this woman had married and moved to California with her husband. But in the twenty years that had elapsed since then her old friendship with the boy—for "boy" he still was to her—had never been broken. During all that time Arnold had written her several times a year—long, rambling letters filled with his plans, despairs, ambitions, hopes, and failures—the incoherent record of an incoherent personality—and the woman had always answered him with short, brisk, friendly letters of her own.

And during all these years, while he remained to her the "boy" that she had taught, her own personality was undergoing a fantastic transformation in his memory. Although she had been a mature and rather spinsterly female when he had known her, and was now a gray-haired woman in the upper fifties, it seemed to him now that she had never been anything but young and beautiful and fair.

And as that picture developed in his mind it seemed to him that he had always loved her—as a man would love a woman—and that the only possible meaning in these casual and friendly letters that she wrote to him lay in the love she bore for him.

Nothing could be done to stop him. For months now he had come to his mother with trembling haste each time that he received one of the letters. He would read them in a trembly voice, finding in the most casual phrases the declarations of a buried love. And his own replies to these friendly notes had become steadily more ardent and intimate, until, at last, they had become the passionate and hysterical professions of a man in love. The effect of this correspondence on the woman was evident—evident to everyone but Arnold himself. At first, her replies had been written in the same friendly tone that had always characterized her notes to him, but a growing uneasiness was apparent. It was evident that in a kindly way she was trying to check this rising tide of passion, divert his emotion into the old channel of fellowship. Then, as his letters increased in the urgent ardor of their confessions, her own had grown steadily more impersonal; the last, in answer to his declaration that he "must see her and would come at once," was decidedly curt. It expressed her cold regret that such a visit as he proposed would be impossible—that she and her family would be "away for the summer"—told him that the journey to California would be long, costly, and unpleasant, and advised him to seek his summer's recreation in some more agreeable and less expensive way.

Even the chilling tenor of this letter failed to quench him. Instead, he "read between the lines," he insisted on finding in these curt phrases the silent eloquence of love, and though months had passed since this last letter, and he had written many ardent times since then, he was even convinced that her protracted silence was just another sign of her love—that she was being suppressed through fear, that she was held in bitter constraint by that tyrannical "brute," her husband—a man of whom he knew nothing, but for whom he had conceived a murderous hatred.

Thus, against all the persuasions of his mother, he had decided to go. And that day when he had fled out of his father's house with bitter imprecations on his lips had marked the final moment of decision. Nothing could be done to stop him, and he went.

He was gone perhaps a month; no one knew exactly how long he was away, for none of his family saw him for about a year. And what the result of that strange meeting may have been, they never heard—and yet never needed to be told.

From that moment on he was completely lost to them; the legend of that last defeat, the ruin of that final and impossible hope was written on him, inscribed on his heart and living in his eyes in letters of unspeakable terror, madness, and despair.

One night a year later, when Eugene had been prowling around the dark and grimy streets of the South Boston slums, he saw a familiar figure in lower Washington Street. It was his cousin, Arnold Pentland. A fine spring rain had been falling all night long, and below the elevated structure the pavements were wet and glistening. Arnold was standing at a corner, looking around with a quick, distracted glance, clutching a tattered bundle of old newspapers under one arm.

Eugene ran across the street, calling to him, "Arnold! Arnold!" The man did not seem to hear at first, then looked around him in a startled way, and at last, as Eugene approached him, calling him by name again, he shrank together and drew back, clutching his bundle of old papers before him with both hands and looking at his cousin with the terror-stricken eyes of a child who has suddenly been attacked.

"Arnold!" Eugene cried again. "*Arnold!* Don't you know me? . . . I'm your cousin—Eugene!" And as he made another step toward the man, his hand outstretched in greeting, Arnold scrambled back with such violent terror that he almost fell, and then, still holding the bundle of old papers before him protectively, stammered:

"Duh-duh-duh-don't know you. . . . Some mistake!"

"Oh, there's no mistake!" the boy cried impatiently. "You know me! I've met you a dozen times at Uncle Bascom's house. . . . Look here, Arnold." He took off his hat so that the man could better see his face. "You know me now, don't you?"

"No!—No!" Arnold gasped, moving away all the time. "Wrong man. . . . Name's not Arnold!"

Eugene stared at him a moment in blank astonishment and then exploded:

"Not Arnold? Of course it's Arnold! Your name's Arnold Pentland, and you're my first cousin. Look here, Arnold—what the hell is this anyway? What are you trying to do?"

"No! . . . No! . . . Mistake, I tell you! . . . Don't know you! Name's not Arnold! . . . Name's Arthur Penn."

"I don't give a damn what you call yourself!" Eugene now cried angrily. "You're Arnold Pentland just the same, and you're not going to get away from me until you admit it! Look here! What kind of trick is this anyway? What are you trying to pull on me?"—

and in his excitement he took the man by his arm and shook him.

Arnold uttered a long, wailing cry of terror and, wrenching free, struggled backward crying:

"You leave me alone now! . . . All of you leave me alone! . . . I never want to see any of you again!"

And, turning, he began to run blindly and heavily away, a grotesque and pitiable figure, clutching his bundle of sodden newspapers, bent over toward the rain.

Eugene watched him go with a feeling of nameless pity, loneliness, and loss—the feeling of a man who for a moment in the huge unnumbered wilderness of life, the roaring jungle of America, sees a face he knows, a kinsman of his blood, and says farewell to him forever. For that moment's vision of that fat, stumbling figure running blindly away from him down a dark, wet street was the last he would ever have. He never saw the man again.

Chickamauga

On the seventh day of August, 1861, I was nineteen
years of age. If I live to the seventh day of August
this year I'll be ninety-five years old. And the way I
feel this mornin' I intend to live. Now I guess you'll
have to admit that that's goin' a good ways back.

I was born up at the Forks of the Toe River in 1842.
Your grandpaw, boy, was born at the same place in
1828. His father, and mine too, Bill Pentland—*your*
great-grandfather, boy—moved into that region way
back right after the Revolutionary War and settled at
the Forks of Toe. The real Indian name fer hit was
Estatoe, but the white men shortened hit to Toe, and
hit's been known as Toe River ever since.

Of course hit was all Indian country in those days.
I've heared that the Cherokees helped Bill Pentland's
father build the first house he lived in, where some of
us was born. I've heared, too, that Bill Pentland's
grandfather came from Scotland back before the Revolution, and that thar was three brothers. That's all
the Pentlands that I ever heared of in this country. If
you ever meet a Pentland anywheres you can rest
assured he's descended from one of those three.

Well, now, as I was tellin' you, upon the seventh
day of August, 1861, I was nineteen years of age. At
seven-thirty in the mornin' of that day I started out
from home and walked the whole way in to
Clingman. Jim Weaver had come over from Big Hick-
ory where he lived the night before and stayed with
me. And now he went along with me. He was the best

friend I had. We had growed up alongside of each
other: now we was to march alongside of each other
fer many a long and weary mile—how many neither
of us knowed that mornin' when we started out.

Hit was a good twenty mile away from where we
lived to Clingman, and I reckon young folks nowadays would consider twenty mile a right smart walk.
But fer people in those days hit wasn't anything at all.
All of us was good walkers. Why Jim Weaver could
keep goin' without stoppin' all day long.

Jim was big and I was little, about the way you see
me now, except that I've shrunk up a bit, but I could
keep up with him anywheres he went. We made hit
into Clingman before twelve o'clock—hit was a hot
day, too—and by three o'clock that afternoon we had
both joined up with the Twenty-ninth. That was my
regiment from then on, right on to the end of the war.
Anyways, I was an enlisted man that night, the day
that I was nineteen years of age, and I didn't see my
home again fer four long years.

Your Uncle Bacchus, boy, was already in Virginny:
we knowed he was thar because we'd had a letter
from him. He joined up right at the start with the
Fourteenth. He'd already been at First Manassas and
I reckon from then on he didn't miss a big fight in
Virginny fer the next four years, except after Antietam
where he got wounded and was laid up fer four
months.

Even way back in those days your Uncle Bacchus
had those queer religious notions that you've heared
about. The Pentlands are good people, but everyone
who ever knowed 'em knows they can go queer on
religion now and then. That's the reputation that
they've always had. And that's the way Back was. He
was a Russellite even in those days: accordin' to his
notions the world was comin' to an end and he was
goin' to be right in on hit when hit happened. That

was the way he had hit figgered out. He was always prophesyin' and predictin' even back before the war, and when the war came, why Back just knowed that this was hit.

Why lawl He wouldn't have missed that war fer anything. Back didn't go to war because he wanted to kill Yankees. He didn't want to kill nobody. He was as tender-hearted as a baby and as brave as a lion. Some fellers told hit on him later how they'd come on him at Gettysburg, shootin' over a stone wall, and his rifle bar'l had got so hot he had to put hit down and rub his hands on the seat of his pants because they got so blistered. He was singin' hymns, they said, with tears a-streamin' down his face—that's the way they told hit, anyway—and every time he fired he'd sing another verse. And I reckon he killed plenty because when Back had a rifle in his hands he didn't miss.

But he was a good man. He didn't want to hurt a fly. And I reckon the reason that he went to war was because he thought he'd be at Armageddon. That's the way he had hit figgered out, you know. When the war came, Back said: "Well, this is hit, and I'm a-goin' to be thar. The hour has come," he said, "when the Lord is goin' to set up His kingdom here on earth and separate the sheep upon the right hand and the goats upon the left—jest like hit was predicted long ago—and I'm a-goin' to be thar when hit happens."

Well, we didn't ask him which side *he* was goin' to be on, but we all knowed which side without havin' to ask. Back was goin' to be on the *sheep* side—that's the way *he* had hit figgered out. And that's the way he had hit figgered out right up to the day of his death ten years ago. He kept prophesyin' and predictin' right up to the end. No matter what happened, no matter what mistakes he made, he kept right on predictin'. First he said the war was goin' to be the Armageddon day. And when that didn't happen he said hit

was goin' to come along in the eighties. And when hit
didn't happen then he moved hit up to the nineties.
And when the war broke out in 1914 and the whole
world had to go, why Bacchus knowed that *that* was
hit.

And no matter how hit all turned out, Back never
would give in or own up he was wrong. He'd say he'd
made a mistake in his figgers somers, but that he'd
found out what hit was and that next time he'd be
right. And that's the way he was up to the time he
died.

I had to laugh when I heared the news of his death,
because of course, accordin' to Back's belief, after you
die nothin' happens to you fer a thousand years. You
jest lay in your grave and sleep until Christ comes and
wakes you up. So that's why I had to laugh. I'd a-give
anything to've been there the next mornin' when Back
woke up and found himself in heaven. I'd've give anything just to've seen the expression on his face. I may
have to wait a bit but I'm goin' to have some fun with
him when I see him. But I'll bet you even then he
won't give in. He'll have some reason fer hit, he'll try
to argue he was right but that he made a little mistake about hit somers in his figgers.

But Back was a good man—a better man than Bacchus Pentland never lived. His only failin' was the
failin' that so many Pentlands have—he went and got
queer religious notions and he wouldn't give them up.

Well, like I say then, Back was in the Fourteenth.
Your Uncle Sam and Uncle George was with the Seventeenth, and all three of them was in Lee's army in
Virginny. I never seed nor heared from either Back or
Sam fer the next four years. I never knowed what had
happened to them or whether they was dead or livin'
until I got back home in '65. And of course I never
heared from George again until they wrote me after
Chancellorsville. And then I knowed that he was

dead. They told hit later when I came back home that hit took seven men to take him. They asked him to surrender. And then they had to kill him because he wouldn't be taken. That's the way he was. He never would give up. When they got to his dead body they told how they had to crawl over a whole heap of dead Yankees before they found him. And then they knowed hit was George. That's the way he was, all right. He never would give in.

He is buried in the Confederate cemetery at Richmond, Virginny. Bacchus went through thar more than twenty years ago on his way to the big reunion up at Gettysburg. He hunted up his grave and found out where he was.

That's where Jim and me thought that we'd be too. I mean with Lee's men, in Virginny. That's where we thought that we was goin' when we joined. But, like I'm goin' to tell you now, hit turned out different from the way we thought.

Bob Saunders was our Captain; L. C. McIntyre our Major; and Leander Briggs the Colonel of our regiment. They kept us thar at Clingman fer two weeks. Then they marched us into Altamont and drilled us fer the next two months. Our drillin' ground was right up and down where Parker Street now is. In those days thar was nothing thar but open fields. Hit's all built up now. To look at hit today you'd never know thar'd ever been an open field thar. But that's where hit was, all right.

Late in October we was ready and they moved us on. The day they marched us out, Martha Patton came in all the way from Zebulon to see Jim Weaver before we went away. He'd known her fer jest two months; he'd met her the very week we joined up and I was with him when he met her. She came from out along Cane River. Thar was a camp revival meetin' goin' on outside of Clingman at the time, and she was visitin' this other gal in Clingman while the revival lasted; and that was how Jim Weaver met her. We was walkin' along one evenin' toward sunset and we passed this house where she was stayin' with this other gal. And both of them was settin' on the porch as we went past. The other gal was fair, and she was dark: she had black hair and eyes, and she was plump and sort of little, and she had the pertiest complexion, and the pertiest white skin and teeth you ever seed; and when she smiled there was a dimple in her cheeks.

Well, neither of us knowed these gals, and so we couldn't stop and talk to them, but when Jim saw the little 'un he stopped short in his tracks like he was shot, and then he looked at her so hard she had to turn her face. Well, then, we walked on down the road a piece and then Jim stopped and turned and looked again, and when he did, why, sure enough, he caught *her* lookin' at him too. And then her face got red—she looked away again.

Well that was where she landed him. He didn't say a word, but Lord! I felt him jerk there like a trout upon the line—and I knowed right then and thar she had him hooked. We turned and walked on down the road a ways, and then he stopped and looked at me and said:

"Did you see that gal back thar?"

"Do you mean the light one or the dark one?"

"You know damn good and well which one I mean," said Jim.

"Yes, I seed her—what about her?" I said.

"Well, nothin'—only I'm a-goin' to marry her," he said.

I knowed then that she had him hooked. And yet I never believed at first that hit would last. Fer Jim had had so many gals—I'd never had a gal in my whole life up to that time, but Lord! Jim would have him a

new gal every other week. We had some fine-lookin'
fellers in our company, but Jim Weaver was the hand-
somest feller that you ever seed. He was tall and lean
and built just right, and he carried himself as straight
as a rod: he had black hair and coal-black eyes, and
when he looked at you he could burn a hole through
you. And I reckon he'd burned a hole right through
the heart of many a gal before he first saw Martha
Patton. He could have had his pick of the whole lot—
a born lady-killer if you ever seed one—and that
was why I never thought that hit'd last.

And maybe hit was a pity that hit did. Fer Jim
Weaver until the day that he met Martha Patton had
been the most happy-go-lucky feller that you ever
seed. He didn't have a care in the whole world—full
of fun—ready fer anything and into every kind of
devilment and foolishness. But from that moment on
he was a different man. And I've always thought that
maybe hit was a pity that hit hit him when hit did—
that hit had to come jest at that time. If hit had only
come a few years later—if hit could only have waited
till the war was over! He'd wanted to go so much—
he'd looked at the whole thing as a big lark—but now!
Well she had him, and he had her: the day they
marched us out of town he had her promise, and in
his watch he had her picture and a little lock of her
black hair, and as they marched us out, and him beside me, we passed her, and she looked at him, and I
felt him jerk again and knowed the look she gave him
had gone through him like a knife.

From that time on he was a different man; from
that time on he was like a man in hell. Hit's funny
how hit all turns out—how none of hit is like what we
expect. Hit's funny how war and a little black-haired
gal will change a man—but that's the story that I'm
goin' to tell you now.

The nearest rail head in those days was eighty mile

away at Locust Gap. They marched us out of town right up the Fairfield Road along the river up past Crestville, and right across the Blue Ridge there, and down the mountain. We made Old Stockade the first day's march and camped thar fer the night. Hit was twenty-four miles of marchin' right across the mountain, with the roads the way they was in those days, too. And let me tell you, fer new men with only two months' trainin' that was doin' good.

We made Locust Gap in three days and a half, and I wish you'd seed the welcome that they gave us! People were hollerin' and shoutin' the whole way. All the women folk and childern were lined up along the road, bands a-playin', boys runnin' along beside us, good shoes, new uniforms, the finest-lookin' set of fellers that you *ever* seed—Lord! you'd a-thought we was goin' to a picnic from the way hit looked. And I reckon that was the way most of us felt about hit, too. We thought we was goin' off to have a lot of fun. If anyone had knowed what he was in fer or could a-seed the passel o' scarecrows that came limpin' back barefoot and half naked four years later, I reckon he'd a-thought twice before he 'listed up.

Lord, when I think of hit! When I try to tell about hit thar jest ain't words enough to tell what hit was like. And when I think of the way I was when I joined up—and the way I was when I came back four years later! When I went away I was an ignorant country boy, so tender-hearted that I wouldn't harm a rabbit. And when I came back after the war was over I could a-stood by and seed a man murdered right before my eyes with no more feelin' than I'd have had fer a stuck hog. I had no more feelin' about human life than I had fer the life of a sparrer. I'd seed a ten-acre field so thick with dead men that you could have walked all over hit without steppin' on the ground a single time.

And that was where I made my big mistake. If I'd only knowed a little more, if I'd only waited jest a little longer after I got home, things would have been all right. That's been the big regret of my whole life. I never had no education. I never had a chance to git one before I went away. And when I came back I could a-had my schoolin' but I didn't take hit. The reason was I never knowed no better: I'd seed so much fightin' and killin' that I didn't care fer nothin'. I jest felt dead and numb like all the brains had been shot out of me. I jest wanted to git me a little patch of land somewheres and settle down and fergit about the world.

That's where I made my big mistake. I didn't wait long enough. I got married too soon, and after that the children came and hit was root, hawg, or die: I had to grub fer hit. But if I'd only waited jest a little while hit would have been all right. In less'n a year hit all cleared up. I got my health back, pulled myself together and got my feet back on the ground, and had more mercy and understandin' in me, jest on account of all the sufferin' I'd seen, than I ever had. And as fer my head, why hit was better than hit ever was: with all I'd seen and knowed I could a-got a schoolin' in no time. But you see I wouldn't wait. I didn't think that hit'd ever come back. I was jest sick of livin'.

But as I say—they marched us down to Locust Gap in less'n four days' time, and then they put us on the cars fer Richmond. We got to Richmond on the mornin' of one day, and up to that very moment we had thought that they was sendin' us to join Lee's army in the north. But the next mornin' we got our orders— and they was sendin' us out west. They had been fightin' in Kentucky: we was in trouble thar; they sent us out to stop the Army of the Cumberland. And that was the last I ever saw of old Virginny. From that time on we fought it out thar in the west and south.

That's where we was, the Twenty-ninth, from then on to the end.

We had no real big fights until the spring of '62. And hit takes a fight to make a soldier of a man. Before that, thar was skirmishin' and raids in Tennessee and in Kentucky. That winter we seed hard marchin' in the cold and wind and rain. We learned to know what hunger was, and what hit was to have to draw your belly in to fit your rations. I reckon by that time we knowed hit wasn't goin' to be a picnic like we thought that hit would be. We was a-learnin' all the time, but we wasn't soldiers yet. It takes a good big fight to make a soldier, and we hadn't had one yet. Early in '62 we almost had one. They marched us to the relief of Donelson—but law! They had taken her before we got thar—and I'm goin' to tell you a good story about that.

U. S. Grant was thar to take her, and we was marchin' to relieve her before old Butcher could git in. We was seven mile away, and hit was comin' on to sundown—we'd been marchin' hard. We got the order to fall out and rest. And that was when I heared the gun and knowed that Donelson had fallen. Thar was no sound of fightin'. Everything was still as Sunday. We was settin' thar aside the road and then I heared a cannon boom. Hit boomed five times, real slow like— Boom!—Boom!—Boom!—Boom!—Boom! And the moment that I heared hit, I had a premonition. I turned to Jim and I said: "Well, thar you are! That's Donelson—and she's surrendered!"

Cap'n Bob Saunders heared me, but he wouldn't believe me and he said: "You're wrong!"

"Well," said Jim, "I hope to God he's right. I wouldn't care if the whole damn war had fallen through. I'm ready to go home."

"Well, he's wrong," said Captain Bob, "and I'll bet money on hit that he is."

Well, I tell you, that jest suited me. That was the way I was in those days—right from the beginnin' of the war to the very end. If thar was any fun or devilment goin' on, any card playin' or gamblin', or any other kind of foolishness, I was right in on hit. I'd a-bet a man that red was green or that day was night, and if a gal had looked at me from a persimmon tree, why, law! I reckon I'd a-clumb the tree to get her. That's jest the way hit was with me all through the war. I never made a bet or played a game of cards in my life before the war or after hit was over, but while the war was goin' on I was ready fer anything.

"How much will you bet?" I said.

"I'll bet you a hundred dollars even money," said Bob Saunders, and no sooner got the words out of his mouth than the bet was on.

We planked the money down right thar and gave hit to Jim to hold the stakes. Well, sir, we didn't have to wait half an hour before a feller on a horse came ridin' up and told us hit was no use goin' any farther —Fort Donelson had fallen.

"What did I tell you?" I said to Cap'n Saunders, and I put the money in my pocket.

Well, the laugh was on him then. I wish you could a-seen the expression on his face—he looked mighty sheepish, I tell you. But he admitted hit, you know, he had to own up.

"You were right," he said. "You won the bet. But— I'll tell you what I'll do!" He put his hand into his pocket and pulled out a roll of bills. "I've got a hundred dollars left—and with me hit's all or nothin'! We'll draw cards fer this last hundred, mine against yorn—high card wins!"

Well, I was ready fer him. I pulled out my hundred, and I said, "Git out the deck!"

So they brought the deck out then and Jim Weaver shuffled hit and held hit while we drawed. Bob Saunders drawed first and he drawed the eight of spades. When I turned my card up I had one of the queens.

Well, sir, you should have seen the look upon Bob Saunders' face. I tell you what, the fellers whooped and hollered till he looked like he was ready to crawl through a hole in the floor. We all had some fun with him, and then, of course, I gave the money back. I never kept a penny in my life I made from gamblin'.

But that's the way hit was with me in those days—I was ready fer hit—fer anything. If any kind of devilment or foolishness came up I was right in on hit with the ringleaders.

Well then, Fort Donelson was the funniest fight that I was ever in because hit was all fun fer me without no fightin'. And that jest suited me. And Stone Mountain was the most peculiar fight that I was in because—well, I'll tell you a strange story and you can figger fer yourself if you ever heared about a fight like *that* before.

Did you ever hear of a battle in which one side never fired a shot and yet won the fight and did more damage and more destruction to the other side than all the guns and cannon in the world could do? Well, that was the battle of Stone Mountain. Now, I was in a lot of battles. But the battle of Stone Mountain was the queerest one of the whole war.

I'll tell you how hit was.

We was up on top of the Mountain and the Yankees was below us tryin' to drive us out and take the Mountain. We couldn't git our guns up thar, we didn't try to—we didn't *have* to git our guns up thar. The only gun I ever seed up thar was a little brass howitzer that we pulled up with ropes, but we never fired a shot with hit. We didn't git a chance to use hit. We no more'n got hit in position before a shell exploded right on top of hit and split that little howitzer plumb in two. Hit jest fell into two parts: you couldn't have made a neater job of hit if you'd cut hit down the middle with a saw. I'll never fergit that little howitzer and the way they split hit plumb in two.

As for the rest of the fightin' on our side, hit was done with rocks and stones. We gathered together a great pile of rocks and stones and boulders all along the top of the Mountain, and when they attacked we waited and let 'em have it.

The Yankees attacked in three lines, one after the other. We waited until the first line was no more'n thirty feet below us—until we could see the whites of their eyes, as the sayin' goes—and then we let 'em have hit. We jest rolled those boulders down on 'em, and I tell you what, hit was an awful thing to watch. I never saw no worse destruction than *that* with guns and cannon during the whole war.

You could hear 'em screamin' and hollerin' until hit made your blood run cold. They kept comin' on and we mowed 'em down by the hundreds. We mowed 'em down without firin' a single shot. We crushed them, wiped them out—jest by rollin' those big rocks and boulders down on them.

There was bigger battles in the war, but Stone Mountain was the queerest one I ever seed.

Fort Donelson came early in the war, and Stone Mountain came later toward the end. And one was funny and the other was peculiar, but thar was fightin' in between that wasn't neither one. I'm goin' to tell you about that.

Fort Donelson was the first big fight that we was in —and as I say, we wasn't really in hit because we couldn't git to her in time. And after Donelson that spring, in April, thar was Shiloh. Well—all that I can tell you is, we was thar on time at Shiloh. Oh Lord, I reckon that we was! Perhaps we had been country boys before, perhaps some of us still made a joke of hit before—but after Shiloh we wasn't country boys no longer. We didn't make a joke about hit after Shiloh. They wiped the smile off of our faces at Shiloh. And after Shiloh we was boys no longer: we was vet'ran men.

From then on hit was fightin' to the end. That's where we learned what hit was like—at Shiloh. From then on we knowed what hit would be until the end.

Jim got wounded thar at Shiloh. Hit wasn't bad— not bad enough to suit him anyways—fer he wanted to go home fer good. Hit was a flesh wound in the leg, but hit was some time before they could git to him, and he was layin' out thar on the field and I reckon that he lost some blood. Anyways, he was unconscious when they picked him up. They carried him back and dressed his wound right thar upon the field. They cleaned hit out, I reckon, and they bandaged hit— thar was so many of 'em they couldn't do much more than that. Oh, I tell you what, in those days thar wasn't much that they could do. I've seen the surgeons workin' underneath an open shed with meat-saws, choppin' off the arms and legs and throwin' 'em out thar in a pile like they was sticks of wood, some-times without no chloroform or nothin', and the screamin' and the hollerin' of the men was enough to make your head turn gray. And that was as much as anyone could do. Hit was live or die and take your chance—and thar was so many of 'em wounded so much worse than Jim that I reckon he was lucky they did anything fer him at all.

I heared 'em tell about hit later, how he come to, a-layin' stretched out thar on an old dirty blanket on the bare floor, and an army surgeon seed him lookin' at his leg all bandaged up and I reckon thought he'd cheer him up and said: "Oh, that ain't nothin'—you'll be up and fightin' Yanks again in two weeks' time."

Well, with that, they said, Jim got to cursin' and a-takin' on something terrible. They said the language he used was enough to make your hair stand up on end. They said he screamed and raved and reached down thar and jerked that bandage off and said—"Like hell I will!" They said the blood spouted up thar like a fountain, and they said that army doctor was so mad he throwed Jim down upon his back and sat on him and he took that bandage, all bloody as hit was, and he tied it back around his leg again and he said: "Goddam you, if you pull that bandage off again, I'll let you bleed to death."

And Jim, they said, came ragin' back at him until you could have heared him fer a mile, and said: "Well, by God, I don't care if I do; I'd rather die than stay here any longer."

They say they had hit back and forth thar until Jim got so weak he couldn't talk no more. I know that when I come to see him a day or two later he was settin' up and I asked him: "Jim, how is your leg? Are you hurt bad?"

And he answered: "Not bad enough. They can take the whole damn leg off," he said, "as far as I'm concerned, and bury hit here at Shiloh if they'll only let me go back home and not come back again. Me and Martha will git along somehow," he said. "I'd rather be a cripple the rest of my life than have to come back and fight in this damn war."

Well, I knowed he meant hit too. I looked at him and seed how much he meant hit, and I knowed thar wasn't anything that I could do. When a man begins to talk that way, thar hain't much you can say to him. Well, sure enough, in a week or two, they let him go upon a two months' furlough and he went limpin' away upon a crutch. He was the happiest man I ever seed. "They gave me two months' leave," he said, "but if they jest let me git back home old Bragg'll have to send his whole damn army before he gits me out of thar again."

Well, he was gone two months or more, and I never knowed what happened—whether he got ashamed of himself when his wound healed up all right, or whether Martha talked him out of hit. But he was back with us again by late July—the grimmest, bitterest-lookin' man you ever seed. He wouldn't talk to me about hit, he wouldn't tell me what had happened, but I knowed from that time on he'd never draw his breath in peace until he left the army and got back home fer good.

Well, that was Shiloh, that was the time we didn't miss, that was where we lost our grin, where we knowed at last what hit would be until the end.

I've told you of three battles now, and one was funny, one was strange, and one was—well, one showed us what war and fightin' could be like. But I'll tell you a fourth one now. And the fourth one was the greatest of the lot.

We seed some big fights in the war. And we was in some bloody battles. But the biggest fight we fought was Chickamauga. The bloodiest fight I ever seed was Chickamauga. Thar was big battles in the war, but thar never was a fight before, thar'll never be a fight again, like Chickamauga. I'm goin' to tell you how hit was at Chickamauga.

All through the spring and summer of that year Old Rosey follered us through Tennessee.

We had him stopped the year before, the time we whupped him at Stone's River at the end of '62. We tard him out so bad he had to wait. He waited thar six months at Murfreesboro. But we knowed he was a-comin' all the time. Old Rosey started at the end of June and drove us out of Shelbyville. We fell back on Tullahoma in rains the like of which you never seed.

The rains that fell the last week in June that year was terrible. But Rosey kept a-comin' on.

He drove us out of Tullahoma too. We fell back across the Cumberland, we pulled back behind the mountain, but he follered us.

I reckon thar was fellers that was quicker when a fight was on, and when they'd seed just what hit was they had to do. But when it came to plannin' and a-figgerin', Old Rosey Rosecrans took the cake. Old Rosey was a fox. Fer sheer natural cunnin' I never knowed the beat of him.

While Bragg was watchin' him at Chattanooga to keep him from gittin' across the Tennessee, he sent some fellers forty mile up stream. And then he'd march 'em back and forth and round the hill and back in front of us again where we could look at 'em, until you'd a-thought that every Yankee in the world was there. But law! All that was just a dodge! He had fellers a-sawin' and a-hammerin', a-buildin' boats, a-blowin' bugles and a-beatin' drums, makin' all the noise they could—you could hear 'em over yonder gittin' ready—and all the time Old Rosey was fifty mile or more down stream, ten mile *past* Chattanooga, a-fixin' to git over way down thar. That was the kind of feller Rosey was.

We reached Chattanooga early in July and waited fer two months. Old Rosey hadn't caught up with us yet. He still had to cross the Cumberland, push his men and pull his trains across the ridges and through the gaps before he got to us. July went by, we had no news of him. "Oh Lord!" said Jim, "perhaps he ain't a-comin'!" I knowed he was a-comin', but I let Jim have his way.

Some of the fellers would git used to hit. A feller'd git into a frame of mind where he wouldn't let hit worry him. He'd let termorrer look out fer hitself. That was the way hit was with me.

With Jim hit was the other way around. Now that he knowed Martha Patton he was a different man. I think he hated the war and army life from the moment that he met her. From that time he was livin' only fer one thing—to go back home and marry that gal. When mail would come and some of us was gittin' letters he'd be the first in line; and if she wrote him why he'd walk away like someone in a dream. And if she failed to write he'd jest go off somers and set down by himself: he'd be in such a state of misery he didn't want to talk to no one. He got the reputation with the fellers fer bein' queer—unsociable—always a-broodin' and a-frettin' about somethin' and a-wantin' to be left alone. And so, after a time, they let him be. He wasn't popular with most of them—but they never knowed what was wrong, they never knowed that he wasn't really the way they thought he was at all. Hit was jest that he was hit so desperate hard, the worst-in-love man that I ever seed. But law! I knowed! I knowed what was the trouble from the start.

Hit's funny how war took a feller. Before the war I was the serious one, and Jim had been the one to play.

I reckon that I'd had to work too hard. We was so poor. Before the war hit almost seemed I never knowed the time I didn't have to work. And when the war came, why I only thought of all the fun and frolic I was goin' to have; and then at last, when I knowed what hit was like, why I was used to hit and didn't care.

I always could git used to things. And I reckon maybe that's the reason that I'm here. I wasn't one to worry much, and no matter how rough the goin' got I always figgered I could hold out if the others could. I let termorrer look out fer hitself. I reckon that you'd have to say I was an optimist. If things got bad, well,

I always figgered that they could be worse; and if they got so bad they couldn't be no worse, why then I'd figger that they couldn't last this way ferever, they'd have to git some better sometime later on.

I reckon toward the end thar, when they got so bad we didn't think they'd ever git no better, I'd reached the place where I jest didn't care. I could still lay down and go to sleep and not worry over what was goin' to come termorrer, because I never *knowed* what was to come and so I didn't let hit worry me. I reckon you'd have to say that was the Pentland in me —our belief in what we call predestination.

Now, Jim was jest the other way. Before the war he was happy as a lark and thought of nothin' except havin' fun. But then the war came and hit changed him so you wouldn't a-knowed he was the same man.

And, as I say, hit didn't happen all at once. Jim was the happiest man I ever seed that mornin' that we started out from home. I reckon he thought of the war as we all did, as a big frolic. We gave hit jest about six months. We figgered we'd be back by then, and of course all that jest suited Jim. I reckon that suited all of us. It would give us all a chance to wear a uniform and to see the world, to shoot some Yankees and to run 'em north, and then to come back home and lord it over those who hadn't been and be a hero and court the gals.

That was the way hit looked to us when we set out from Zebulon. We never thought about the winter. We never thought about the mud and cold and rain. We never knowed what hit would be to have to march on an empty belly, to have to march barefoot with frozen feet and with no coat upon your back, to have to lay down on bare ground and try to sleep with no coverin' above you, and thankful half the time if you could find dry ground to sleep upon, and too tard the rest of hit to care. We never knowed or

thought about such things as these. We never knowed
how hit would be there in the cedar thickets beside
Chickamauga Creek. And if we had a-knowed, if
someone had a-told us, why I reckon that none of us
would a-cared. We was too young and ignorant to
care. And as fer *knowin'*—law! The only trouble about
knowin' is that you've got to know what knowin's *like*
before you know what knowin' *is*. Thar's no one that
can tell you. You've got to know hit fer yourself.

Well, like I say, we'd been fightin' all this time and
still thar was no sign of the war endin'. Old Rosey jest
kept a-follerin' us and— "Lord!" Jim would say, "will
it never end?"

I never knowed myself. We'd been fightin fer two
years, and I'd given over knowin' long ago. With Jim
hit was different. He'd been a-prayin' and a-hopin'
from the first that soon hit would be over and that he
could go back and get that gal. And at first, fer a year
or more, I tried to cheer him up. I told him that it
couldn't last forever. But after a while hit wasn't no
use to tell him that. He wouldn't believe me any
longer.

Because Old Rosey kept a-comin' on. We'd whup
him and we'd stop him fer a while, but then he'd git
his wind, he'd be on our trail again, he'd drive us
back.—"Oh Lord!" said Jim, "will hit never stop?"

That summer I been tellin' you about, he drove us
down through Tennessee. He drove us out of Shelbyville, and we fell back on Tullahoma, to the passes of
the hills. When we pulled back across the Cumberland I said to Jim: "Now we've got him. He'll have to
cross the mountains now to git at us. And when he
does, we'll have him. That's all that Bragg's been
waitin' fer. We'll whup the daylights out of him this
time," I said, "and after that thar'll be nothin' left of
him. We'll be home by Christmas, Jim—you wait and
see."

And Jim just looked at me and shook his head and said: "Lord, Lord, I don't believe this war'll ever end!"

Hit wasn't that he was afraid—or, if he was, hit made a wildcat of him in the fightin'. Jim could get fightin' mad like no one else I ever seed. He could do things, take chances no one else I ever knowed would take. But I reckon hit was jest because he was so desperate. He hated hit so much. He couldn't git used to hit the way the others could. He couldn't take hit as hit came. Hit wasn't so much that he was afraid to die. I guess hit was that he was still so full of livin'. He didn't want to die because he wanted to live so much. And he wanted to live so much because he was in love.

. . . So, like I say, Old Rosey finally pushed us back across the Cumberland. We was in Chattanooga in July, and fer a few weeks hit was quiet thar. But all the time I knowed that Rosey would keep comin' on. We got wind of him again along in August. He had started after us again. He pushed his trains across the Cumberland, with the roads so bad, what with the rains, his wagons sunk down to the axle hubs. But he got 'em over, came down in the valley, then across the ridge, and early in September he was on our heels again.

We cleared out of Chattanooga on the eighth. And our tail end was pullin' out at one end of the town as Rosey came in through the other. We dropped down around the mountain south of town and Rosey thought he had us on the run again.

But this time he was fooled. We was ready fer him now, a-pickin' out our spot and layin' low. Old Rosey follered us. He sent McCook around down toward the south to head us off. He thought he had us in retreat but when McCook got thar we wasn't thar at all. We'd come down south of town and taken our positions along Chickamauga Creek. McCook had gone too far. Thomas was follerin' us from the north and when McCook tried to git back to join Thomas, he couldn't pass us, fer we blocked the way. They had to fight us or be cut in two.

We was in position on the Chickamauga on the seventeenth. The Yankees streamed in on the eighteenth, and took their position in the woods a-facin' us. We had our backs to Lookout Mountain and the Chickamauga Creek. The Yankees had their line thar in the woods before us on a rise, with Missionary Ridge behind them to the east.

The Battle of Chickamauga was fought in a cedar thicket. That cedar thicket, from what I knowed of hit, was about three miles long and one mile wide. We fought fer two days all up and down that thicket and to and fro across hit. When the fight started that cedar thicket was so thick and dense you could a-took a butcher knife and drove hit in thar anywheres and hit would a-stuck. And when that fight was over that cedar thicket had been so destroyed by shot and shell you could a-looked in thar anywheres with your naked eye and seed a black snake run a hundred yards away. If you'd a-looked at that cedar thicket the day after that fight was over you'd a-wondered how a hummin' bird the size of your thumbnail could a-flown through thar without bein' torn into pieces by the fire. And yet more than half of us who went into that thicket came out of hit alive and told the tale. You wouldn't have thought that hit was possible. But I was thar and seed hit, and hit was.

A little after midnight—hit may have been about two o'clock that mornin', while we lay there waitin' for the fight we knowed was bound to come next day —Jim woke me up. I woke up like a flash—you got used to hit in those days—and though hit was so dark you could hardly see your hand a foot away, I

knowed his face at once. He was white as a ghost and
he had got thin as a rail in that last year's campaign.
In the dark his face looked white as paper. He dug his
hand into my arm so hard hit hurt. I roused up sharp-
like; then I seed him and knowed who hit was.

"John!" he said—"John!"—and he dug his fingers in
my arm so hard he made hit ache—"John! I've seed
him! He was here again!"

I tell you what, the way he said hit made my blood
run cold. They say we Pentlands are a superstitious
people, and perhaps we are. They told hit how they
saw my brother George a-comin' up the hill one day
at sunset, how they all went out upon the porch and
waited fer him, how everyone, the children and the
grown-ups alike, all seed him as he clumb the hill,
and how he passed behind a tree and disappeared as
if the ground had swallered him—and how they got
the news ten days later that he'd been killed at Chancellorsville on that very day and hour. I've heared
these stories and I know the others all believe them,
but I never put no stock in them myself. And yet, I
tell you what! The sight of that white face and those
black eyes a-burnin' at me in the dark—the way he
said hit and the way hit was—fer I could feel the men
around me and hear somethin' movin' in the wood—I
heared a trace chain rattle and hit was enough to
make your blood run cold! I grabbed hold of him—
I shook him by the arm—I didn't want the rest of 'em
to hear—I told him to hush up——

"John, he was here!" he said.

I never asked him what he meant—I knowed too
well to ask. It was the third time he'd seed hit in a
month—a man upon a horse. I didn't want to hear no
more—I told him that hit was a dream and I told him
to go back to sleep.

"I tell you, John, hit was no dream!" he said. "Oh
John, I heared hit—and I heared his horse—and I

seed him sittin' thar as plain as day—and he never said a word to me—he jest sat thar lookin' down, and then he turned and rode away into the woods. . . . John, John, I heared him and I don't know what hit means!"

Well, whether he seed hit or imagined hit or dreamed hit, I don't know. But the sight of his black eyes a-burnin' holes through me in the dark made me feel almost as if I'd seed hit too. I told him to lay down by me—and still I seed his eyes a-blazin' thar. I know he didn't sleep a wink the rest of that whole night. I closed my eyes and tried to make him think that I was sleepin' but hit was no use—we lay thar wide awake. And both of us was glad when mornin' came.

The fight began upon our right at ten o'clock. We couldn't find out what was happenin': the woods thar was so close and thick we never knowed fer two days what had happened, and we didn't know fer certain then. We never knowed how many we was fightin' or how many we had lost. I've heared them say that even Old Rosey himself didn't know jest what had happened when he rode back into town next day, and didn't know that Thomas was still standin' like a rock. And if Old Rosey didn't know no more than this about hit, what could a common soldier know? We fought back and forth across that cedar thicket fer two days, and thar was times when you would be right up on top of them before you even knowed that they was thar. And that's the way the fightin' went— the bloodiest fightin' that was ever knowed, until that cedar thicket was soaked red with blood, and thar was hardly a place left in thar where a sparrer could have perched.

And as I say, we heared 'em fightin' out upon our right at ten o'clock, and then the fightin' came our way. I heared later that this fightin' started when the Yanks come down to the Creek and run into a bunch of Forrest's men and drove 'em back. And then they had hit back and forth until they got drove back themselves, and that's the way we had hit all day long. We'd attack and then they'd throw us back, then they'd attack and we'd beat them off. And that was the way hit went from mornin' till night. We piled up there upon their left: they mowed us down with canister and grape until the very grass was soakin' with our blood, but we kept comin' on. We must have charged a dozen times that day—I was in four of 'em myself. We fought back and forth across that wood until there wasn't a piece of hit as big as the palm of your hand we hadn't fought on. We busted through their right at two-thirty in the afternoon and got way over past the Widder Glenn's, where Rosey had his quarters, and beat 'em back until we got the whole way cross the Lafayette Road and took possession of the road. And then they drove us out again. And we kept comin' on, and both sides were still at hit after darkness fell.

We fought back and forth across that road all day with first one side and then tother holdin' hit until that road hitself was soaked in blood. They called that road the Bloody Lane, and that was jest the name fer hit.

We kept fightin' fer an hour or more after hit had gotten dark, and you could see the rifles flashin' in the woods, but then hit all died down. I tell you what, that night was somethin' to remember and to marvel at as long as you live. The fight had set the wood afire in places, and you could see the smoke and flames and hear the screamin' and the hollerin' of the wounded until hit made your blood run cold. We got as many as we could—but some we didn't even try to git—we jest let 'em lay. It was an awful thing to hear. I reckon many a wounded man was jest left to die or burn to death because we couldn't git 'em out.

You could see the nurses and the stretcher-bearers movin' through the woods, and each side huntin' fer hits dead. You could see them movin' in the smoke an' flames, an' you could see the dead men layin' there as thick as wheat, with their corpse-like faces an' black powder on their lips, an' a little bit of moonlight comin' through the trees, and all of hit more like a nightmare out of hell than anything I ever knowed before.

But we had other work to do. All through the night we could hear the Yanks a-choppin' and a-thrashin' round, and we knowed that they was fellin' trees to block us when we went fer them next mornin'. Fer we knowed the fight was only jest begun. We figgered that we'd had the best of hit, but we knowed no one had won the battle yet. We knowed the second day would beat the first.

Jim knowed hit too. Poor Jim, he didn't sleep that night—he never seed the man upon the horse that night—he jest sat there, a-grippin' his knees and starin', and a-sayin': "Lord God, Lord God, when will hit ever end?"

Then mornin' came at last. This time we knowed jest where we was and what hit was we had to do. Our line was fixed by that time. Bragg knowed at last where Rosey had his line, and Rosey knowed where he was. So we waited there, both sides, till mornin' came. Hit was a foggy mornin' with mist upon the ground. Around ten o'clock when the mist began to rise, we got the order and we went chargin' through the wood again.

We knowed the fight was goin' to be upon the right —upon our right, that is—on Rosey's left. And we knowed that Thomas was in charge of Rosey's left.

And we all knowed that hit was easier to crack a flint rock with your teeth than to make old Thomas budge. But we went after him, and I tell you what, that was a fight! The first day's fight had been like playin' marbles when compared to this.

We hit old Thomas on his left at half-past ten, and Breckenridge came sweepin' round and turned old Thomas's flank and came in at his back, and then we had hit hot and heavy. Old Thomas whupped his men around like he would crack a rawhide whup and drove Breckenridge back around the flank again, but we was back on top of him before you knowed the first attack was over.

The fight went ragin' down the flank, down to the center of Old Rosey's army and back and forth across the left, and all up and down old Thomas's line. We'd hit him right and left and in the middle, and he'd come back at us and throw us back again. And we went ragin' back and forth thar like two bloody lions with that cedar thicket so tore up, so bloody and so thick with dead by that time, that hit looked as if all hell had broken loose in thar.

Rosey kept a-whuppin' men around off of his right, to help old Thomas on the left to stave us off. And then we'd hit old Thomas left of center and we'd bang him in the middle and we'd hit him on his left again, and he'd whup those Yankees back and forth off of the right into his flanks and middle as we went fer him, until we run those Yankees ragged. We had them gallopin' back and forth like kangaroos, and in the end that was the thing that cooked their goose.

The worst fightin' had been on the left, on Thomas's line, but to hold us thar they'd thinned their right out and had failed to close in on the center of their line. And at two o'clock that afternoon when Longstreet seed the gap in Wood's position on the right, he took five brigades of us and poured us through. That whupped them. That broke their line and smashed their whole right all to smithereens. We went after them like a pack of ragin' devils. We killed 'em and we took 'em by the thousands, and those we didn't kill and take right thar went streamin' back across the Ridge as if all hell was at their heels.

That was a rout if ever I heared tell of one! They went streamin' back across the Ridge—hit was each man fer himself and the devil take the hindmost. They caught Rosey comin' up—he rode into them—he tried to check 'em, face 'em round, and get 'em to come on again—hit was like tryin' to swim the Mississippi upstream on a boneyard mule! They swept him back with them as if he'd been a wooden chip. They went streamin' into Rossville like the rag-tag of creation—the worst whupped army that you ever seed, and Old Rosey was along with all the rest!

He knowed hit was all up with him, or thought he knowed hit, for everybody told him the Army of the Cumberland had been blowed to smithereens and that hit was a general rout. And Old Rosey turned and rode to Chattanooga, and he was a beaten man. I've heared tell that when he rode up to his headquarters thar in Chattanooga they had to help him from his horse, and that he walked into the house all dazed and fuddled-like, like he never knowed what had happened to him—and that he jest sat thar struck dumb and never spoke.

This was at four o'clock of that same afternoon. And then the news was brought to him that Thomas was still thar upon the field and wouldn't budge. Old Thomas stayed thar like a rock. We'd smashed the right, we'd sent it flyin' back across the Ridge, the whole Yankee right was broken into bits and streamin' back to Rossville for dear life. Then we bent old Thomas back upon his left. We thought we had him, he'd have to leave the field or else surrender. But old

Thomas turned and fell back along the Ridge and put his back against the wall thar, and he wouldn't budge.

Longstreet pulled us back at three o'clock when we had broken up the right and sent them streamin' back across the Ridge. We thought that hit was over then. We moved back stumblin' like men walkin' in a dream. And I turned to Jim—I put my arm around him, and I said: "Jim, what did I say? I knowed hit, we've licked 'em and this is the end!" I never even knowed if he heared me. He went stumblin' on beside me with his face as white as paper and his lips black with the powder of the cartridge-bite, mumblin' and mutterin' to himself like someone talkin' in a dream. And we fell back to position, and they told us all to rest. And we leaned thar on our rifles like men who hardly knowed if they had come out of that hell alive or dead.

"Oh Jim, we've got 'em and this is the end!" I said.

He leaned thar swayin' on his rifle, starin' through the wood. He jest leaned and swayed thar, and he never said a word, and those great eyes of his a-burnin' through the wood.

"Jim, don't you hear me?"—and I shook him by the arm. "Hit's over, man! We've licked 'em and the fight is over!—Can't you understand?"

And then I heared them shoutin' on the right, the word came down the line again, and Jim—poor Jim!—he raised his head and listened, and "Oh God!" he said, "we've got to go again!"

Well, hit was true. The word had come that Thomas had lined up upon the Ridge, and we had to go fer him again. After that I never exactly knowed what happened. Hit was like fightin' in a bloody dream—like doin' somethin' in a nightmare—only the nightmare was like death and hell. Longstreet threw us up that hill five times, I think, before darkness came. We'd charge up to the very muzzles of their guns, and they'd mow us down like grass, and we'd come stumblin' back—or what was left of us—and form again at the foot of the hill, and then come on again. We'd charge right up the Ridge and drive 'em through the gap and fight 'em with cold steel, and they'd come back again and we'd brain each other with the butt end of our guns. Then they'd throw us back and we'd re-form and come on after 'em again.

The last charge happened jest at dark. We came along and stripped the ammunition off the dead—we took hit from the wounded—we had nothin' left ourselves. Then we hit the first line—and we drove them back. We hit the second and swept over them. We were goin' up to take the third and last—they waited till they saw the color of our eyes before they let us have hit. Hit was like a river of red-hot lead had poured down on us: the line melted thar like snow. Jim stumbled and spun round as if somethin' had whupped him like a top. He fell right toward me, with his eyes wide open and the blood a-pourin' from his mouth. I took one look at him and then stepped over him like he was a log. Thar was no more to see or think of now—no more to reach—except that line. We reached hit and they let us have hit—and we stumbled back.

And yet we knowed that we had won a victory. That's what they told us later—and we knowed hit must be so because when daybreak came next mornin' the Yankees was all gone. They had all retreated into town, and we was left there by the Creek at Chickamauga in possession of the field.

I don't know how many men got killed. I don't know which side lost the most. I only know you could have walked across the dead men without settin' foot upon the ground. I only know that cedar thicket which had been so dense and thick two days before you could've drove a knife into hit and hit would of stuck, had been so shot to pieces that you could've looked in thar on Monday mornin' with your naked eye and seed a black snake run a hundred yards away.

I don't know how many men we lost or how many of the Yankees we may have killed. The Generals on both sides can figger all that out to suit themselves. But I know that when that fight was over you could have looked in thar and wondered how a hummin' bird could've flown through that cedar thicket and come out alive. And yet that happened, yes, and something more than hummin' birds—fer men came out, alive.

And on that Monday mornin', when I went back up the Ridge to where Jim lay, thar just beside him on a little torn piece of bough, I heard a redbird sing. I turned Jim over and got his watch, his pocket-knife, and what few papers and belongin's that he had, and some letters that he'd had from Martha Patton. And I put them in my pocket.

And then I got up and looked around. It all seemed funny after hit had happened, like something that had happened in a dream. Fer Jim had wanted so desperate hard to live, and hit had never mattered half so much to me, and now I was a-standin' thar with Jim's watch and Martha Patton's letters in my pocket and a-listenin' to that little redbird sing.

And I would go all through the war and go back home and marry Martha later on, and fellers like poor Jim was layin' thar at Chickamauga Creek.

Hit's all so strange now when you think of hit. Hit all turned out so different from the way we thought. And that was long ago, and I'll be ninety-five years old if I am livin' on the seventh day of August, of this present year. Now that's goin' back a long ways, hain't hit? And yet hit all comes back to me as clear as if hit happened yesterday. And then hit all will go away and be as strange as if hit happened in a dream.

But I have been in some big battles I can tell you. I've seen strange things and been in bloody fights. But the biggest fight that I was ever in—the bloodiest battle anyone has ever fought—was at Chickamauga in that cedar thicket—at Chickamauga Creek in that great war.

The Return of the Prodigal

1. *The Thing Imagined*

Eugene Gant was a writer, and in the great world he had attained some little fame with his books. After a while, indeed, he became quite a famous person. His work was known, and everywhere he went he found that his name had preceded him. Everywhere, that is, except where he would most have wished it—at home.

The reason for this anomaly was not far to seek. His first novel had been based in large measure upon a knowledge of people derived from his boyhood in a little town. When the book came out, the townsfolk read it and thought they recognized themselves in the portraits he had drawn, and almost to a man the town rose up against him. He received threatening letters. He was warned never to show his face again in the precincts from which his very life had sprung.

He had not expected anything like this, and the shock of it had a profound effect upon him. He took it hard. And for seven years thereafter he did not go home again. He became an exile and a wanderer.

And through all these seven years when he did not go back, his thoughts went back forever. At night as he walked the streets of distant cities or tossed sleepless in his bed in foreign lands, he would think of home, recalling every feature of the little town's familiar visage, and wondering what reception he would get at home if he should decide at last to visit it again.

He thought of this so often with the intensity of nostalgic longing that in the end his feelings built up in his mind an image which seemed to him more true than anything that he had ever actually experienced. After that it became an image that never varied. It came back to haunt him a thousand times—this image of what it would be like if he did go home again:

One blustery night toward the end of October a man was walking swiftly down a street in the little town of Altamont in the hill district of Old Catawba. The hour was late, and a small, cold rain was falling, swept by occasional gusts of wind. Save for this solitary pedestrian, the street was bare of life.

The street itself was one of those shabby and nondescript streets whereon the passage of swift change and departed grandeur is strikingly apparent. Even at this dreary season and hour it was possible to see that the street had known a time of greater prosperity than it now enjoyed and that it had once been a pleasant place in which to live. The houses were for the most part frame structures in the style of that ugly, confused, and rather pretentious architecture which flourished forty or fifty years ago, and, so late at night, they were darkened and deserted looking. Many of them were set back in yards spacious enough to give an illusion of moderate opulence and security, and they stood beneath ancient trees, through the bare branches of which the wind howled mournfully. But even in the darkness one could see on what hard times the houses and the street had fallen. The gaunt and many-gabled structures, beaten and swept by the cold rain, seemed to sag and to be warped by age and disrepair, and to confer there dismally like a congress of old crones in the bleak nakedness of night and storm that surrounded them. In the dreary concealments of the dark, one knew by certain instinct that the old houses had fallen upon grievous times and had been unpainted for many years, and even if one's intuition had not conveyed this, the strangely mixed and broken character of the street would have afforded telling evidence of the fate which had befallen it. Here and there the old design of pleasant lawns had been brutally deformed by the intrusion of small, cheap, raw, and ugly structures of brick and cement blocks. These represented a variety of enterprises: one or two were grocery stores, one was a garage, some were small shops which dealt in automobile accessories, and one, the most pretentious of the lot, was a salesroom for a motor car agency. In the harsh light of a corner lamp, broken by the stiff shadows of bare, tangled boughs, the powerful and perfect shapes of the new automobiles glittered splendidly, but in this splendor there was, curiously, a kind of terrible, cold, and desolate bleakness which was even more cruel, lonely, and forbidding than all the other dismal bleakness of the dark old street.

The man, who was the only evidence of life the street provided at this hour, seemed to take only a casual and indifferent interest in his surroundings. He was carrying a small suitcase, and from his appearance he might have been taken for a stranger, but his manner—the certain purpose in his stride, and the swift, rather detached glances he took from time to time at objects along the way—indicated that the scene was by no means an unfamiliar one but had at some period in his life been well known to him.

Arrived at length before an old house set midway down the street, he paused, set down his suitcase on the pavement, and for the first time showed signs of doubt and indecision. For some moments he stood looking with nervous and distracted intentness at the dark house as if trying to read upon its blank and gloomy visage some portent of the life within, or to decipher in one of its gaunt and ugly lineaments some answer to the question in his mind. For some time he stood this way, but at length, with an impatient movement, he picked up his suitcase, mounted the brief flight of concrete steps that went up to the yard, advanced swiftly along the walk and up the steps onto the porch, set down his suitcase at the door, and after a final instant of disturbed hesitancy shook his head, impatiently and almost angrily, and rang the bell.

The bell sent through the old dark hall within, lit dimly at the farther end by one small light, a sharp and vital thring of sound that drew from the man a shocked and involuntary movement, almost of protest and surprise. For a moment his jaw muscles knotted grimly; then, thrusting his hands doggedly into the pockets of his raincoat, he lowered his head and waited.

—They flee us, who beforetime did us seek, with desolate pauses sounding between our chambers, in old chapters of the night that sag and creak and pass and stir and come again. They flee us who beforetime did us seek. And now, in an old house of life, forever in the dark mid-pause and watches of the night, we sit alone and wait.

What things are these, what shells and curios of outworn custom, what relics here of old, forgotten time? Festoons of gathered string and twines of thread, and boxes filled with many buttons, and bundles of old letters covered with scrawled and faded writings of the dead, and on a warped old cupboard, shelved with broken and mended crockery, an old wooden clock where Time his fatal, unperturbed measure keeps, while through the night the rats of time and silence gnaw the timbers of the old house of life.

A woman sits here among such things as these, a woman old in years, and binded to the past, remem-

bering while storm shakes the house and all the festoons of hung string sway gently and the glasses
rattle, the way the dust rose on a certain day, and the
way the sun was shining, and the sound of many
voices that are dead, and how sometimes in these
mid-watches of the night a word will come, and how
she hears a step that comes and goes forever, and old
doors that sag and creak, and something passing in
the old house of life and time in which she waits
alone.

The naked, sudden shock of the bell broke with
explosive force against her reverie. The old woman
started as if someone had spoken suddenly across her
shoulder. Her swollen, misshapen feet were drawn
quickly from the edge of the open oven door where
she had been holding them for warmth, and, glancing
around and upward sharply with the sudden attentive-
ness of a startled bird, she cried out instinctively, although no one was there: "Hah? What say?"

Then, peering through her glasses at the wooden
clock, she got up slowly, stood for a moment holding
her broad, work-roughened hands clasped loosely at
the waist, and after a few seconds' troubled indecision
went out into the hall and toward the closed front
door, peering uncertainly and with a puzzled, troubled look upon her face as she approached. Arrived at
the door, she paused again and, still holding her
hands in their loose clasp across her waist, she waited
a moment in uncertain and troubled meditation.
Then, grasping the heavy brass knob of the door, she
opened it cautiously a few inches and, prying out into
the dark with curious, startled face, she repeated to
the man she saw standing there the same words that
she had spoken to herself in solitude a minute or two
before: "Hah? What say?"—and immediately, with a
note of sharp suspicion in her voice: "What do you
want?"

He made no answer for a moment, but had there been light enough for her to observe the look upon his face she might have seen him start and change expression, and be about to speak, and check himself with an almost convulsive movement of control. Finally he said quietly:

"A room."

"What's that?" she said, peering at him suspiciously and almost accusingly. "A room, you say?" Then, sharply, after a brief pause: "Who sent you?"

The man hesitated, then said: "Someone I met in town. A man in the lunchroom. I told him I had to put up somewhere overnight, and he gave me your address."

She answered him as before, repeating his words in the same suspicious manner, yet her tone also had in it now a certain quality of swift reflection, as if she were not so much questioning him as considering his words. "A man—lunchroom—say he told you?" she said quickly. And then instantly, as if for the first time recognizing and accepting the purpose of this nocturnal visit, she added: "Oh, yes! MacDonald! He often sends me people. . . . Well, come in," she said, and opened the door and stood aside for him to enter. "You say you want a room?" she went on now more tolerantly. "How long do you intend to stay?"

"Just overnight," he said. "I've got to go on in the morning."

Something in his tone awoke a quick and troubled recollection in her. In the dim light of the hall she peered sharply and rather painfully at him with a troubled expression on her face, and, speaking with the same abrupt and almost challenging inquiry that had characterized her former speech but now with an added tinge of doubt, she said: "Say you're a stranger here?"—although he had said nothing of the sort. "I guess you're here on business, then?"

"Well—not exactly," he answered hesitantly. "I guess you could almost call me a stranger, though. I've been away from here so long. But I came from this part of the country."

"Well, I was thinkin'," she began in a doubtful but somewhat more assured tone, "there was somethin' about your voice. I don't know what it was, but—" she smiled a tremulous yet somewhat friendly smile—"it seemed like I must have heard it somewhere. I knew you must have come from somewheres around here. I knew you couldn't be a Northern man—you don't have that way of talkin'. . . . Well, then, come in," she said conciliatingly, as if satisfied with the result of her investigation, "if it's only a room for the night you want, I guess I can fix you up. You'll have to take things as you find them," she said bluntly. "I used to be in the roomin'-house business, but I'm not young enough or strong enough to take the interest in it I once did. This house is gettin' old and run-down. It's got too big for me. I can't look after it like I used to. But I try to keep everything clean, and if you're satisfied with things the way they are, why—" she folded her hands across her waist in a loose, reflective gesture and considered judicially for a moment—"why," she said, "I reckon you can have the room for fifty cents."

"It's little enough," she thought, "but still it looks as if that's about all he's able to pay, an' things have got to such a state nowadays it's either take what you can get an' get somethin', or take nothin' at all an' lose everything. Yes, he's a pretty seedy-lookin' customer, all right," she went on thinking. "A fly-by-night sort of feller if I ever saw one. But then I reckon MacDonald had a chance to size him up, an' if MacDonald sent him I guess it's all right. An', anyway, that's the only kind that ever comes here nowadays. The better class all have their automobiles an' want to get out in the

mountains. And besides, no one wants to come to an
old, cold, run-down sort of place like this if they can
afford to go to a hotel. So I'd better let him in, I guess,
an' take what little he can pay. It's better than nothin'
at all."

During the course of this reflection she was peering
through her glasses at him sharply and intently, and
with a somewhat puzzled and troubled expression on
her face. The figure that her old, worn, and enfeebled
eyes made out in the dim, bleak light of the hall was
certainly far from prepossessing. It was that of an
uncommonly tall man, heavily built, and shabbily
dressed in garments which were badly in need of
pressing, and which, as she phrased it to herself,
"looked as if he'd come the whole way across the country in a day coach." His face was covered with the
heavy black furze of a week-old beard, and, although
the features were neither large nor coarse, they had,
somewhere in life, suffered a severe battering. The
nose, which was short, tilted, and pugnacious-
looking, had been broken across the ridge and was
badly set, and there was a scar which ran slant-wise
across the base of the nose. This disfigurement gave
the man's face a somewhat savage appearance, an
impression which was reinforced by the look in his
eyes. His eyes, which were brown, had a curiously
harsh and dark and hurt look in them, as though the
man had been deeply wounded by life and was trying
to hide the fact with a show of fierce and naked trucu-
lence as challenging as an angry word.

Nevertheless, it was the cold anger in his eyes that
somehow finally reassured the old woman. As he returned her prying stare with his direct and angry look
she felt vaguely comforted, and reflected: "Well, he's
a rough-lookin' customer, sure enough, but then he
looks honest—nothin' hang-dog about him—an' I
reckon it's all right."

And, aloud, she repeated: "Well, then, come on. If you're satisfied with things the way they are, I guess I can let you have this room here."

Then turning, she led the way into a room which opened from the hall to the right and switched on the dingy light. It was a large front room, gaunt in proportions like the house, high-ceilinged, cheerless, bare and clean and cold, with whitewashed walls. There was a black old fireplace, fresh-painted and unused, which gave a bleak enhancement to the cold white bareness of the room. A clean but threadbare carpet covered the worn planking of the floor. In one corner there was a cheap dresser with an oval mirror, in another a small washstand with a bowl and pitcher and a rack of towels, and in the ugly bay window which fronted the street side of the house there was a nondescript small table covered with a white cloth. Opposite the door stood a clean but uninviting white iron bed.

The old woman stood for a moment with her hands clasped loosely at her waist as she surveyed the room with a reflective stare.

"Well," she remarked at last with an air of tranquil and indifferent concession, "I reckon you'll find it pretty cold in here, but then there's no one in the house but one roomer and myself, an' I can't afford to keep fires burnin' in a house like this when there's nothin' comin' in. But you'll find things clean enough," she added quietly, "an' there's lots of good, warm covers on the bed. You'll sleep warm enough, an' if you're gettin' up to make an early start tomorrow, I don't guess you'll want to sit up late anyway."

"No, ma'am," he answered, in a tone that was at once harsh and hurt. "I'll get along all right. And I'll pay you now," he said, "in case I don't see you in the morning when I leave."

He fished into his pockets for a coin and gave it to

her. She accepted it with the calm indifference of old,
patient, unperturbed people, and then remained standing there in a reflective pause while she gave the room
a final meditative look before leaving him.

"Well, then," she said, "I guess you've got all you
need. You'll find clean towels on the washstand rack,
and the bathroom's upstairs at the end of the first hallway to the left."

"Thank you, ma'am," he answered in the same tone
as before. "I'll try not to disturb anyone."

"There's no one to disturb," she said quietly. "I
sleep at the back of the house away from everything,
an' as for Mr. Gilmer—he's the only steady roomer
I've got left—he's been here for years, an' he's so quiet
I hardly know when he's in the house. Besides, he
sleeps so sound he won't even know you're here. He's
still out, but he ought to be comin' in any minute now.
So you needn't worry about disturbin' us. An' no one
will disturb you either," she said, looking straight at
him suddenly and smiling the pale, tremulous smile of
an old woman with false teeth. "For there's one thing
sure—this is as quiet a house as you could find. So if
you hear anyone comin' in, you needn't worry; it's
only Mr. Gilmer goin' to his room.'"

"Thank you," the man said coldly. "Everything's all
right. And now," he added, turning away as if anxious
to terminate a more protracted conversation, "I'm
going to turn in. It's past your bedtime, too, and I
won't keep you up, ma'am, any longer."

"Yes," she said hastily, turning to go, yet still regarding him with a puzzled, indecisive look. "Well, then, if
there's anything else you need——"

"No, ma'am," he said. "I'll be all right. Good night
to you."

"Good night," she answered, and, after one more
parting glance around the cold walls of the room, she
went out quietly and closed the door behind her.

For a moment after she was gone, the man stood motionless and made no sound. Then he looked about him slowly, rubbing his hand reflectively across the rough furze-stubble of his beard. His traveling gaze at length rested on his reflected image in the dresser mirror, and for a brief instant he regarded himself intently, with a kind of stupid and surprised wonder. And suddenly his features were contorted by a grimace as anguished and instinctive as a cornered animal's.

Almost instantly, however, it was gone. He ran his hands through his disheveled hair and shook his head angrily as though throwing off a hurt. Then quickly and impatiently he took off his coat, flung it down across a chair, sat down upon the bed, bent and swiftly untied his muddy shoes and removed them, and then sat there numbly in a stupor for some minutes, staring before him blindly at the wall. The cold, white bareness of the room stole over him and seemed to hold his spirit in a spell.

At length he stirred. For a moment his lips moved suddenly. Slowly he looked around the bare white walls with an expression of dawning recognition and disbelief. Then, shaking his head and shrugging his thick shoulders with an involuntary and convulsive shudder, he got up abruptly, switched off the light, and, without removing the rest of his clothes, lay down upon the bed and drew a quilt across his body.

And then, while storm beat against the house and cold silence filled it, he lay there, flat and rigid on his back, staring up with fixed eyes into blackness. But at last the drug of cold, dark silence possessed him, his eyes closed, and he slept.

In the old house of time and silence there is something that creaks forever in the night, something that moves and creaks forever, and that never can be still.

The man awoke instantly, and instantly it was as if he had never slept at all. Instantly it was as if he had never been absent from the house, had never been away from home.

Strong, unreasoning terror gripped him, numb horror clove his breath, the cold, still silence laid its hand upon his heart. For in his brain it seemed a long-forgotten voice had just re-echoed, in his heart a word, and in his ear it seemed a footfall, soft and instant, had just passed.

"Is anybody there?" he said.

Storm beat about the house, and darkness filled it. There was nothing but cold silence and the million drumming hoof-beats of small rain.

"But I heard it!" his mind repeated. "I heard a voice now lost, belonging to a name now seldom spoken. I heard a step that passed here—that of a phantom stranger and a friend—and with it was a voice that spoke to me, saying the one word, 'Brother!'

"Is it the storm," he said to himself, "that has a million voices? Is it the rain? Is it the darkness that fills an old house of life and gives a tongue to silence, a voice to something that moves and creaks forever in the night? Or is it the terror of cold silence that makes of my returning no return, and of me an alien in this house, where my very mother has forgotten me? Oh, is it the cold and living silence of strong terror moving in the house at night that stabs into the living heart of man the phantom daggers of old time and memory? Is there a tongue to silence and the dark?——"

Light and instant as the rain a footfall passed above him.

"Who's there?" he said.

Storm beat upon the house, and silence filled it. Strong darkness prowled there and the bare boughs creaked, and something viewless as the dark had come into the house, and suddenly he heard it again and knew that it was there.

Above his head, in Ben's old room—the room of his brother, Ben, now dead these many years, and, like himself, forgotten too—he heard a light, odd step, as nimble as a bird's, as soft as ashes, and as quick as rain.

And with the step he heard once more the old familiar voice, saying softly:

"Brother! Brother! . . . What did you come home for? . . . You know now that you can't go home again!"

2. *The Real Thing*

Eugene Gant had been seven years from home, and many times in those long years of absence he had debated with himself, saying: "I will go home again. I shall lay bare my purposes about the book, say my piece, speak so that no man living in the world can doubt me. Oh, I shall tell them till the thing is crystal clear when I go home again."

Concerning the town's bitter and ancient quarrel with him, he knew that there was much to say that could be said. He also knew that there was much to say that never could be spoken. But time passes, and puts halters to debate. And one day, when his seven years were up, he packed his bag and started out for home.

Each man of us has his own America, his own stretch, from which, here outward, the patterns are familiar as his mother's face and the prospect is all his. Eugene's began at Gettysburg, his father's earth; then southward through Hagerstown, and down the Valley of Virginia.

First, the great barns, the wide sweep and noble

roll of Pennsylvania fields, the neat-kept houses. Lower down, still wide fields, still neat-kept houses, white fences and painted barns, a grace and sweetness that still lingers in the Valley of Virginia. But now, for the first time, the hodden drab of nigger gray also appears—gray barns, gray sheds, gray shacks and lean-tos sturdy to the weather that had given them this patina to make up for the lack of paint. Now, too, the gashed and familiar red of common clay. To Eugene Gant returning home it was all most beautiful, seen so with the eyes of absence.

The rains of spring were heavy through Virginia, the land was sodden and everywhere was spotted with wet pools of light. It was almost the time of apple blossoms, and faintly there was the smell of rain and apple blossoms on the air.

Through the Valley of Virginia he went down very slowly. And slowly the rains lifted, and one day, in sun and light, the blue veil round the shouldering ramparts of the great Blue Ridge appeared.

Quickly, now, the hills drew in out of wide valley-dom, and signs of old kept spaciousness vanished into the blue immediate. Here was another life, another language of its own—the life and language of creek, hill, and hollow, of gulch and notch and ridge and knob, and of cabins nestling in their little patches of bottom land.

And suddenly Eugene was back in space and color and in time, the weather of his youth was round him, he was home again.

Following some deep, unreasoning urge that sought to delay the moment and put off the final impact of his return, he took a circuitous course that carried him southwestward from Virginia into Tennessee, then south again, beyond the high wall of the mountains, to Knoxville. From there the road to Altamont is long and roundabout. Almost at once it starts to mount the ramparts of the Great Smokies. It winds in and out, and goes by rocky waters boiling at the bottom of steep knolls, then climbs, climbs, winds and climbs. May is late and cold among the upper timber. Torn filaments of mist wash slowly round the shoulders of the hills. Here the chestnut blight is evident: ruined, in the blasted sweeps, the great sentries of the heights appear.

Very steep, now, the road went up across the final crest of the mountains. The ruined hulks of the enormous chestnut trees stood bleakly on the slopes. High up on the eroded hillsides, denuded of their growth, were the raw scars of mica pits. Beyond, stretching into limitless vistas, were the blue and rugged undulations of a lost and forgotten world. And suddenly a roadside sign—Eugene was back in Old Catawba, and the road started down again, to Zebulon.

Zebulon—the lost world. Zebulon—the syllables that shaped the very clay of his mother's ancestral earth.

And all at once he heard his mother's voice echo across the years: "Son! Son! . . . Where are you, boy? I'll vow—where has he gone?" And with it came faint echoes of the bell that came and went like cloud shadows passing on a hill, and like the lost voices of his kinsmen in the mountains long ago. With it returned old memories of his mother's endless stories about her people, stories of Marches long ago, of bleak dusk and rutted clay, of things that happened at sunset in the mountains when the westering red was pale, ragged, cold, and desolate, and winter was howling in the oak.

And with the echo of his mother's voice, that had seemed to fill all the days of his childhood with its unending monotone, there returned to him an immediate sense of everything that he had ever known: the front porch of the old house in Altamont where he had lived, the coarse and cool sound of Black's cow munching grass in the alleyway, along the edges of the backyard fence, the mid-morning sound of sawn ice out in the hot street of summer, the turbaned slatterns of good housewives awaiting noon, the smell of turnip greens, and, upon the corner up above, the screeching halt of the street car, and the sound of absence after it had gone, then the liquid smack of leather on the pavement as the men came home at noon for dinner, and the slam of screen doors and the quiet greetings; and, inside the house, the cool, stale smell of the old parlor, and the coffined, rich piano smell, the tinkling glasspoints of the chandelier, the stereopticon of Gettysburg, the wax fruit on the mantel underneath its glass hood, and he himself reclining on his father's couch, buried in a book, his imagination soaring with Grimm, and with thoughts of witches, a fair princess, fairies, elves, and gnomes, and of a magic castle on a rock.

Then a memory of one particular day, and his mother's voice again:

"Child! Child! . . . I'll vow—where is that boy? . . . Son! Son! Where are you? . . . Oh, here! Boy, here's your Uncle Bacchus. He comes from Zebulon, where all your folks—*my* folks—were from. Father lived for years in Zebulon, where he was born a hundred years ago—an' Uncle Bacchus, he was my father's brother."

And then the voice of Uncle Bacchus, drawling, quiet as the sifting of the winter ash, impregnant with all time and memory, and in it suggestive overtones of the voices of lost kinsmen long ago: "I knowed the minute that I seed him, 'Liza—fer he looks like you." The voice was benevolent, all-sure, triumphant, unforgettable—as hateful as the sound of good and unctuous voices that speak softly while men drown. It was the very death-watch of a voice, the voice of one who waits and watches, all-triumphant, while others die, and then keeps vigil by the dead in a cabin in the hills, and drawls the death-watch out to the accompaniment of crackling pine-knots on the hearth and the slow crumbling of the ash.

"Your Uncle Bacchus, child, from Zebulon——"

So memory returned with Eugene Gant's return. And this was Zebulon. Now down the stretch of road he went his own way home. The tallest hills in all the eastern part of North America soared on every side. The way wound steeply down by blighted chestnut trees and brawling waters into the mountain fastnesses of old Zebulon.

And the voice of Uncle Bacchus came back again:

"Yore grandpaw, son, was my own brother. He was born, like all of us, on the South Toe out in Zebulon. He married yore grandmaw thar and settled down and raised a family. His paw before him—my paw, too—he come in thar long years before. I've heerd him tell it was wild country then. Thar was Cherokees when yore great-grandpaw first come in thar. Yes, sir. And he hunted, fished, and laid traps fer bear. He growed or trapped everything he et. He was a great hunter, and one time they say he run the hounds the whole way over into Tennessee."

Then his mother's voice again:

"That's the way it was, all right. I've heard father tell about it a thousand times. . . . You must go out there some day, son. It's many years since I was there, but dozens of my people are still livin' out in Zebulon. There's Uncle John, an' Thad an' Sid, an' Bern, Luke, an' James—they're all there with the families they have raised. . . . Well, now, I tell you what—Uncle Bacchus is right about it. It was a wild place back in those days. Why, father used to tell us how much wild life there was even in his time. But look here—

why, wasn't I readin' about it just the other day?—an article, you know—says the wild life has all gone now."

The county seat of Zebulon is a little town. Eugene decided to stay overnight and see if he could hunt out any of his mother's people. There was no hotel, but he found a boarding house. And the moment he began to make inquiries about the Pentlands, his mother's family, he seemed to run into people everywhere who said they were relatives of his. Most of them he had never seen before, or even heard of, but as soon as he identified himself they all appeared to know who he was, and the first show of suspicion and mountain aloofness with which they had greeted him when they thought him a stranger quickly melted into friendly interest when they placed him as "Eliza Pentland's boy." One man in particular proved most obliging.

"Why, hell," he said, "we've all heard of you from your cousin Thad. He lives a mile from town. And your Uncle Johnny and Bern and Sid—the whole crowd of them are out upon the Toe. They'll want to see you. I can drive you out tomorrow. My name is Joe Pentland, and we're fifth cousins. Everybody's kinfolks here. There are only fifteen thousand people in Zebulon County, and we're all related somehow. . . . So you're goin' home again? Well, it's all blown over now. The people who were mad about the book have forgotten it. They'll be glad to see you. . . . Well, you won't find this much of a town after the cities you have seen. Six hundred people, a main street, a few stores and a bank, a church or two—that's all there is. . . . Yes, you can get cigarettes in the drug store. It's still open—this is Saturday night. You'd better wear your coat. We're thirty-seven hundred feet up here—we've got a thousand feet on

Altamont—you'll find it cooler than it is down there.
. . . I'll go with you."

The night had the chill cool of mountain May, and
as the two men walked along, a nerve, half ecstasy,
was set atremble in Eugene's blood. The country
street was fronted by a few brick stores, their monot-
ony broken only by the harsh rawness of the Baptist
Church. A light was burning inside the church, and
the single squat and ugly window that faced the
street depicted Christ giving mercy in the bleak colors
of raw glass. The drug store was on the corner at the
crossroads. Next door was a lunchroom. Three or four
ancient and very muddy Fords were parked slanting
at the curb before the drug store. A few feet away,
outside the lunchroom, there was a huddled group of
men in overalls, attentive, watching, like men looking
at a game of cards. From the center of the group
came a few low words—drawling, mountain-quiet,
somehow ominous. Eugene's companions spoke casually to one of the men:

"What is it, Bob?"

The answer came evasive, easy, mountain-quiet
again:

"Oh, I don't know. A little argument, I guess."

"Who was that?" asked Eugene as they entered the
drug store.

"That was Bob Creasman. Said there was some argument going on. Ted Reed's there—he's my cousin—
and he's drunk again. It happens every Saturday
night. A bunch of 'em was at the quarry this
afternoon, and they've been drinkin' corn. I guess
they're arguin' a bit. . . . What's yours? A Coca-
Cola? . . . Make it two cokes and a couple of packs
of Chesterfields."

Five minutes later, as the two men emerged from
the drug store, there was a just-perceptible stir in the
attentive group of men outside.

"Wait a minute," said Joe Pentland. "Let's see what's goin' on."

There was the same quietness as before, but the waiting men were now drawn back against the lunch-room window, and in front of them two others stood and faced each other. One of them was in overalls, and he was saying:

"Now, Ted. . . ."

The other was more urbanely clothed in dark trousers and a white shirt without a collar. His hat was pushed to the back of his head, and he just stood there staring heavily, his sullen face, sleepy-eyed, thrust forward, silent, waiting.

"Now, Ted," the one in overalls repeated. "I'm warnin' ye. . . . You're goin' too fer now. . . . Now leave me be."

Drowsy-eyed, swart-visaged, and unspeaking, a little sagging at the jowls, a little petulant like a plump child, darkly and coarsely handsome, with his head thrust forward, the other listens sullenly, while the men, attentive, feeding, wait.

"You leave me be now, Ted. . . . I'm not lookin' fer no trouble, so you leave me be."

Still sullen and unspeaking, the swart visage waits.

"Ted, now, I'm tellin' ye. . . . When ye cut me up six years ago, yore family an' yore kinfolks begged you out of hit. . . . Now you leave me be. . . . I'm not lookin' fer no trouble with ye, Ted, but you're goin' too fer now. . . . You leave me be."

"It's Ted Reed and Emmet Rogers," Joe whispers hoarsely in Eugene's ear, "and they've started in again. They had a fight six years ago. Ted cut Emmet up, and now they always get this way on Saturday night. Ted, he gets to drinkin' and acts big—but pshaw! he wouldn't hurt a fly. He ain't got the kind of guts it takes to be *real* mean. Besides, Will Saggs is

here—the one there in the white shirt—he's the cop.
Will's scared—you can see that. Not scared of Ted,
though. See that big man standin' back of Will—that's
Lewis Blake, Ted's cousin. That's who Will's afraid of.
Lewis is the kind that won't take nothin' off of
nobody, and if it wasn't for him Will Saggs would
break this up. . . . *Wait* a minute! Something's happening!"

A quick flurry, and——

"Now, goddam you, Ted, you leave me be!"

The two men are apart now, Ted circling the other,
and slowly his hand goes back upon his hip.

"Look out!"—shouted from the crowd. "He's got his
gun!"

There is the dull wink of blue metal at Ted Reed's
hips, the overalled line fades back, and every waiting
man now jumps for cover. The two principals are left
alone.

"Go on and shoot, goddam you! I'm not afraid of
you!"

To Eugene, who has dodged back into the recessed
entrance of the drug store, someone calls out sharply:
"Better git behind a car there at the curb, man! You
ain't got no protection in that doorway!"

Moving with the urgency of instant fear, Eugene
dives across the expanse of open pavement just as the
explosion of the first shot blasts the air. The bullet
whistles right past his nose as he ducks behind a car.
Cautiously he peers around the side to see Emmet
moving slowly with a strange grin on his face, circling
slowly to the shot, mocking his antagonist with the
gun, his big hands spread palms outward in a gesture
of invitation.

"Go on, goddam you, shoot! You bastard, I'm not
scared of you!"

The second shot blows out a tire on the car Eugene

has retreated to. He crouches lower—another shot—the sharp hiss of escaping air from another tire, and Emmet's whine, derisive, scornful:

"Why, go on and shoot, goddam you!"

A fourth shot——

"Go on! Go on! Goddam you, I'm not——"

A fifth—and silence.

Then Ted Reed comes walking slowly past the row of cars. Men step out from behind them and say quietly:

"What's wrong, Ted?"

Sullenly, the gun held straight downward at his thigh: "Oh, he tried to git smart with me."

Other voices now, calling to each other:

"Where'd he git 'im?"

"Right underneath the eye. He never knowed what hit 'im."

"You'd better go on, Ted. They'll be lookin' fer you now."

Still sullen: "The bastard wasn't goin' to git smart with me. . . . Who's this?"—stopping to look Eugene up and down.

Joe Pentland, quickly: "Must be a cousin of yours, Ted. Leastways, he's a cousin of mine. You know—the feller who wrote that book."

With a slow and sullen grin Ted shifts the gun and offers his hand. The hand of murder is thick flesh, strong, a little sticky, cool and moist.

"Why, sure, I know about you. I know your folks. But, by God, you'd better never put *this* in a book! Because if you do——"

Other voices, coaxingly: "You better go along now, Ted, before the sheriff gits here. . . . Go on, you fool, go on."

"Because if you do—" with a shake of the head and a throaty laugh—"you and me's goin' to git together!"

The voices breaking in again: "You're in fer it this time, Ted. You carried it too fer this time."

"Hell, you couldn't git a jury here in Zebulon to convict a Reed!"

"Go on, now. They'll be looking fer ye."

"They don't make jails that can hold a Reed!"

"Go on. Go on."

And he was gone, alone, and with his gun still in his hand—gone right down the middle of the quiet street, still sullen-jowled and sleepy-eyed—leaving a circle of blue-denimed men, and a thing there on the pavement which, two minutes before, had been one of their native kind.

Eugene saw it all, and turned away with a leaden sickness in his heart. And once again he heard the echoes of his mother's voice, saying:

"The wild life has all gone now."

At last Eugene was home again in Altamont, and at first it was good to be home again. How many times in those seven years had he dreamed and thought of going home and wondered what it would be like! Now he was back, and saw, felt, knew it as it really was—and nothing was the way he had imagined it. Indeed, there was very little that was even as he remembered it.

Of course there were some things that had not changed, some things that were still the same. He heard again all the small familiar sounds of his boyhood: the sounds of night, of voices raised in final greetings, saying "Good night" as screen doors slammed—"Good night," far off, and the receding thunderdrone of a racing motor—"Good night," and the last street car going—"Good night," and the rustle of the maple leaves around the street light on the corner. Again he heard in the still-night distance the barking of a dog, the shifting of the engines in the yards, the heavy thunder of the wheels along the river's edge, the clanking rumble of the long freights, and far off, wind-broken, mournful, the faint tolling of the bell. He saw again the first blue light of morning break against the rim of eastern hills, and heard the first cock's crow just as he had heard it a thousand times in childhood.

Niggertown was also still the same, with the branchmire running in the nigger depths, yellow, rank with nigger sewage. And the smells were just the same—the sour reek from the iron laundry pots mixed in with the branchmire smell and the acrid tang of woodsmoke from the nigger shacks. So, too, no doubt, were the smells the same inside of nigger-shackdom— the smells of pork, urine, nigger funk, and darkness. He remembered all of this with the acid etchings of a thousand wintry mornings, when, twenty-five years ago, with the canvas strap around his neck and the galling weight of the bag forever pulling at him, he had gone down to Niggertown upon his paper route and had heard, a hundred times repeated every morning, the level smack of ink-fresh news against the shanty doors and the drowsy moan of funky wenches in the sleeping jungle depths.

These things were still the same. They would never change. But for the rest, well——

"Hello, there, Gene! I see you've put on weight! How are you, boy?"

"Oh, fine. Glad to see you. *You* haven't changed much."

"Have you seen Jim yet?"

"No. He came by the house last night, but I wasn't there."

"Well, Jim Orton's been looking for you—he and

Ed Sladen, Hershel Brye, Holmes Benson, Brady Chalmers, Erwin Hines. . . . Why, say! Here's Jim now, and all the rest of them."

A chorus of voices, laughing and calling out greetings as they all piled out of the car that had pulled up at the curb:

"Here he is! . . . All right, we've got him now! . . . So you decided to come home again? . . . What was it you said about me in the book—that I concealed the essential vulgarity of my nature behind a hearty laugh?"

"Now look here, Jim—I—I——"

"I—I—hell!"

"I didn't mean——"

"The hell you didn't!"

"Let me explain——"

"Explain nothing! Why hell, man, what is there to explain? You didn't even get started in that book. If you were going to write *that* kind of book, why didn't you let me know? I could have told you dirt on some of the people in this town that you never even heard about. . . . Look at his face! . . . We've got him now! . . . Hell, son, don't look so backed. It's all forgotten now. A lot of them around here were pretty hot about it for a while. Two or three of them were out to get you—or said they were."

Laughter, then a sly voice:

"Have you seen Dan Fagan yet?"

"No, I haven't. Why?"

"Oh, nothing. I just wondered. Only——"

"Hell, he won't do nothing! No one will. The only ones who are mad today are those you left out!"

More laughter.

"Hell, it's true! The rest of 'em are proud of it! . . . We're all proud of you, son. We're glad that you came home. You've been away too long. Stay with us now."

"Why, hello, son! Glad to see you back! . . . You'll find many changes. The town has improved a lot since you were here. I guess the new Courthouse and the County Hall were put up since you left. Cost four million dollars. Have you seen the tunnel they bored under the mountain for that new roadway out of town? Cost two million more. And the High School and the Junior College, and the new streets, and all the new improvements? . . . And look at the Square here. I think it's pretty now the way they've laid it out, with flower beds and benches for the people. That's the thing this town needs most—some parks, some new amusements. If we hope to bring tourists here and make this a tourist town, we've got to give them some amusements. I've always said that. But you get a bunch of messheads in at City Hall and they can't see it. . . . Fact is, tourists don't stay here any more. They used to come and stay a month. You ought to know—you wrote about them sitting on the porches of the boarding houses. They'd come and sit and rock upon the porches, and they'd stay a month, people from all over—Memphis, Jacksonville, Atlanta, New Orleans. But we don't get them any more. They've all got cars now, and there are good roads everywhere, so they just stay overnight and then hit it for the mountains. You can't blame them—we've got no amusements. . . . Why, I can remember when this was a *sporting* center. The big swells all came here, the millionaires and racing men. And we had seventeen saloons—Malone's, and Creasman's, and Tim O'Connell's, and Blake's, and Carlton Leathergood's— your father used to go in there, he was a friend of Leathergood's. Do you remember Leathergood's tall, pock-marked, yellow nigger and his spotted dog? All gone now—dead, forgotten. . . . Here's where your father's shop used to stand. Do you remember the angel on the porch, the draymen sitting on the wooden steps, your father standing in the door, and the old calaboose across the street? It's pretty now, the way they've got all the grass and flower beds where the old calaboose used to be, but somehow the whole Square looks funny, empty at one end. And it's strange to see this sixteen-story building where your father's old marble shop once stood. But, say what you will, they've certainly improved things a lot. . . . Well, good-bye. The whole town wants to see you. I won't keep you. Come to see me sometime. My office is on the eleventh floor—right over where your father's workbench used to be. I'll show you a view you never dreamed of when your father's shop was here."

The return of the prodigal, and the whole town broken into greetings, while the on-coming, never-ceasing younger generation just gaped, curiously a-stare:

"He's back. . . . Have you seen him yet? . . . Which one is he?"

"Don't you see him there, talking to all those people? . . . There—over *there*—before the shoe-shine shop."

A girl's voice, disappointed: "Oh-h! Is that him? . . . Why, he's *old!*"

"Oh, Eugene's not so *very* old. He's thirty-six. He only seems old to you, honey. . . . Why I remember him when he was a snotty-nosed little kid, running around the street selling *Saturday Evening Posts,* and delivering a route in Niggertown for the *Courier.*"

"But—why, he's fat around the waist. . . . And look! He just took his hat off. Why, he's getting bald on top! . . . Oh-h, I never thought——"

"What did you think? He's thirty-six years old, and he never was very much to look at, anyway. He's just Eugene Gant, a snot-nosed kid who used to carry a paper route in Niggertown, and whose mother ran a boarding house, and whose father had a tombstone shop upon the Square. . . . And now just look at him! The snot-nosed kid who went away and wrote a book or two—and look there, will you!—look at all those people crowding round him! They called him every name they could think of, and now they're crawling over one another just to shake his hand."

And across the street:

"Hello, Gene!"

"Oh hello—ah—hello—ah——"

"Come on, now: hello-ah what?"

"Why, hello—ah——"

"Boy, I'll beat your head in if you don't call me by my name. Look at me. Now, what is it? Hello-ah *what?*"

"Why, ah—ah——"

"Come on, now! . . . Well, tell me this: who was it that called you 'Jocko' in that book?"

"Why—ah—ah—Sid! Sidney Purtle!"

"By God, you better *had!*"

"Why Sid, how are you? Hell, I knew you the minute you spoke to me!"

"The hell you did!"

"Only I couldn't quite . . . Oh, hello, Carl. Hello, Vic. Hello, Harry, Doc, Ike——"

He felt someone plucking at his sleeve and turned:

"Yes, ma'am?"

The lady spoke through artificial teeth, close-lipped, prim, and very hurriedly:

"Eugene I know you don't remember me I'm Long Wilson's mother who used to be in school with you at Plum Street School Miss Lizzy Moody was your teacher and——"

"Oh yes, Mrs. Wilson. How is Long?"

"He's very well thank you I won't keep you now I

see you're busy with your friends I know everyone wants to see you you must be rushed to death but sometime when you aren't busy I'd like to talk to you my daughter-in-law is very talented she paints sculptures and writes plays she's dying to meet you she's written a book and she says the experience of her life is so much like yours that she's sure you'd both have a lot in common if you could only get together to talk about it——"

"Oh, I'd love to. I'd love to, Mrs. Wilson."

"She's sure if she could talk to you you'd be able to give her some suggestions about her book and help her to find a publisher I know you're bothered with so many people that you've hardly any time to call your own but if you could only talk to her——"

"Oh, I'd be glad to."

"She's a very in-ter-est-ing person and if you'd only let us see you sometime I know——"

"Oh, I will. I will. Thank you so much, Mrs. Wilson. I will. I will. I will."

And at home:

"Mama, have there been any calls?"

"Why, child, the telephone's been goin' *all* day long. I've never known the like of it. Sue Black called up an' says for you to ring her back—an' Roy Hitchebrand, an' Howard Bartlett, an'—oh yes, that's so—a lady from out along Big Homing. Says she's written a book an' she's comin' in to see you. Says she wants you to read it an' criticize it for her an' tell her how to make it good so it will sell. . . . An' yes—that's so now— Fred Patton called up for the Rotary Club an' wants to know if you will speak to them at lunch next Tuesday. I think you ought to do that, son. They're good, substantial men, all of them, with a high standin' in the community. That's the kind of people you ought to be in with if you're goin' to keep on writin' books.

. . . An'—oh yes!—someone called up from the Veterans' Hospital—a girl named Lake, or Lape, or somethin' like that—says she used to be in the same class with you at Plum Street School, an' she's in charge of the Recreation Center for the veterans—says a lot of 'em have read your books an' want to see you an' won't you be the guest of honor on Saturday night. I wish you'd do that, child. I reckon the poor fellers, most of 'em, are far from home, an' many of 'em will never go back again to where they came from—it might cheer 'em up. . . . An' yes, that's so!—Sam Colton called up for the alumni committee of the university, an' they want you to speak to 'em at the big alumni rally next week at the Country Club. You ought to go, child. They're your old friends an' classmates, an' they want to see you. An' yes!—what about it, now!—why, you're to speak on the same program with "Our Dick"—Senator Richard L. Williams of the United States Senate, if you please! As Sam said, you and him are the two most famous alumni of the university that the town has yet produced. Hm-m! . . . Then there was Jimmy Stevenson, he called up and wanted you to come to a steak dinner to be given by the Business Men's Convention out at Sharpe's Cabin on the Beetree Creek, nine miles from Gudgerton. I'd certainly go if I were you. I've never seen the place, but they say Ed Sharpe certainly has a beautiful cabin, the best one around here—an' as the feller says, right in the heart of Nature's Wonderland, in the center of these glorious hills. I know the section well, for that's where father an' mother went to live ninety years ago, just after they were married—they moved there from Zebulon—didn't stay, of course—I reckon the pull of Zebulon an' all their kinfolks there was too much for 'em—but you couldn't pick a prettier spot if you hunted all over for it, right out in the heart of nature, with old Craggy Tavern in the background.

That's the place I'd go, boy, if I was a writer an'
wanted to get inspiration. Get close to Nature, as the
feller says, an' you'll get close to God. . . . An', yes—
two young fellers called up from over in Tennessee—
said they're the Blakely boys. You've heard of the
famous Blakely Canners. Why, I hear that they own
almost every farm in three counties there, an' they've
got factories everywhere, through Tennessee, an' way
down South, an' all out through the Middle West—
why, they're worth millions. Says—oh, just a boy, you
know—but says, real slylike, 'Is this Miss Delia?'—
givin' me the name you gave me in the book. Well, I
just played right along with him—'Well, now,' I says,
'I don't know about that. My name's Eliza. Now I've
heard that I've been called Delia, but you mustn't
believe all that you read,' I says. 'For all you know, I
may be human just like everybody else. Now,' I says,
'I looked real good and hard at myself this mornin' in
the mirror, an' if there are any horns stickin' out of my
head, why I must've missed 'em, I didn't see any. Of
course I'm growin' old, an' maybe my eyesight's failin'
me,' I says, 'but you're young an' ought to have good
eyes, so why don't you come an' have a look an' tell
me what you think.' Well, sir, he laughed right out
across the phone as big as you please, an' says, 'Well,
you're all right! I think you're wonderful! An' I'm
tryin' to be a writer—even if my father does put up
tomatoes—an' I think your son's one of the best
writers that we have.' Well, I didn't let on, of course.
Father always taught us that it was vulgar an'
unrefined to brag about your own, so I just said,
'Well, now, I don't know about that. But you come on
an' look at him. Up to the time he was twelve years
old,' I says, 'he was a good, normal sort of boy like
everybody else. Now what happened to him after
that,' I says—you see, I thought I'd have a little fun
with him—'what happened after that I don't know—

I'm not responsible. But you come an' take a look at him. Maybe you'll get surprised. Maybe you'll find he doesn't have horns, either.' Well, he laughed right out an' said, 'You're all right! An' I'm goin' to take you up on that. My brother an' I are drivin' over tomorrow afternoon—an' we're goin' to bring him back with us,' he says. 'If he wants a cabin like I hear he does, I've got one here that I can give him, so we're goin' to bring him back,' he says. Well, you can't do that, of course, child, but be nice to them. He spoke like a very well-brought-up sort of boy—an' the Blakelys are the kind of people that you ought to know. . . . An' after that a lot of girls called up an' said they heard you needed someone to type for you—said they'd like to do it, and knew how to type good. One of 'em said she'd be willin' to do it for nothin'—says she wants to be a writer, an' knew she'd learn so much from you an' what an inspiration it would be. Hm! pshaw!—I cut her off mighty quick, I can tell you! Sounded funny to me—wantin' to work for nothin', an' all that gushy talk about inspiration. I knew what *she* was after, all right. You watch out, son—don't let any of these silly women rope you in. . . . Yes, that's so. Cash Hopkins was here askin' about you. Of course he's just a plain, workin' sort of man. He used to do jobs for your father, but your father liked him, an' he's always been our friend, interested in all of you. . . . Mr. Higginson was here, too. He's an Episcopal minister that came to town several years ago for his health—an' what about it!—he's been your friend right from the start. When all the preachers were denouncin' you, an' sayin' you'd disgraced us all, an' everyone was down on you an' said if you ever came back here they'd kill you—he *defended* you, sir! He stood right up for you! He read everything you wrote an' he said, 'That boy should have been a preacher. He's got more of the true gos-

pel in his books than all of us preachers put together!'
Oh, he came right out for you, you know. 'It's we who
have failed,' he said, 'not him!' Child, I hope you'll be
nice to Mr. Higginson. He's been your friend from the
first, an', as the sayin' goes, he's a scholar an' a Chris-
tian gentleman. . . . An', law, what about it! I'm
sorry you were not here to see it. I'll vow, I had to
turn my head away to keep from laughin'. Why, Ernest Pegram, if you please, in his big car—all rared
back there in a brand-new Cadillac as fat as a pig, an'
with a big cigar stickin' out of his mouth. Why, of
course; he's *rich* now! He's well-fixed—every last one
of the Pegrams is! You see, when Will Pegram died
two years ago up there in the North somewhere, he
was a wealthy man, a big official in some large corporation. You see, he was the only one of the Pegrams
who got away. But, poor Will! I can remember just as
well the day he left here more than forty years ago—
this corporation had given him a job down in the
eastern part of the state, an', as the sayin' goes, he
didn't have an extra shirt to put on his back. An' here
he dies two years ago an' leaves close to a million
dollars. So they're well-fixed! Of course, Will had no
childern, an' his brothers an' sisters got it all. He left
Ernest a flat hundred thousand—that's what it was, all
right, because I read it in the papers, an' Ernest told
me so himself. The others came in for their share, too.
Here the rest of us are broke, the whole town ruined,
everyone has lost everything they had—as the Bible
says, 'How have the mighty fallen!'—but the Pegrams
don't have to worry from now on. So Ernest drives up
an' stops before the house this afternoon in his big,
new car, smokin' his fine cigar. 'Why, Ernest,' I says, 'I
don't think I ever saw you lookin' better. Are you still
workin' at your plumbin' trade?' I says. Of course I
knew he wasn't—I just wanted to hear what he would

say. 'No, Eliza,' he says—oh, the biggest thing you ever saw, puffin' away at his cigar. 'No,' he says. 'I've reached the age,' he says, 'when I figgered it was about time to retire.' Pshaw! *Retire!* I had to turn my head away to keep from laughin'. Who ever heard of a plumber retirin'? What did *he* ever have to retire *on*— that's what *I'd* like to know—if it hadn't been for Will? But—oh yes, see here, now—says: 'You tell Gene,' he says, 'that I haven't got a thing to do. My time is free,' he says, 'an' if there's any place he wants to go, any place where I can take him, why, my car is here,' he says, 'an' it's at his disposal.' You know how good-hearted he's always been. I reckon he was thinkin' of the days when he used to live next to us on Wood-son Street, an' how he watched all you childern grow up. The Pegrams have always been our friends an' taken a great interest in your career. I wish, son, that you'd go to see them all while you're here. They'll be glad to see you. But when I saw Ernest there in his big car, puffin' away on his cigar, an' lookin' fat enough, as the sayin' goes, to pop right out of his britches, an' tellin' me he had retired—well, I just had to turn my head away an' laugh. . . . Well, in all my life I've never seen the beat of it! There's been a steady string of them here all day long, an' the telephone has just rung constantly. I'll vow—it seems to me that everyone in town has either been here or called up today. . . . An', oh yes! There are two of 'em out in the sun parlor now—old Cap'n Fitzgerald and a Miss Morgan, a trained nurse. I don't know what they want. They've been waitin' for an hour, so I wish you'd just step out an' say hello to 'em. . . . An' yes! There's three more in the front parlor—a lady who says she's from Charles-ton an' had read your books an' was just passin' through town an' heard you were here an' wanted to shake hands with you, an' that young Tipton that you used to know, an'—oh yes! that's so!—the reporter from the paper, he's there, too. I guess he wants to write you up, so you'd better go right in. . . . I'll vow! There goes that phone again! Just a minute, son —I'll answer it."

On Leprechauns

An Armenian friend of ours, a Mr. Vladimir Adzigian of South Brooklyn, has mentioned among the defects of our literary style a certain coldness and economy of tone and manner, which, while it makes for precision and temperance, is likely to err too much on the side of understatement. This critic feels—and rightly, too, we think—that our work would profit if it had a little more exuberance, a more impulsive warmth, even a little exaggeration here and there. "For," says he, "exaggeration is in itself a form of enthusiasm, and enthusiasm, in my opinion, is the quality that your work, together with almost all American writing, lacks." This cultivated gentleman then goes on to say that here in America we have never overcome the repressive influences of our Puritan ancestry, and he thinks we will never completely realize ourselves until we do.

While admitting the truth of our friend's observations and conceding regretfully that our own style does suffer from a kind of puritanic sparseness, an almost frigid restraint, we think we might interpose a few mild, although apologetic, reservations to the general tenor of his remarks. In the first place, if our style does suffer from a puritanic frigidity, it is because we, in our own person, suffer from the same defect. And however much we may regret it, however much we may want to burst through the barriers of our reserve to a warm and free communication with the universe, it is probably better to reflect the color of our soul—

even though that color be cold and hard—than to assume a false, unwarranted spontaneity that we do not have. Moreover, even if we could overcome the constrained reserve of our nature and break through to a more impulsive spontaneity, we should hesitate to attempt it, because we have so many friends and readers whose own sense of propriety and personal modesty would be affronted if we did.

Chief among these people are our Irish friends, whom we number by the hundreds. Our admiration and affection for the Irish is, we believe, well known. In addition to the traditional affection for the race in which every American boy is brought up, and which is as natural to him as a sore toe, we have had the privilege time and again in our written works of expressing—as soberly and temperately as any man could, it seemed to us, and certainly far too soberly and temperately to suit the tastes of Mr. Adzigian— what seemed to us to be the shining and distinguishing qualities of the race, its great and lasting contributions to our nation's life.

We have found frequent occasion to pay tribute to their sterling honesty, the devotion of their public service, their brilliant skill in politics and government, which have given them a record of unselfish and incorruptible administration that is, we believe, unequaled by any other people in the world. Where else in the world may a people be found who will so cheerfully and uncomplainingly take over the onerous and thankless burden of running the government, and whose devotion to the principles of law and order, sobriety, reasonable conciliation, and selfless and unseeking consecration to the common weal are as high, loyal, and untarnished in their idealism as are those of the Irish? Where else, among all the peoples who make up the vast polyglot of American life, will another people be found whose patriotism is not only one hundred per cent American, but maintains a constant average of one hundred and thirty-seven per cent?

We have considered it not only a duty but an agreeable privilege to refer to these well-known facts on several occasions, and if we finally desisted, it was largely because of the quiet protests of our Irish friends themselves.

For, said they, the only reward they ever desired or hoped for was the knowledge of public duty modestly done and honorably completed. Virtue was its own exceeding great reward. There were, it was true, among other peoples, certain odious demagogues who were always making public speeches in their own behalf, and slapping themselves proudly on their own breasts; there were even those contemptible characters who regarded politics as a means of feathering their own nests out of the common funds. As for themselves, however, all they asked was the joyful privilege of serving their state or their city as well as they could, giving to their country the last full measure of devotion. That was reward enough, and the knowledge that one had given his *all* for his country should be sufficient for any man. Certainly the thought of public acknowledgment for such a noble and idealistic service was odious, and would we please not affront their deepest and most sacred feelings by speaking of it further?

Since the matter was presented to us in this way by many of our dear Irish friends, we consented reluctantly to refrain from a further public display of our enthusiasm rather than incur the quiet reproaches of a people who, as is well known, are among the shyest and most modest races in the world. In matters of literary judgment, however, we trust we may be allowed a more full and free expression of our emotions, since every race, no matter how innately modest, how consecrated to a public trust, may be justly proud of its artistic achievements, and justly boastful of all its men of genius.

We take it as a matter of general consent that Ireland has always swarmed with geniuses. Old Erin has been for centuries running over with them—has, in fact, had so many of this glorious type that it has been necessary to establish a kind of emigration service for the exportation of Irish geniuses to other nations which, though bigger, are lamentably deficient in their genius supply.

The leading customer for the importation of Irish geniuses has been our own fair land. In fact, we do not believe it any extravagant exaggeration to say that where genius is concerned the Irish brand tops the list with us. Here in America we'd rather have one good, bona-fide, Irish genius than a half-dozen Polish, Swedish, Czecho-Slovakian, or Hungarian specimens, no matter what their reputations.

It is true that visiting Englishmen are still in considerable demand, and ply a thriving trade before the Culture Clubs and Female Forums of the Corn Belt. Almost any ninth-rate scribbler from Great Britain can still come over here and insult the country with the choicest and most indecipherable sneers in his whole Oxford vocabulary, and command prices from his adoring audiences that no American could dream of asking.

Yes, there is still a good market for the English genius, but among the *haut ton,* so to say, the true sophisticates of culture, the Irish bards and storytellers come first. A bad English writer may still put in a profitable six or eight months and eat and drink his way across the pampas from Portland, Maine, to Tacoma, Washington, at the expense of this great, benevolent, and culture-loving people. But to do so requires considerable traveling, and the English genius cannot always pick his spots; he must occasionally prepare

himself for the uncomfortable exigencies of one-night
stands, bad accommodations, and poor food.

An Irish genius is faced with none of these embar-
rassing possibilities. He can pick his spots and do as
he damn pleases. He can remain in New York in the
perfumed salons of the art-loving plutocracy, and can
always have the very best of everything at no cost to
himself, provided he exercises only a very small degree of caution and has sense enough to know upon
which side his cake is caviared. An Englishman may
have to stand an occasional round of drinks, or stay
with the second-best family in Hamtramck, Michigan,
but a visiting Irishman—never! A visiting Englishman
may have to have at least the vestige of a reputation
—to have received the endorsement of Hugh
Walpole, or to have in his pocket a letter of introduction from J. B. Priestley—but a visiting Irishman
needs nothing. It is naturally preferable if someone
has heard of him before, but it is by no means essential. The main thing is that he be a visiting Irish
writer, and, of course, all visiting Irish writers are
geniuses, and not only geniuses, but the most Extra-
Special, A-Number-1, Eighteen-Carat Geniuses in existence.

After that, no introduction is necessary. He can just
call himself Sean O'Mulligan or Seamus O'Toole or
some other whimsical appellative of this nature, and
everything will be all right. He needs only to get off
the boat and announce to the reporters that he is the
author of an untranslated and untranslatable epic,
written in pure Gaelic (he disdains, of course, to use
the English speech, unless it be to cash a check; otherwise he abhors the race that has cruelly, bloodily, and
damnably oppressed Old Erin for a thousand years,
etc., etc., etc.), and from that time on his path is
smooth, his bed is roses.

If, in addition, he will only come down the gangplank muttering through his whiskers something about "a green leprechaun which they do be sayin' an old man in the west was afther seein' on the hill behint his house, year afther year, bedad," or some other elfin talk of this nature, by which the bearded adults of this race strive to convince themselves and other people that they are really just a lot of little boys, the whole thing will be lapped up greedily, will travel the round of the salons, and be hailed as a perfect masterpiece of whimsey, just too Irish, quaint, and delightful for words. Many a visiting Irish bard has established a reputation, achieved celebrity, and eaten and drunk his way into the Great American Heart on no better grounds than this.

It may be perfectly true, of course, that while all this is going on—while the Irish genius is muttering through his whiskers about the fairies and the leprechauns, and is being coddled in the silken laps of the adoring plutocracy as a reward for his whimsical caprice—some poor, benighted bastard of a native son, some gaunt-eyed yokel from Nebraska, Texas, Tennessee, or Minnesota, may be eating his heart out in a Greenwich Village garret, opening canned beans at midnight, and wreaking out the vision of his life here in America with all the passion, fury, terror, suffering, poverty, cruelty, and neglect which a young man in this abundant land may know. It may be true, we say, that while the visiting Seans and Seamuses are chirping on Park Avenue about their leprechauns to an adoring audience of silken wenches, some wild-eyed native youth may be pounding at the wall of his garret with bloody knuckles, wondering where, when, and how in God's name, in a swarming city of eight millions, he can find a woman, or even slake his hunger for a moment with the bought and bitter briefness of a whore.

Yes, while the lovely legs cross slowly, and slide the

silken thighs, while the fragrant bellies heave in unction to the elfin blandishments of Sean, a boy may be
burning in the night, burning in the lone, stern
watches of darkness, and giving a tongue to silence
that will shape a new language long after silken
thighs and Sean and Seamus are no more.

But have no perturbations, gentle reader. When the
boy has won through from the agony of silence to an
uttered fame, when his toiling and imperiled soul has
beat its way to shore, when by his own unaided effort
he stands safe on land, you may depend on it that he
will be at once encumbered with the help he no
longer needs. Lovely legs and silken thighs and fragrant bellies will then heave amorously for *him,* as
they do now for Sean, and every little whore of wealth
and fashion will contend for the honors of the bed
that poverty had bachelored and that fame has filled.
The youth, once left to rot and starve, will now be
fawned upon and honeyed over by the very apes of
fashion who previously ignored him, and who now
seek to make him their ape. And the treachery of their
adoration will be more odious than the treachery of
their neglect, for it stands written in Fame's lexicon
that he who lets himself be whored by fashion will be
whored by time.

Perhaps the reader may detect in these grave lines a
color of some bitterness. Perhaps he may be shocked
to realize that there is some slight neglect among the
people of this present age, in this enlightened and art-
loving nation, toward the young native artist. It is
conceivable that the reader may espy here, in this true
picture of our native customs, some tincture of injustice, some snobbery of fashion, some conceit of taste.
But there are high authorities on these matters who

will quickly inform the reader that if he thinks any of these things he is seriously mistaken.

It is necessary to look at what George Webber learned in college to call "The Deeper and More Significant Aspects of the Situation." Seen in this light, things which may have seemed a little difficult and puzzling become beautifully clear. Elsewhere I have told the story of George Webber's life in considerable detail, and in that chronicle I have shown that the usual reception of our young native artist during the years of his apprenticeship is a good, swift kick in the teeth, followed by a good, swift kick in the seat of the pants that will send him flying out of doors onto the pavement. The reason why this happens to the poor, young, native son, while Sean and Seamus eat and drink and wench it to their heart's content, is not because anyone means to be cruel or indifferent, but because great men and lovely women of the Cultured Classes have found out long since that the best thing that could possibly happen to a poor young man of native stock and talent is to get a few good kicks in the face. They know that he can come to his full maturity only through adversity, so they kick him out of doors just to help him along.

In this way he is prevented from getting soft. People who live in luxury, on assured incomes, have very stern and Spartan notions about getting soft. To be sure, everyone is willing to sympathize with a young man's early struggles after he has had them, but, obviously, there can be no sympathy unless he *has* had them.

Any enlightened millionaire can explain "The Deeper and More Significant Aspects of the Situation." It is really a part of what we call "The American Dream." It belongs to our ideal of rugged individualism. The more often one gets kicked in the teeth, the more rugged he becomes. It is our method of doing things, and such a simple and direct expression of our life that we have even invented a name for it. We speak of it proudly as "The American Way."

Portrait of a Literary Critic

The personality of the celebrated Dr. Turner—or Dr. Hugo Twelvetrees Turner as he was generally known to the reading public—was not an unfamiliar one to George Webber, the novelist. Dr. Turner's wider reputation had been well known to the public for fifteen years or more. And for ten years he had been the guiding spirit of the splendid journal he had himself established, the *Fortnightly Cycle of Reading, Writing, and the Allied Arts.*

The establishment of the *Fortnightly Cycle* marked, as one critic says, "one of the most important literary events of our time," and life without it, another offered, would have been "simply unthinkable." *The Cycle* came into being at the time when the critical field was more or less divided between the somewhat prosaic conservatism of the *Saturday Review of Literature* and the rather mannered preciosity of *The Dial.* Between the two, Dr. Turner and *The Cycle* struck a happy medium; the position of *The Cycle* might be best classified as middle-of-the-road, and Dr. Turner himself might be described as the nation's leading critical practitioner of middle-of-the-roadism. Here, really, lay his greatest contribution.

It is true that there were certain skeptics who stubbornly disputed Dr. Turner's right to such a title. These critics, instead of being reassured by the broad yet sane liberalism of the Doctor's views, were seriously alarmed by it: they professed to see in Dr. Turner's critical opinions a tendency toward a disturbing—nay dangerous!—radicalism. Such a judgment was simply ridiculous. Dr. Turner's position was neither too far to the right nor too far to the left, but "a little left of center." With this definition he would himself have instantly agreed; the phrasing would have pleased him.

True, there had been a period in Dr. Turner's rich career when his position had been much more conservative than it now was. But to his everlasting credit let it be said that his views had grown broader as the years went on; the years had brought increase of tolerance, depth of knowledge, width of understanding; ripeness with this valiant soul was all.

There had been a time when Dr. Turner had dismissed the works of some of the more modern writers as being the productions of "a group of dirty little boys." Indeed the first use of this delightfully homely and pungent phrase may be safely accredited to Dr. Turner himself. People on Beacon Hill read it with appreciative chuckles, gentlemen in clubs slapped the *Fortnightly Cycle* on their thighs and cried out "Capital!" It was just the way they themselves had always felt about these moderns, except that they had never found quite the words to put it so; but this man now, this What's-His-Name, this Turner—oh, Capital! Capital! It was evident that a fearless, new, and salutary force had come into the Nation's Letters.

A little later on, however, Dr. Turner's "dirty little boy" had been qualified somewhat by the adjectival words, "who scrawls bad words which he hopes may shock his elders upon the walls of privies."

This was even better! A pleasing image was thus conveyed to the readers of Dr. Turner's *Fortnightly Cycle* that brought much unction to their souls. For what could be more comforting to a devoted reader of the *Fortnightly Cycle* than the reassuring sense that just as he was settling down to attend to one of the most inevitable of the natural functions, he might look up and read with an amused and tolerating eye certain words that various dirty little boys like Anatole France, George Bernard Shaw, Theodore Dreiser, Sherwood Anderson, and D. H. Lawrence had scrawled up there with the intention of shocking him.

If Dr. Turner had made no further contribution to literature, his position would have been secure. But more, much more, was yet to come. For even at this early stage one of the salient qualities of Dr. Turner's talent had revealed itself. He was always able to keep at least two jumps ahead, not only of his own critics, but of his own admirers. Thus it was Dr. Turner who first made the astonishing discovery that Sex is Dull. The news at first stunned the readers of the *Fortnightly Cycle*, who had begun to be seriously alarmed about the whole matter, shocked, appalled, and finally reduced to a state of sputtering indignation by "This —this Sort of Thing, now; Sort of Thing they're writing nowadays; this, this—why, this Filth! This fellow Lawrence, now!"

Dr. Turner put these perturbed spirits to rest. Dr. Turner was neither appalled, shocked, nor incensed by anything he read about sex. He didn't get indignant. He knew a trick worth six of these. Dr. Turner was amused. Or would have been amused, that is, if he had not found the whole business so excessively boring. Even as early as 1924, he was writing the following in comment on a recent book of D. H. Lawrence:

"This preoccupation with Sex—really not unlike the preoccupation of a naughty little boy with certain four-letter words which he surreptitiously scrawls upon the sides of barns—(observe how the earlier exuberances of the Doctor are here subtly modified) —would on the whole be mildly amusing to an adult intelligence who had presumed that these were things that one had lived through and forgotten in one's salad days, if it were not for the fact that the author contrives to make the whole business so appallingly dull.

The readers of the *Fortnightly Cycle* were at first amazed, then simply enchanted by this information. They had been dismayed and sore perplexed—but now! Why, hah-hah-hah, the whole thing was very funny, wasn't it? The extreme seriousness of the fellow about the Kind of Thing they had themselves forgotten since their sophomore days—would really be quite amusing if he had not contrived to make it so abysmally Dull!

There was more, much more, to come. The whole tormented complex of the 'twenties was upon good Dr. Turner. People everywhere were bewildered by the kaleidoscopic swiftness with which things changed. It was a trial that might well have floored a less valiant spirit than that of Dr. Turner. Hardly a week went by without its discovery of a new great poet. Scarcely an issue of the *Fortnightly Cycle* appeared without proclaiming to the world some new novel to equal *War and Peace*. And not a month passed without producing some new and sensational movement in the bewildering flux of fashion. Charlie Chaplin was discovered to be, not primarily a comedian at all, but the greatest tragic actor of the time (learned adepts of the arts assured the nation that his proper role was Hamlet). The true art-expression of America was the comic strip (the productions of the Copleys, Whistlers, Sargents, Bellowses, and Lies could never hold a candle to it). The only theater that was truly native and worth preserving was the burlesque show. The only music that was real was Jazz. There had been only one writer in America: his name was Twain, and he had been defeated just because he

was—American; he was so good just because he was
—American; but if he had not been American he
could have been—*so* good! Aside from this, the only
worthwhile writing in the land was what the advertis-
ing writers wrote; this was the true expression of the
Yankee clime—all else had failed us, all was dross.

The madness grew from week to week. With every
revolution of the clock the Chaos of the Cultures
grew. But through it all the soul of Dr. Turner kept its
feet. Turner hewed true and took the Middle Way. To
all things in their course, in their true proportion, he
was just.

True, he had lapses. In culture's armies he was not
always foremost to the front. But he caught up. He
always caught up. If there were sometimes errors in
his calculations, he always rectified them before it was
too late. If he made mistakes—like the man he was,
he gallantly forgot them.

It was inspiring just to watch his growth. In 1923,
for instance, he referred to the *Ulysses* of James Joyce
as "that encyclopædia of filth which has become the
bible of our younger intellectuals"; in 1925, more tolerantly, as "that bible of our younger intellectuals
which differs from the real one in that it manages to
be so consistently dull"; in 1929 (behold this man!) as
"that amazing *tour de force* which has had more
influence on our young writers than any other work of
our generation"; and in 1933, when Justice Woolsey
handed down the famous decision that made the sale
of *Ulysses* legally permissible throughout these
United States (in a notable editorial that covered the
entire front page of the *Fortnightly Cycle*), as "a
magnificent vindication of artistic integrity . . . the
most notable triumph over the forces of bigotry and
intolerance that has been scored in the Republic of
Letters in our time."

Similarly, when one of the earlier books of William

Faulkner appeared, Dr. Turner greeted it with an editorial that was entitled, "The School of Bad Taste." He wrote:

"One wonders what our bright young men will do for material now that the supply of four-letter words and putrescent situations has been so exhausted that further efforts in this direction can only rouse the jaded reader to a state of apathy. Is it too much to hope that our young writers may grow tired of their own monsters and turn their talents to a possible investigation of—dare we hope it?—normal life?"

A few years later, however, when Mr. Faulkner's *Sanctuary* appeared, the Doctor had so altered his views that, after likening the author to Poe in "the quality of his brooding imagination . . . his sense of the macabre . . . his power to evoke stark fear, sheer horror, as no other writer of his time has done," he concluded his article by saying darkly to his readers, "This man may go far."

Thus, although Dr. Turner was occasionally out of step, he always fell in again before the Top Sergeant perceived his fault. Moreover, once he got into the fore, he had a very brave and thrilling way of announcing his position to his readers as if he had been in the crow's nest all along and had cried "Land Ho!" at the very moment when the faint shore of some new and brave America was first visible.

These, then, were among the Doctor's more daring discoveries. Some of the more conservative of his following were made uneasy by such risky venturesomeness, but they should not have been alarmed. For, if the Doctor ever stuck his neck out, it was only when he had it safely armor-plated: his bolder sorties out among the new and strange were always well-hedged round by flanking guards of reservations. Upon more familiar ground, however, the Doctor would go the whole hog in a way that warmed the soul. His praises of the Joyces, Faulkners, Eliots, and Lawrences were always fenced in by parentheses of safe reserve; even the Dreisers and the Lewises had their moderating checks; but when the Millays, Glasgows, Cabells, Nathans, and Morleys were his meat, he spoke out of the fullness of his heart—then it was, in vulgar phrase, that the Doctor really went to town.

And, curiously enough, it was just here, when Dr. Turner was on what he himself was fond of classifying as "safe ground," that his judgment was likely to grow giddy and was prone to err. This exuberance later caused him some embarrassment. Thus, at various stages of his editorial career, he had described Christopher Morley as being the possessor of "the most delightful prose style that the familiar essay has known since the days of his true contemporary and, may I say, *almost* his equal, Charles Lamb. Aside from Lamb there is no other essayist since Montaigne's time to match him." Of Ellen Glasgow he wrote: "She is not only our greatest living novelist, but one of the greatest novelists that ever lived," and that lady's many works he characterized as ". . . in their entirety comprising a picture of a whole society that, for variety and scope, has no parallel in literature except the *Comédie Humaine*, and that, in the perfection of their form and style, achieve a faultless artistry that Balzac's cruder talent never reached." The whimsy-whamsy of Robert Nathan he pronounced "sheer genius. There's no other word for it; it's sheer elfin genius of a kind that not even Barrie has attained, and that has no rival in our language unless perchance it be the elfin loveliness of the Titania-Oberon scenes in *A Midsummer Night's Dream*." Of the baroque pilgrimage of Mr. Cabell in his Province of Cockaigne he wrote: "He is our greatest ironist, with the greatest prose style in the language—perhaps the only Pure Artist that we have." And of a young gentleman who wrote a book about a bridge in South America he said: "A great writer—certainly the greatest writer that the Younger Generation has produced. And the book! Ah, what a book! A book to be treasured, cherished, and re-read; a book to put upon your shelves beside *War and Peace, Don Quixote, Moby Dick, Candide* . . . and withal a book, that, without one touch of the dreary and degrading realism that disfigures the work of most of our younger writers, is so essentially, splendidly American . . . as American as Washington, Lincoln, or the Rocky Mountains, since in its story are implicit the two qualities that are most characteristic of our folk: Democracy through Love; Love through Democracy."

The world being the grim place it sometimes is, it is sorrowful but not surprising to relate that there were a few wicked spirits who took a cruel delight in unearthing these lush phrases years after they had first been uttered, and after they had lain decently interred in old copies of the *Fortnightly Cycle* for so long that presumably they were as dead as most of the books that had evoked them. Then the worthy Doctor had to pretend he did not know that they were there, or else eat them, and of all the forms of diet this is the toughest and least palatable.

But on the whole the Doctor came through nobly. The sea at times was stormy and the waves ran very high, but the staunch ship that was Turner weathered through.

Among his followers, it is true, there were some whose tendencies were so conservative that they deplored the catholicity of the Doctor's tastes. And among his enemies there were some who were cruel enough to suggest that he wanted to be all things to all men, that Turner was not only the proper, but the inevitable, name for him, that the corkscrew shaped his course, and that if he went around the corner he would run into himself on the way back. Dr. Turner's answer to both these groups was simple, dignified, and complete: "In the Republic of Letters," said he, "of which I am a humble citizen, there are, I am glad to say, no factions, groups, or class distinctions. It is a true Democracy, perhaps the only one that now exists. And as long as I am privileged to belong to it, in however modest a capacity, I hope I shall be worthy of it, too, and broad enough to see all sides."

In appearance, Dr. Turner was scarcely prepossessing. He was so much below the middle height that at first sight it seemed that one of Singer's Midgets had enjoyed a run of extra growth. His little bread-crumb of a body (for in appearance he suggested nothing so much as a piece of well-done toast) was surmounted by a head of normal size which appeared too large for the meager figure that supported it. His face resembled somewhat that of the little man one so often sees in political cartoons, and which bears the caption "The Common People." It was such a face as one might see upon the streets a hundred times a day, and never think of later: it might have belonged to a bank clerk, a bookkeeper, an insurance agent, or someone going home to Plainfield on the 5:15.

George Webber was himself one of the good Doctor's more belated discoveries. When the author's first book, *Home to Our Mountains*, appeared, Dr. Turner had not been favorably impressed. The review in the *Fortnightly Cycle* had been a very gem of bland dismissal: "No doubt the thing is well enough," said Dr. Turner, "but after all, old Rabelais is really so much better"—a conclusion which the unhappy author was by no means minded to dispute.

Six years later, upon the eve of publication of Webber's second book, the good Doctor was still undecided just what he was going to do about it or him.

Three weeks before the book was released for general
sale, the Doctor met Webber's publisher and, after
confessing that he had read an advance copy of the
new work, he added grimly: "I haven't yet made up
my mind about Webber. But," said he bodingly, "I'll
make it up within a week or two." Between then and
the time the book came out, Dr. Turner apparently
felt the telepathy of moderating influences—"You can
always tell," as he was wont to say, "when Things are
in the Air"—so that when his critique ultimately appeared, it was much more favorable than Webber or
his publisher had dared to hope. Not that the Doctor
was thoroughly persuaded, but he took a more con-
ciliating tone. The book, he averred, "could hardly be
called a novel"—he did not trouble to explain what
could—it was really "a Spiritual Autobiography."
Then, having arrived at this sounding definition, he
discussed the volume freely in spiritual-autobiographi-
cal terms, and on the whole was pretty favorable
about it, too, having neatly furnished forth a special
little nest for Webber without in any way impinging
on the jealous precincts of more splendid birds on
more important boughs.

The way for a rapprochement was thus opened
gracefully and when George Webber first met the
Doctor some months later their greetings were of a
friendly kind. Indeed the good Doctor was so very
friendly that he insisted forthwith on taking Webber
home with him, and would accept no refusal. So they
went, and the manner of their going was very much
like that of an ocean liner being warped from its berth
and down the river and out to sea by a busy little tug.

"Darling," said Dr. Turner to his wife when at last
they reached the house, "I want you to meet Mr.
Webber. Oh, pshaw, now! I can't get used to all this
Mister stuff. I'm going to call you George!" cried Dr.
Turner with an air of bluff heartiness that was simply

irresistible. "I know so many people that you know, and have heard them call you George for so many years, that no other name seems possible."

Webber murmured that he was enchanted to be thus addressed, meanwhile feeling a little helpless and confused under the hypnotic influence of Mrs. Turner, who, holding him by the hand, was looking steadily into his eyes with a slow, strange smile.

"You!" she said at length. "You!" she repeated slowly and deliberately, and then concluded simply, "You wrote the book."

Webber felt vague, not knowing just how to answer this, but managed to mumble that he had. The lady's reply was to continue to hold him by the hand and to regard him steadily with a fixed smile that seemed to harbor some dawning mirth to which no one else was a party.

"You!" she said presently again. "I don't know, but somehow you make me laugh. You amuse me. There is something about you that is like—is like—an Elf!"

"Yes," said Dr. Turner quickly, and, meeting Webber's bewildered eye, he went on with an air of hasty explanation in the manner of people steering away from well-known reefs: "My wife was *awfully* interested in that book of yours. *Awfully*. Of course, we *all* were," he went on rapidly. "Matter of fact, I wrote three full columns on it," he went on with just a tinge of nervous constraint, as if he hoped this fact would make everything all right. "I believe it was the longest review I have done since *An American Tragedy*. I was *awfully* interested in it. Did you see my review by any chance?" he asked, and then quickly, before Webber could answer: "I was really *awfully* interested. I called your book a kind of Spiritual Autobiography. I mean," he added quickly as Webber opened his mouth as if to speak, "it really made me think of *Wilhelm Meister*. Not—" the Doctor instantly cried, as Webber started to open his mouth again—"not that that was all of it. Of course there were passages in it that were *very* much like *War and Peace*. I remember saying to Mrs. Turner at the time, 'You know, there are times when he is very much like Tolstoi.'"

"And like—an Elf," said Mrs. Turner at this point, never for a moment relinquishing her grasp on Webber's hand, and continuing to smile steadily at him in a slow, strange way. "So like an Elf," she said, and laughed merrily.

"And, of course," said Dr. Turner rapidly, "there's the *Moby Dick* influence, too. I know I told my wife at the time that there were passages, magnificent passages," cried Dr. Turner, "that were much like Herman Melville."

"And like an Elf!" the wife said.

"But *more* like *Moby Dick!*" the Doctor said decidedly.

"And still *more*," thought Webber, whose mind was at last beginning to work slowly, "oh, much, *much* more like a whale!"

In this way, after so long and perilous a voyage, the storm-tossed mariner, George Webber, was brought to port by the good Dr. Turner. And if he was not berthed among the mighty liners, at least he now had anchorage in the slips where some of the smaller vessels in the Turnerian haven were.

The Lion at Morning

❦

It was morning, shining morning, bright motes of morning in the month of May, when James awoke. An old man in a big room in a great house in the East Seventies near Central Park. A little, wiry, bright-eyed man in the great master's chamber of one of those lavish, fatly sumptuous, limestone-and-marble, mansard-roof, bastard-French-chateau atrocities which rich men were forever building for their wives some forty or fifty years ago. But this was 1929, and shining morning in the month of May, when James awoke.

He awoke as he did everything, very cleanly, abruptly, and aggressively, with a kind of grim pugnacity. He would not *fool* with slumber: once he was done with sleep, he was *done* with it. He liked comfort and the best of everything, but he hated softness, sloth, and feeble indecision. There was a proper time and place for everything—a time for work; a time for sport, travel, pleasure, and society; a time for a good dinner, brandy, and a good cigar; and last of all, a time for sleep. James knew when the time for everything should be.

For when a thing was finished it was finished. This applied to sleep as well as to every other useful, pleasant thing in life. He had discharged his debt to sleep and darkness for eight hours, now he was done with it. He paid sleep off as he would sign a check—cleanly, sharply, vigorously, with a final flourish of the pen—

169

Pay to the order of—*Sleep*—Eight - - - - - - and $\frac{no}{100}$ hrs.

—James Wyman, Sr.

There you are, sir! You are satisfied, I hope? Good!
The matter's settled! But, come now! No silly
business, if you please, of yawning sleepily, stretching
out luxuriously, rolling over on your other side, and
mumbling some damned nonsense about "just five minutes more," or some such stuff as that! And none of
this business of pulling cobwebs from your brain, getting your eyes unglued, brushing the filaments of
sleep away, trying to wake up, come out of it, remember where you are! No! Wake up at once! Come out
of it cleanly! Be done with it the moment your eyes
are open! Get up and go about your work—day's beginning, night is over, sleep-time's done!

James awoke like this. He was a small and wiry
figure of a man, aged seventy-four, with a cold
fighter's face. It was not a hard face, in no respect a
brutal, savage, or distempered face—no, on the whole
it was a rather pleasant face, certainly a very decisive
face, and just as certainly a fighting face.

The face was very bright, and had a brisk, sharp,
and rather frosty look. The eyes were very blue,
frosty-looking, and as cold and straight as steel. The
hair was white and close-cropped, likewise the mustache. The nose was long and cold and definite, the
whole structure of the face slightly concave, the
straight, grim mouth touched faintly at the edges with
the eternal suggestion of a grin—a grin that was good-
humored enough, but also straight, hard, cold, naturally truculent. It was the face of a man who hated fear
and despised those who were afraid, which could respect another face that looked right back at it and told
it to go to hell, and feel contempt for the face that
trembled and the eye that shifted from its own cold

steel; a face which could be savage, ruthless, merciless to what it hated and despised, and gravely generous, loyal, and devoted to what it liked; a face which could be intolerant, arrogant, insensitive, and occasionally unjust; but a face which could not be mean.

James lay still for a moment with his cold blue eyes wide awake and staring at the ceiling. Then he looked at his watch. It lacked only a few minutes of eight o'clock, his invariable time for rising every morning in the city for the past fifty years. In the country, save for Sundays, he rose one hour and fifteen minutes earlier. He fumbled in the bosom of his nightshirt and scratched himself hairily and reflectively. He had worn a nightshirt all his life, as his father had before him, and as any sensible man would do. He had enough of the discomforts of clothing during the business day. When he went to bed he wasn't going to put on a damned monkey suit with bright green stripes all over it, rope himself in around the belly like a sack of meal, and incase his legs in trousers. No! The place to wear pants was on the street and in the office. When he went to bed he wanted all the free space he could get for his legs and belly.

He swung to a sitting posture, worked his toes into his bedroom slippers, got up, walked across the room, and stood looking out the window at the street. For a moment he felt giddy: the clear mind reeled a little, the knees felt weak, he shook his head impatiently, and breathed deep; pushed the heavy, corded curtains as far back as they would go, opened the window wider. His heart was pumping hard; the thin, grim smile around the firm mouth deepened. Seventy-four! Well, then—what? And for a moment, still holding to the heavy curtain with the veined old hand, he stood looking out into the street. Few people were about and stirring. Across the street, in a big limestone-and-marble mansion similar to his own, a housemaid on

her knees was mopping marble steps. A rickety-look-
ing wagon drawn by a shaggy little horse went
rattling by. Six doors away a taxi drilled past in the
early morning of Fifth Avenue; and, beyond, old
James could see the trees and shrubs of Central Park
just greening into May. Here in his own street, before
the ugly, lavish houses, there were a few trees, all
spangled with young green. Bright, shining morning
slanted on the house fronts of the street, and from the
tender, living green of the young trees the bird song
rose.

A fine morning, then, and, from Nature, May, and
sunlight it borrowed a too pleasant coloring, James
thought, for such a damned ugly street. It was a typi-
cal street of the rich in the East Seventies—a hodgepodge of pretentious architectures. The starkly bleak
and solid ugliness of brownstone fronts was interrupted here and there by lavish bastard-French cha-
teaux like his, and in the middle of the block by the
pale salmon brick façade, the fashionable flat front,
and the green canopy of a new apartment house.

He turned, still smiling grimly. Out in the hall the
deep-toned grandfather clock was striking eight
through morning's quietness, and on the last stroke
the handle of the great walnut door was turned, his
valet entered.

The man said, "Good morning, sir," in a quiet tone.
James grunted "Morning" in reply, and without another word walked across the room into the bathroom,
and after a moment flushed the toilet noisily, then
washed his hands in the old streaked-marble basin,
turned the tumbling water on full blast into the big
old-fashioned ivory-yellow tub, and, while the tub
filled, surveyed himself in the mirror, craning his
neck, and rubbing his hand reflectively across the
wiry gray stubble of his beard. He got his shaving

things out of the cabinet and set them up in readiness, stropped his old straight razor vigorously, and with an air of satisfaction tested its deadly whetted blade, laid his razor down beside the other shaving things, turned off the water, stripped the nightshirt off over his head, stepped into the tub, and let himself down gingerly and with an easeful grunt into the water.

It took him four minutes to bathe and dry himself, and just six more to lather his face, crane cautiously, and shave the tough gray stubble of his beard as smooth as a grained wood. By the time he had finished, cleaned his old, worn razor with tender pride, and put his shaving things away again, it was eight-ten.

As he re-entered his bedroom in his dressing gown, the servant had just finished laying out his clothes. From the old walnut dresser or bureau, the man had taken socks, fresh underwear, a clean shirt, cufflinks, and a collar; and from the huge old walnut wardrobe a suit of dark clothes, a black necktie, and a pair of shoes. James would have none of "this new-fangled furniture" in his room. By this he meant that he would have neither the modern style of recent years, nor the passionately revived Colonial. His bedroom was furnished with massive Victorian pieces that had come from his father's bedroom many years before. The high and hideous old dresser, or bureau, had a tall mirror with a carved, towering, cornice-like frame of wood, and a slab of gray-streaked marble, indented and sunk between some little boxlike drawers (God knows what these were for, but probably for collar buttons, shirt studs, cufflinks, collars, and what he called "thing-ma-jigs"); below were some ponderous walnut drawers with brass knobs, which held his shirts, socks, underwear and nightshirts. The huge walnut wardrobe was at least ten feet tall; and there was a monstrous walnut table with thick curved legs and a top of the same hideous gray-streaked marble that the bureau had.

James crossed the room to the chair beside the bed, threw off his dressing gown, and, grunting a little and holding on to the man with one hand for support, thrust first one wiry shank, and then the other, into a pair of long half-weight flannel drawers, buttoned a light flannel undershirt across his hairy chest, put on his white starched shirt and buttoned it, got the starched cuffs linked together, and looked around for his trousers, which the man was holding for him, when he changed his mind suddenly, and said:

"Wait a minute! Where's that gray suit—the one I got last year? I think I'll wear it to-day."

The valet's eyes were startled, his quiet voice touched just traceably with surprise:

"The *gray*, sir?"

"I said gray, didn't I?" said James grimly, and looked at him with a naked challenge of the cold blue eyes.

"Very well, sir," the man answered quietly; but for a moment their eyes met, and although the face of each was grave, and that of James a trifle grim and truculent, there was also a sharp enkindled twinkle in the eyes of each, a kind of "tickled" quality that would not speak, because there was no need to speak.

Gravely, imperturbably, the man went to the doors of the great walnut wardrobe, opened them, and took out a neat, double-breasted suit of light gray—a decidedly gay and skittish suit for James, whose apparel was habitually dark and sober. Still imperturbable, the man came back, laid out the coat, held out the trousers to his master, and gravely held the trouser ends as James grunted and thrust gingerly into them. The servant did not speak again until James had

hitched his braces over his square shoulders and was
buttoning up the neat buttons of the vest.

"And the necktie, sir?" the man inquired. "You will
not be wearing the dark one now, I suppose."

"No," said James, hesitated for a moment, then
looked the man pugnaciously in the eye and said:
"Give me a light one—something that goes with this
suit of clothes—something gay."

"Yes, sir," the man answered calmly; and again their
eyes met, their faces grave and stern, but in their eyes
again the sly, enkindled twinkle of their recognition.

It was not until James was carefully knotting under
his wing collar a distinctly fashionable cravat of light
spring gray, slashed smartly with black stripes, that
the man found occasion to say smoothly:

"It's a fine morning, isn't it, sir?"

"It is! Yes, sir!" said James firmly and grimly, and
looked at his servant truculently again; but again
there was the enkindled sparkle in their eyes, and the
man was smiling quietly behind his master's back as
James marched sprucely from his chamber.

Outside the master's door the hall was dark and
heavy, cushioned to the tread, still with silence, sleep,
and morning, filled with walnut light and the slow
tocking of the clock.

James glanced toward the door of his wife's chamber. The huge walnut door was also eloquent with
silence, steep, inviolable repose. He smiled grimly and
went down lavish marble stairs. They swept down
with magnificence: the ghostly feet of memory and
old event thronged on them—the rustle of silk and
satin and the gleam of naked shoulders, proud tiaras,
bustles, dog-collars of hard diamonds, ropes of pearls.

He smiled grimly to himself and with displeasure.
Damned old barn! From the great reception hall at
the bottom he looked in at the lush magnificence of

the huge salon: at the red carpet, velvet to the tread; at the fat red-plush chairs with gold backs and gilded arms; at the straight, flimsy, ugly, brutally uncomfortable little chairs of gold, with faded coverings of silk; at the huge mirrors with gilt frames, also a little faded; at the French clock, a mass of fat gilt cupids, gew-gaws, thing-ma-jigs; at the damned ugly tables, cabinets, glass cases, all loaded down with more thing-ma-jigs, gew-gaws, china figures, vases, fat gilt cupids.

Junk!

Well, this was what they wanted forty years ago—what they *thought* they wanted, anyway—what the *women* wanted—what *she* wanted. He had let her have it! He had always hated it. He had said often and grimly that the only comfortable room in the whole damned place was his bathroom; the only easy chair, the stool. They had tried to change *that* a year ago: he wouldn't let them!

As for the rest of it, it was no home. It was a kind of frigid mausoleum for what people used to call "Society." It had been built for that purpose forty years ago, when people went in for that kind of thing, and when everyone was trying to outdo his neighbor in ugliness, vulgarity, lavish pretentiousness—in strident costliness, blind waste, and arrogant expense.

As such, no doubt, it had served its purpose well! It had cost him a quarter of a million dollars, but he doubted if he'd get a hundred thousand if he put it on the block tomorrow. You couldn't even keep the damned barn warm! And now? And for the future? Well, *she* would outlive him. The Parrotts always lived longer than the Wymans. What would happen? He didn't have to die and go to heaven to find out the answer to that one! She'd try to swing it for a while, then she'd find out! It'd be *her* money then—she'd run

the show, and she'd find out! She'd give a reception
or two, attempt a party in the old grand manner, try
to revive dog-collardom—and find out dog-collardom
was dead forever!

She'd get a few old hags, their skinny necks and
bony arms encrusted with their jewelry; a few dodder-
ing old fools, creaking at the joints and lisping
through their artificial teeth—all trying to revive the
ghostly pomps of Mrs. Astor! She'd get a few furiously
bored young people, there at grandma's imperative
command, wondering when in God's name the ghastly
business would be over, when they could decently
escape from the Morgue and flee to glittering spots of
music, dancing, noise, and alcohol—and she'd find
out!

Grimly, he fancied he could already hear her anguished screech when bills came in and she discovered
what it cost, discovered further that it was *her* money
she was spending now, and that money didn't grow on
trees—or if it did, it was her *own* tree now, the *Parrott* tree.

That made a difference, didn't it? For the Parrotts,
he reflected grimly, were known for their tender solici-
tude where their *own* tree was concerned—whether it
was a family tree or a money tree. Her father—
damned old fool!—had spent the last twenty years of
his life writing a single book. And what a book! *The
Beginnings of the New England Tradition: A History
of the Parrott Family.* Great God, had anyone ever
heard of such conceited bilge as that since time
began! And he—James Wyman, Sr.—had had to persuade one of his publishing acquaintances to print the
damned thing; and then he had had to endure the
gibes, the digs, the witticisms of all his friends at the
club—or else listen to the Parrott screech. Of the two
evils he had taken, he thought, the lesser one. Swift

ridicule, he had concluded, was better than slow torture; a silly book is soon forgotten, but a woman's tongue cannot be stilled.

Well, *she'd* find out, he thought, and grimly paused upon the marble flags of the reception hall, and grimly stared into the faded splendors of the great salon. He thought he foresaw the anguished progress of events already: The screech of pained astonishment when she saw the bills—the bills for coal alone—those ten-ton truck loads, car loads, barge loads, train loads of black coal required just to keep the grave-damp chill of this damned tomb reduced to a degree of semi-frigidness from October until May. And the caretakers, the nightwatchmen, the housekeepers, and so on, required to keep it guarded, watched and mended, dusted off—from May until October—when the family was away! As if anyone was going to walk off with the damned thing! Oh, if someone only would!—if a parliament of public-spirited second-story men, yeggmen, dynamiters, roof-and-cellar men, elegant silk-hatted Raffleses, and plain common-garden burglars in secret session assembled would only, in their large benevolence of soul, agree to enter, search, seize, and take away everything they could lay their hands on while the family was out of town: if they would only turn up before the barn at night in five-ton trucks, armored motor cars, swift sedans: if they would only come with any vehicle they had—wheelbarrows, furniture vans, or covered wagons—and walk out with every bit of junk in sight—all of the damned plush chairs, and gilt French clocks; all of the vases, statuettes, and figurines; all of the painted china, crimson carpets, agonizing chairs and hideous tables; all of the gew-gaws and thing-ma-jigs, the imposing sets of unread books and the bad portraits of the ancestors, including the atrocious one of Parrott, Sr., author of *The Beginnings of the New*

England Tradition—the old fool!—and while they
were about it, also overpower, gag, chloroform, and
spirit away into oblivion all of the caretakers, housekeepers, nightwatchmen, and——

"Breakfast is served, sir!"

At the soft, the whispered, the oh-most-elegant,
refined, and sugared tones, James started. As if shocked
with an electric current, he turned and stared grimly
into the unctuous, oily visage of his butler, Mr. Warren.

—and yes! above all, and by all means, if some
kind-hearted gang of kidnappers would only remove
out of his hearing, sight, and memory forever the
pompous person and the odious presence of Old Sugarlips——

"Coming," James said curtly.

"Very good, sir," Sugarlips replied with maddening
unctuousness. Then the butler turned solemnly and
departed down the hall—departed with the pompous
waddle of his big, fat buttocks, his bulging and ob-
scenely sensual calves; departed like the disgusting fat
old woman that he was, with his oily face and his fat
lips set in an expression of simpering propriety——

—Oh, if only Sugarlips would depart for good! If
only noble-hearted kidnappers would do their merciful work! If only he—James Wyman, Sr.—could somehow free himself from Sugarlips, somehow detach this
fat Old Woman of the Sea from his life, so that he
could enjoy a moment's peace and privacy in his own
house without being told that something was "Very
good, sir," enjoy a moment's rest and relaxation without Sugarlips "Begging your pardon, Sir," sit down at
his own table to feed himself in his own way without
feeling Sugarlips' damned moist breath upon his neck,
eat as he chose and what he chose and help himself
the way he chose without having every movement
censured by the interrogation of that fishy eye, the
infuriating assurance of "Allow me, sir."

If only he—James Wyman, Sr.—free, white, and—
seventy-four!—a free American citizen, by God!—
could come and go the way he chose to come and go,
sit where he wanted, eat as he wished to eat, do as he
pleased and as a free man had a right to do—without
having all the acts, engagements, and arrangements of
his personal and most private life subjected to the
constant supervision of a fool! He was tired; he was
ill, he knew; he was getting sour and crotchety—yes,
he knew all this—but, Great God! Great God!—he
was an old man and he wanted to be left alone! He'd
seen and known it all, now—he'd tried all the arguments, found all the answers, done all the things he
should have done—that the world of his time, his
wife, his family, and Society, had expected of him—
even *this*—and Great God! why had he done them?
Was it worth it? He stared in again among the faded
splendors of the great salon, and for a moment his
cold blue eyes were clouded by the shade of baffled
doubt. He had wanted a home to live in, hadn't he?—
a place of warmth, of light, a dwelling place of love
and deep security—he had had all the means of getting it, hadn't he?—wealth, courage, character, and
intelligence—and he had come to this? Somewhere,
somehow, he had missed out in life, something had
been put over on him. But where? And how? How
and where had he failed?

He had been one of the conspicuous men of his
time and generation—conspicuous not alone for his
material achievements, but conspicuous for character,
honesty, integrity, and fair-dealing in the world of
money-getting, pirate-hearted, and red-handed Yan-
keedom. Of all the men of that time and generation,
he was among the first. There were great names in
America today—names great for wealth, for power,
for ruthlessness, for their stupendous aggrandize-
ments. And he knew the way most of those names

were tainted with dishonor, those names of men who
had so ruthlessly exploited life, destroyed their fellows, betrayed mankind and their own country. Those
names, he knew, would be a stench in the nostrils of
future generations, a shame and a disgrace to the un-
fortunate children and grandchildren who would have
to acknowledge them; and from this shameful taint he
knew that his own name was triumphantly secure.
And yet something had gone wrong! Where? How?

He was no whiner; he was a brave man and a
fighter; and he knew that wherever lay the fault, the
fault, dear Brutus, lay not in his stars, but in himself!
But—(James stared grimly in among the faded splendors of the great salon)—his life had come to *this!*
And why? Why? Why?

Had all gone ill then? By no means! There had
been high effort, great accomplishment. There had
been true friendship; rooted, deep affection; the
confident regard of Kings and Presidents, statesmen,
men of letters, great industrialists, other leading
bankers and financiers like himself.

He had yielded to no man to his own dishonor; he
had yielded to many with fair-dealing, generous
concession, unresentful pardon. He had fought hardest
when the odds were all against him, but had eased
pressure when he was on top; he had not withheld the
stroke in battle, but he had not exulted over a fallen
foe.

No, the slate was clean, the mirror was unclouded—
yet, he had come to *this*. An old man, living with an
old wife, in an old dead graveyard of a house—
alone.

Old James looked in upon the faded gilt of morning
with a baffled eye. Where had it gone to, then—all of
the passion and the fire of youth, and the proud singing; all of the faith, the hope, the clean belief of fifty
years ago? Where had it gone to, then—the strength,

the faith, the wisdom, the sound health and substance of his lost America? Had it been only a dream, then? No, it was no dream—"for he lay broad awaking"—or, if dream, then such a dream as men have lived a million years to dream—to hope for—to achieve. But where now?

Gone—all gone—gone like phantasmal images of smoke, the shining bright reality of that deathless dream submerged in ruin. In the great world all around him now he saw black chaos exploding into unpurposeful and blatant power; confusion swarming through the earth, the howling jargons of a million tongues, each one dissimilar, none speaking to another; brute corruption crowned with glory, privilege enthroned. Where once there had been the patient hard confusion of honest doubt, the worried perturbation of strong faith, was now the vile smirk of a passive acceptance, the cheap sneer of the weakling lip, the feeble gibe of the ignoble vanquished, gibing their own treason and their lack of faith, the fatted heart no longer sound enough for battle, the clouded and beclamored mind no longer clear enough for truth, the bleared eye murked with rotten mockeries. The thin venom of the tongues just sneered and said —"Well, what are you going to do about it?"—and so were lost, all joined together in the corrupt defenses of their shame and cowardice—all kneeling basely at the feet of their own traitors, all bent in obscene reverence before their own monsters, all yielding, all submissive to the gods of money-getting and of mockery, all bent forward to kiss the dyer's bloody hand subdued to its own dye. So was his lost America rotted out. Gone, now, the faith, the youth, the morning, and the passion: the gold, the singing, and the dream—all vanished like phantasmal smoke, and come to *this*!

And *from* this, too! For had he not sold out somewhere along the line? But where? Where? Where?

The *hour*, the *moment*, and the actual point of *crisis*—where?

Had not he who was James Wyman fifty years ago —young and brave and an American who had the faith, and felt the strength and heard the singing, who had seen the plains, the rivers, and the mountains, the quiet blueness in a farmhand's eyes, and had heard the voices in the darkness talking, known how the land went, and the shapes of things, and known, too, that the dream was something more than dream, the great hope something more than hope—had not he, James Wyman, who had seen and heard and felt and known all these things, as all men in this land have known them—had he not sold out somewhere down the line?—taken what the others had to give?—believed what others had to say?—accepted what they had to offer? And what was that? Dog-collardom, vulgarity, and empty show, the hypocrisies and shrill pretenses of a clownlike aristocracy, the swinish gluttonies of last year's hog all varnished over with his this-year's coat-of-arms, the no-questions-asked philosophy of money-sewerdom, proud noses lifted with refined disdain at uncouth table manners, but not too nice or dainty to appraise with charity the full, rich droppings of a scoundrel's bank account.

Yes, he had so accepted, he had been so persuaded, he had so believed; or, so believing that he so believed, had so sold out somewhere, being young along the line—and so had come to *this:* an old man, living with an old wife, in an old graveyard of a house—alone.

And, looking grimly in upon the faded gilt of morning in the great salon, James reflected that not even morning entered here. No, nothing young and sweet and fresh and alive and shining could exist here. Even light, the crystal shining light of spring, of morning, and of May, was staled and deadened here. It forced its way in dustily, it thrust in through the reluctant folds of the plush curtains, it came in in mote-filled beams of dusty light, it was old and dead before it got here—like the plush, the gilt, the carpets, the chairs and tables, the gew-gaws, bric-a-brac, and thing-ma-jigs—as musty, stale, and full of death as all the things it fell upon.

No, it was not like Morning, really, by the time it had forced its painful entrance in that room. Rather, James reflected grimly, it was like the Morning After —it was—it was—well, it was like After the Ball Is Over.

The whole house, he thought, was like After the Ball Is Over. It had always been like that. "After the Ball," he thought, would be an excellent name for the damned thing: that had always been the effect it had produced on him. It had never been a home, never a place to come back to at night, and find rest and peace and warmth and homeliness and comfort. No, it had always been the cold mausoleum of departed guests; a great, frigid, splendid, and completely life-less temple to the memory of the glittering and fash-ionable parties which should have been given here last night, but which probably had not occurred. Thus, the great house was haunted constantly by the haughty ghosts of stuffed-shirtdom and dog-collardom; but by the presences of living warmth, fa-miliar usage, genial homeliness—never! The great mar-ble steps with their magnificent sweep, the marble entrance hall, the great salon, always seemed to be congealing mournfully, fading again into a melan-choly staleness, mustiness, and frigid loneliness after the rustling silks and satins, the blazing chandeliers, the refined and cultivated voices, the silvery laughter and the champagne bubbles, the dog-collars, ropes of pearls, bare backs, stiff shirts, and glowing shoulders of last night's splendid gathering had departed.

All that was needed to complete the illusion was a corps of caterer's men—twenty or thirty swarthy little fellows in monkey suits marching in to clear up the litter of the party—the empty champagne glasses, salad dishes, the cigar butts; the ashes on the carpet, and the filaments of colored paper hanging from the chandeliers—tattered remnants of the ball.

James sighed a little, then turned brusquely and marched down the hall into the great dining room.

The dining room, too, was splendid and magnificent —cold, cold, cold—like eating in a tomb. The room was on the west side of the house: the morning sun had not yet entered here. The great table was a somber polished slab, the large buffet, resplendent as a coffin, set with massive plate. At one end of the enormous table, a great high-backed chair, of carved and somber darkness, a big plate, a great heavy knife and fork and spoon, the slender elegance of a silver coffee pot, a fragile purity of cups and saucers, another plate domed richly with an enormous silver warming-cover, a glass of orange juice, and stiff, heavy, spotless napery.

James seated himself down there, a lonely little figure at the end of the enormous table—and surveyed the feast. First he looked at the glass of orange juice, raised it to his lips, shuddered, and set it down. Then, gingerly, he lifted the great silver warming-lid and peered beneath the cover: three thin brown slices of dry toast lay chastely on a big white plate. James let the silver cover fall with a large clatter. Sugarlips appeared. James poured black fluid from the coffee pot into his cup and tasted it: a slight convulsion twisted his firm mouth, he said:

"What is this stuff?"

"Coffee, sir," said Sugarlips.

"Coffee?" said James coldly.

"A new coffee, sir," breathed Sugarlips, "that has no caffein in it."

James made no answer, but his cold blue eyes were bright and hard, and, nodding toward the covered dish, he spoke coldly, tonelessly, as before:

"And this?"

"Your toast, sir," breathed Sugarlips moistly.

"*My* toast?" James inquired, in the same cold and unpersuaded tone.

"Yes, sir," breathed Sugarlips. "*Your* toast—dry toast, sir."

"Oh, no," said James grimly, "you're wrong there. It's not *my* toast—dry toast has never been *my* toast! . . . What's this?" he said with brutal suddenness, jerking his head toward the glass of orange juice.

"Your fruit juice, sir," breathed Sugarlips.

"Oh, no," said James, more cold and grim than ever. "It's not my fruit juice. You're wrong again! You never saw me drink it yet." For a moment he surveyed the butler with blue blazing eyes. Cold fury choked him. "Look here," he rasped suddenly, "what the hell's the meaning of all this? Where's my breakfast? You told me it was ready!"

"Begging your pardon, sir—" Sugarlips began, dilating his full lips moistly.

"Begging my pardon, hell!" cried James, and threw his napkin to the floor. "I don't want my pardon begged—I want my breakfast! Where is it?"

"Yes, sir," Sugarlips began, and moistened his full lips nervously—"but the doctor, sir—the diet he prescribed, sir! . . . It was the mistress's orders that you get it, sir."

"Whose breakfast is this, anyway?" said James, "Mine or your mistress's?"

"Why, *yours*, sir," Sugarlips hastily agreed.

"Who's *eating* it?" James went on brusquely. "Your mistress or me?"

"Why, you are, sir," said Sugarlips. "Of course, sir!"

"Then bring it to me!" shouted James. "At once!
When I need anyone's help to tell me what I have to
eat, I'll let you know!"

"Yes sir, yes sir," Sugarlips breathed, all of a twitter
now. "Then you desire——"

"You know what I desire," James yelled. "I desire
my breakfast! At once! Now! Right away! . . . The
same breakfast that I always have! The breakfast that
I've had for forty years! The breakfast that my father
had before me! The breakfast that a working man has
got to have—as it was in the beginning, is now, and
ever shall be! Amen!" James shouted. "Namely, a dish
of oatmeal, four slices of buttered toast, a plate of
ham and eggs, and a pot of coffee—strong black
coffee—*real* coffee!" James shouted. "Do you understand?"

"Y-y-yes, sir," stammered Sugarlips. "P-p-perfectly,
sir."

"Then go and get it! . . . Have you got any real
coffee in the house?" he demanded sharply.

"Of course, sir."

"Then bring it!" James cried, and struck the table.
"At once! Now! . . . And hurry up with it! I'll be late
to the bank as it is!" He picked up the folded pages of
The Times beside his plate and opened it with a vi-
cious rattle— "And take this slop away!" he barked,
as an afterthought, indicating the rejected breakfast
with a curt nod. "Do what you like with it—throw it
down the sink—but take it away!" And he went back
savagely to the crisp pages of *The Times* again.

The coffee came in, Sugarlips poured it, and James
was just on the point of drinking it when something
happened. He bent forward sharply, ready with the
cup of real right coffee almost to his lips, grunted
suddenly with surprise, put the cup down sharply,

and leaned forward with the paper tightly gripped in his two hands, reading intently. What he read—what caught and held his startled interest—ran as follows:

ACTRESS SUES SUNDAY SCHOOL SUPERINTENDENT, CLAIMING HEART BALM

Notice of suit was filed yesterday before Mr. Justice McGonigle in an action for breach of promise brought by Mrs. Margaret Hall Davis, 37, against W. Wainwright Parsons, 58. Mr. Parsons is well known as the author of many books on religious subjects, and for the past fifteen years he has been Superintendent of the Church School at the fashionable Episcopal Church of St. Balthazar, whose vestrymen include such leading citizens of New York as Mr. James Wyman, Sr., the banker, and. . . .

Old James swore softly to himself at this linking of his own name with such a scandal. He skimmed swiftly through the list of his fellow vestrymen and read on avidly:

Mr. Parsons could not be found last night at the University Club, where he lives. Officials at the club said he had occupied his rooms there until three days ago, when he departed, leaving no address. Members of the club, when questioned, expressed surprise when informed of Mrs. Davis's suit. Mr. Parsons, they said, was a bachelor of quiet habits, and no one had ever heard of his alleged connection with the actress.

Mrs. Davis, interviewed at her Riverside Drive apartment, answered questions willingly. She is a comely blonde of mature charms, and was formerly, she said, a member of the Ziegfeld Follies, and later a performer on the musical comedy stage. She said that she met the elderly Mr. Parsons two years ago, during a week-end at Atlantic City. Their friendship, she asserted, developed rapidly. Mr. Parsons proposed marriage to her, she claims, a year ago, but requested a postponement until New Year's Day, pleading business and financial difficulties and the illness of a member of his family as reasons for the delay. To this the pretty divorcee agreed, she says, and as a result of his ardent persuasions consented to a temporary alliance prior to their marriage. Since the first of last October, she asserted, they have occupied the Riverside Drive apartment jointly, and were known to the landlord and the other tenants of the building as "Mr. and Mrs. Parsons."

As the time for their marriage approached, the woman alleges, Mr. Parsons pleaded further complications in his personal affairs, and asked for another postponement until Easter. To this she also agreed, still confident of the sincerity of his intentions. Early in March, however, he left the apartment, telling her he had been called to Boston on business, but would return in a few days. Since that time, she says, she has not seen him, and all efforts to communicate with him have been fruitless. The woman further asserts that, in reply to repeated letters from her, Mr. Parsons finally wrote her three weeks ago, stating it would now be impossible for him to fulfill his promise of marriage and suggesting that "for the good of all concerned, we call the whole thing off."

This, Mrs. Davis asserted, she is unwilling to do.

"I loved Willy," she declared, with tears in her eyes. "God is my witness that I loved him with the deepest, purest love a woman ever had to give a man. And Willy loved me, loves me still. I know he does. I am *sure* of it! If you could only see the letters that he wrote me—I have dozens of them here"—she indicated a thick packet of letters on the table, tied with a pink ribbon—"the most passionate and romantic letters any lover ever wrote," she declared. "Willy was a wonderful lover—so gentle, so tender, so poetic—and always such a perfect gentleman! I can not give him up!" she passionately declared. "I *will* not! I love him still in spite of everything that has happened. I am willing to forgive all, forget all—if only he will come back to me."

The actress is suing for damages for one hundred thousand dollars. The firm of Hoggenheimer, Blaustein, Glutz, and Levy, of 111 Broadway, are her legal representatives.

Mr. Parsons is well known for his books in the religious field. According to Who's Who, he was born in Lima, Ohio, April 19, 1871, the son of the Reverend Samuel

Abner Parsons, and the late Martha Elizabeth Bushmiller Parsons. Educated at De Pauw University, and later at the Union Theological Seminary, he was himself ordained to the ministry in 1897, and during the next ten years filled successive pulpits in Fort Wayne, Indiana, Pottstown, Pennsylvania, and Elizabeth, New Jersey. In 1907, he retired from the ministry to devote his entire time to literary activity. Always a prolific writer, and gifted with a facile pen, his success in this field was rapid. He is the author of more than a score of books on devotional subjects, several of which have run through repeated editions, and one of which, a travel book, *Afoot in the Holy Land,* enjoyed a tremendous sale not only in this country but abroad. Some of his other works, according to *Who's Who,* are as follows:

Following After the Master (1907); *Almost Thou Persuadest Me* (1908); *Job's Comforters* (1909); *Who Follows in His Train* (1910); *For They Shall See God* (1912); *Jordan and the Marne* (1915); *Armageddon and Verdun* (1917); *Christianity and the Fuller Life* (1921); *The Way of Temptation* (1927); *The Song of Solomon* (1927); *Behold, He Cometh* (1928).

James saw the item just as he had been bending forward to sip his coffee. The name of W. Wainwright Parsons leaped out at him and hit him in the eye. Down went the coffee cup with a bang. James read on. It was not reading so much as a kind of lightning-like absorption. He tore through the column, ripping splintered fragments from the thing—all he needed!— until he had it clear and blazing in his mind. Then for a moment, after he had finished, he sat completely motionless, with a look of utter stupefaction on his face. Finally he raised the outspread paper in both hands, banged it down emphatically on the table, leaned back in his great chair, stared straight and far and viewlessly across the enormous polished vista of the table, and said slowly and with emphasis:

"I'll—be—God—damned!"

Just then Sugarlips came in with the oatmeal, smoking hot, and slid it unctuously before him. James slashed thick cream all over it, spread sugar with a copious spoon, and dug in savagely. At the third mouthful he paused again, picked up the paper in one old hand and stared at it, flung it down with an impatient growl, took another mouthful of hot oatmeal, couldn't keep away from the accursed paper—took it finally and propped it up against the coffee pot with the accusing article staring blank and square in his cold eye, and then re-read it slowly, carefully, precisely, word for word and comma for comma, and between mouthfuls of hot oatmeal let out a running commentary of low-muttered growls:

" 'I loved Willy——' "

"Why, the damned——!"

" 'Willy was a wonderful lover—so gentle, so tender, so poetic——' "

"Why—that damned mealy-mouthed, butter-lipped, two-faced——!"

"Mr. Parsons is well known as the author of many books on religious subjects——"

James dug savagely into the oatmeal and swallowed. *"Religious subjects! Bah!"*

"Superintendent . . . Church School . . . fashionable Episcopal Church of St. Balthazar . . . whose vestrymen include . . . Mr. James Wyman, Sr.——"

James groaned, picked up the offending paper, folded it, and banged it down with the story out of sight. The ham and eggs had come and he ate savagely, in a preoccupied silence, broken by an occasional angry growl. When he got up to go, he had composed himself, but his bright blue eyes were as hard and cold as glacial ice and the suggestion of a faint grim grin about the edges of his mouth was sharper, finer, more deadly than it had ever been before.

He looked at the paper, growled impatiently,

started for the door, paused, turned round, looked back, came back growling, picked up the paper, thrust it angrily into his pocket, and marched down the enormous hall. He paused at the entrance, took a derby hat and placed it firmly, a trifle jauntily, and at an angle on his well-shaped head, stepped down and opened the enormous front door, went out and down the street at a brisk pace, turned left, and so into Fifth Avenue.

To one side, the Park and young greening trees; in the roadway, the traffic beginning to thicken and drill past; everywhere, people thronging and hurrying; directly ahead, the frontal blaze and cliff of the terrific city, and morning, shining morning, on the tall towers —while an old man with cold-blazing eyes went sprucely swinging through the canyoned slant, muttering to himself:

—Following After the Master—*Bah!*

—Almost Thou Persuadest Me—*Bah!*

—The Way of Temptation——

Suddenly he whipped the folded newspaper out of his pocket, turned it over, and peered intently at the story again, comparing dates. The faint grim grin around the edges of his mouth relaxed a little.

—The Song of Solomon——

The grin spread over his face, suffusing it with color, and his old eyes twinkled as, still peering intently, he re-read the last line of the story.

—Behold, He Cometh——

With a jaunty motion he slapped the folded paper against his thigh, and, chuckling to himself with a full return of his good humor, he muttered:

"By God! I didn't know he had it in him!"

God's Lonely Man

My life, more than that of anyone I know, has been spent in solitude and wandering. Why this is true, or how it happened, I cannot say; yet it is so. From my fifteenth year—save for a single interval—I have lived about as solitary a life as a modern man can have. I mean by this that the number of hours, days, months, and years that I have spent alone has been immense and extraordinary. I propose, therefore, to describe the experience of human loneliness exactly as I have known it.

The reason that impels me to do this is not that I think my knowledge of loneliness different in kind from that of other men. Quite the contrary. The whole conviction of my life now rests upon the belief that loneliness, far from being a rare and curious phenomenon, peculiar to myself and to a few other solitary men, is the central and inevitable fact of human existence. When we examine the moments, acts, and statements of all kinds of people—not only the grief and ecstasy of the greatest poets, but also the huge unhappiness of the average soul, as evidenced by the innumerable strident words of abuse, hatred, contempt, mistrust, and scorn that forever grate upon our ears as the manswarm passes us in the streets—we find, I think, that they are all suffering from the same thing. The final cause of their complaint is loneliness.

But if my experience of loneliness has not been different in kind from that of other men, I suspect it has been sharper in intensity. This gives me the best authority in the world to write of this, our general complaint, for I believe I know more about it than anyone of my generation. In saying this, I am merely stating a fact as I see it, though I realize that it may sound like arrogance or vanity. But before anyone jumps to that conclusion, let him consider how strange it would be to meet with arrogance in one who has lived alone as much as I. The surest cure for vanity is loneliness. For, more than other men, we who dwell in the heart of solitude are always the victims of self-doubt. Forever and forever in our loneliness, shameful feelings of inferiority will rise up suddenly to overwhelm us in a poisonous flood of horror, disbelief, and desolation, to sicken and corrupt our health and confidence, to spread pollution at the very root of strong, exultant joy. And the eternal paradox of it is that if a man is to know the triumphant labor of creation, he must for long periods resign himself to loneliness, and suffer loneliness to rob him of the health, the confidence, the belief and joy which are essential to creative work.

To live alone as I have lived, a man should have the confidence of God, the tranquil faith of a monastic saint, the stern impregnability of Gibraltar. Lacking these, there are times when anything, everything, all or nothing, the most trivial incidents, the most casual words, can in an instant strip me of my armor, palsy my hand, constrict my heart with frozen horror, and fill my bowels with the gray substance of shuddering impotence. Sometimes it is nothing but a shadow passing on the sun; sometimes nothing but the torrid milky light of August, or the naked, sprawling ugliness and squalid decencies of streets in Brooklyn fading in the weary vistas of that milky light and evoking the intolerable misery of countless drab and nameless lives. Sometimes it is just the barren horror of raw concrete, or the heat blazing on a million beetles of machinery darting through the torrid streets, or the cindered weariness of parking spaces, or the slamming smash and racket of the El, or the driven manswarm of the earth, thrusting on forever in exacerbated fury, going nowhere in a hurry.

Again, it may be just a phrase, a look, a gesture. It may be the cold, disdainful inclination of the head with which a precious, kept, exquisite princeling of Park Avenue acknowledges an introduction, as if to say: "You are nothing." Or it may be a sneering reference and dismissal by a critic in a high-class weekly magazine. Or a letter from a woman saying I am lost and ruined, my talent vanished, all my efforts false and worthless—since I have forsaken the truth, vision, and reality which are so beautifully her own.

And sometimes it is less than these—nothing I can touch or see or hear or definitely remember. It may be so vague as to be a kind of hideous weather of the soul, subtly compounded of all the hunger, fury, and impossible desire my life has ever known. Or, again, it may be a half-forgotten memory of the cold wintry red of waning Sunday afternoons in Cambridge, and of a pallid, sensitive, æsthetic face that held me once in earnest discourse on such a Sunday afternoon in Cambridge, telling me that all my youthful hopes were pitiful delusions and that all my life would come to naught, and the red and waning light of March was reflected on the pallid face with a desolate impotence that instantly quenched all the young ardors of my blood.

Beneath the evocations of these lights and weathers, and the cold, disdainful words of precious, sneering, and contemptuous people, all of the joy and singing of the day goes out like an extinguished candle, hope seems lost to me forever, and every truth that I have ever found and known seems false. At such a time the lonely man will feel that all the evidence of his own senses has betrayed him, and that nothing really lives and moves on earth but creatures of the death-in-life—those of the cold, constricted heart and the sterile loins, who exist forever in the red waning light of March and Sunday afternoon.

All this hideous doubt, despair, and dark confusion of the soul a lonely man must know, for he is united to no image save that which he creates himself, he is bolstered by no other knowledge save that which he can gather for himself with the vision of his own eyes and brain. He is sustained and cheered and aided by no party, he is given comfort by no creed, he has no faith in him except his own. And often that faith deserts him, leaving him shaken and filled with impotence. And then it seems to him that his life has come to nothing, that he is ruined, lost, and broken past redemption, and that morning—bright, shining morning, with its promise of new beginnings—will never come upon the earth again as it did once.

He knows that dark time is flowing by him like a river. The huge, dark wall of loneliness is around him now. It encloses and presses in upon him, and he cannot escape. And the cancerous plant of memory is feeding at his entrails, recalling hundreds of forgotten faces and ten thousand vanished days, until all life seems as strange and insubstantial as a dream. Time flows by him like a river, and he waits in his little room like a creature held captive by an evil spell. And he will hear, far off, the murmurous drone of the great earth, and feel that he has been forgotten, that his powers are wasting from him while the river flows, and that all his life has come to nothing. He feels that his strength is gone, his power withered, while he sits there drugged and fettered in the prison of his loneliness.

Then suddenly, one day, for no apparent reason, his faith and his belief in life will come back to him in a tidal flood. It will rise up in him with a jubilant and invincible power, bursting a window in the world's great wall and restoring everything to shapes of deathless brightness. Made miraculously whole and secure in himself, he will plunge once more into the triumphant labor of creation. All his old strength is his again: he knows what he knows, he is what he is, he has found what he has found. And he will say the truth that is in him, speak it even though the whole world deny it, affirm it though a million men cry out that it is false.

At such a moment of triumphant confidence, with this feeling in me, I dare now assert that I have known Loneliness as well as any man, and will now write of him as if he were my very brother, which he is. I will paint him for you with such fidelity to his true figure that no man who reads will ever doubt his visage when Loneliness comes to him hereafter.

The most tragic, sublime, and beautiful expression of human loneliness which I have ever read is the Book of Job; the grandest and most philosophical, Ecclesiastes. Here I must point out a fact which is so much at variance with everything I was told as a child concerning loneliness and the tragic underweft of life that, when I first discovered it, I was astounded and incredulous, doubting the overwhelming weight of evidence that had revealed it to me. But there it was, as solid as a rock, not to be shaken or denied; and as the years passed, the truth of this discovery became part of the structure of my life.

The fact is this: the lonely man, who is also the tragic man, is invariably the man who loves life dearly —which is to say, the joyful man. In these statements there is no paradox whatever. The one condition implies the other, and makes it necessary. The essence of human tragedy is in loneliness, not in conflict, no matter what the arguments of the theater may assert. And just as the great tragic writer (I say, "the tragic writer" as distinguished from "the writer of tragedies," for certain nations, the Roman and French among them, have had no great tragic writers, for Vergil and Racine were none, but rather great writers of tragedy), just as the great tragic writer—Job, Sophocles, Dante, Milton, Swift, Dostoevski—has always been the lonely man, so has he also been the man who loved life best and had the deepest sense of joy. The real quality and substance of human joy is to be found in the works of these great tragic writers as nowhere else in all the records of man's life upon the earth. In proof of this, I can give here one conclusive illustration:

In my childhood, any mention of the Book of Job evoked instantly in my mind a long train of gloomy, gray, and unbrokenly dismal associations. This has been true, I suspect, with most of us. Such phrases as "Job's comforter," and "the patience of Job," and "the afflictions of Job," have become part of our common idiom and are used to refer to people whose woes seem uncountable and unceasing, who have suffered long and silently, and whose gloom has never been interrupted by a ray of hope or joy. All these associations had united to make for me a picture of the Book of Job that was grim, bleak, and constant in its misery. When I first read it as a child, it seemed to me that the record of Job's tribulations was relieved only by a kind of gloomy and unwilling humor—a humor not intended by the author, but supplied by my own exasperation, for my childish sense of proportion and justice was at length so put upon by this dreary tidal flood of calamities that I had to laugh in protest.

But any reader of intelligence and experience who has read that great book in his mature years will realize how false such a picture is. For the Book of Job, far from being dreary, gray, and dismal, is woven entire, more than any single piece of writing I can recall, from the sensuous, flashing, infinitely various, and gloriously palpable material of great poetry; and it wears at the heart of its tremendous chant of everlasting sorrow the exulting song of everlasting joy.

In this there is nothing strange or curious, but only what is inevitable and right. For the tragic writer knows that joy is rooted at the heart of sorrow, that ecstasy is shot through with the sudden crimson thread of pain, that the knife-thrust of intolerable desire and the wild, brief glory of possession are pierced most bitterly, at the very instant of man's greatest victory, by the premonitory sense of loss and death. So seen and so felt, the best and worst that the human heart can know are merely different aspects of the same thing, and are interwoven, both together, into the tragic web of life.

It is the sense of death and loneliness, the knowledge of the brevity of his days, and the huge impending burden of his sorrow, growing always, never lessening, that makes joy glorious, tragic, and unutterably precious to a man like Job. Beauty comes and passes, is lost the moment that we touch it, can no more be stayed or held than one can stay the flowing of a river. Out of this pain of loss, this bitter ecstasy of brief having, this fatal glory of the single moment, the tragic writer will therefore make a song for joy. That, at least, he may keep and treasure always. And his song is full of grief, because he knows that joy is fleeting, gone the instant that we have it, and that is why it is so precious, gaining its full glory from the very things that limit and destroy it.

He knows that joy gains its glory out of sorrow, bitter sorrow, and man's loneliness, and that it is haunted always with the certainty of death, dark death, which stops our tongues, our eyes, our living

breath, with the twin oblivions of dust and nothing-
ness. Therefore a man like Job will make a chant for
sorrow, too, but it will still be a song for joy as well,
and one more strange and beautiful than any other
that man has ever sung:

Hast thou given the horse strength? hast thou clothed
his neck with thunder?
Canst thou make him afraid as a grasshopper? the glory
of his nostrils is terrible.
He paweth in the valley, and rejoiceth in his strength:
he goeth on to meet the armed men.
He mocketh at fear, and is not affrighted; neither turneth
he back from the sword.
The quiver rattleth against him, the glittering spear and
the shield.
He swalloweth the ground with fierceness and rage;
neither believeth he that it is the sound of the trumpet.
He saith among the trumpets, Ha, ha; and he smelleth
the battle afar off, the thunder of the captains, and the
shouting.

That is joy—joy solemn and triumphant; stern,
lonely, everlasting joy, which has in it the full depth
and humility of man's wonder, his sense of glory, and
his feeling of awe before the mystery of the universe.
An exultant cry is torn from our lips as we read the
lines about that glorious horse, and the joy we feel is
wild and strange, lonely and dark like death, and
grander than the delicate and lovely joy that men like
Herrick and Theocritus described, great poets though
they were.

Just as the Book of Job and the sermon of Ecclesiastes are, each in its own way, supreme histories of
man's loneliness, so do all the books of the Old Testament, in their entirety, provide the most final and profound literature of human loneliness that the world
has known. It is astonishing with what a coherent

unity of spirit and belief the life of loneliness is recorded in those many books—how it finds its full expression in the chants, songs, prophecies, and chronicles of so many men, all so various, and each so individual, each revealing some new image of man's secret and most lonely heart, and all combining to produce a single image of his loneliness that is matchless in its grandeur and magnificence.

Thus, in a dozen books of the Old Testament—in Job, Ecclesiastes, and the Song of Solomon, in Psalms, Proverbs, and Isaiah; in words of praise and words of lamentation; in songs of triumph and in chants of sorrow, bondage, and despair; in boasts of pride and arrogant assertion, and in stricken confessions of humility and fear; in warning, promise, and in prophecy; in love, hate, grief, death, loss, revenge, and resignation; in wild, singing jubilation and in bitter sorrow—the lonely man has wrought out in a swelling and tremendous chorus the final vision of his life.

The total, all-contributary unity of this conception of man's loneliness in the books of the Old Testament becomes even more astonishing when we begin to read the New. For, just as the Old Testament becomes the chronicle of the life of loneliness, the gospels of the New Testament, with the same miraculous and unswerving unity, become the chronicle of the life of love. What Christ is saying always, what he never swerves from saying, what he says a thousand times and in a thousand different ways, but always with a central unity of belief, is this: "I am my Father's son, and you are my brothers." And the unity that binds us all together, that makes this earth a family, and all men brothers and the sons of God, is love.

The central purpose of Christ's life, therefore, is to destroy the life of loneliness and to establish here on earth the life of love. The evidence to support this is

clear and overwhelming. It should be obvious to everyone that when Christ says: "Blessed are the poor in
spirit: for theirs is the kingdom of heaven," "Blessed
are they that mourn: for they shall be comforted,"
"Blessed are the meek: for they shall inherit the
earth," "Blessed are they which do hunger and thirst
after righteousness: for they shall be filled," "Blessed
are the merciful: for they shall obtain mercy," and
"Blessed are the pure in heart: for they shall see God"
—Christ is not here extolling the qualities of humility,
sorrow, meekness, righteousness, mercy, and purity as
virtues sufficient in themselves, but he promises to
men who have these virtues the richest reward that
men were ever offered.

And what is that reward? It is a reward that promises not only the inheritance of the earth, but the kingdom of heaven as well. It tells men that they shall not
live and die in loneliness, that their sorrow will not go
unassuaged, their prayers unheard, their hunger and
thirst unfed, their love unrequited: but that, through
love, they shall destroy the walls of loneliness forever;
and even if the evil and unrighteous of this earth shall
grind them down into the dust, yet if they bear all
things meekly and with love, they will enter into a
fellowship of joy, a brotherhood of love, such as no
men on earth ever knew before.

Such was the final intention of Christ's life, the purpose of his teaching. And its total import was that the
life of loneliness could be destroyed forever by the
life of love. Or such, at least, has been the meaning
which I read into his life. For in these recent years
when I have lived alone so much, and known loneliness so well, I have gone back many times and read
the story of this man's words and life to see if I could
find in them a meaning for myself, a way of life that
would be better than the one I had. I read what he
had said, not in a mood of piety or holiness, not from

a sense of sin, a feeling of contrition, or because his promise of a heavenly reward meant very much to me. But I tried to read his bare words nakedly and simply, as it seems to me he must have uttered them, and as I have read the words of other men—of Homer, Donne, and Whitman, and the writer of Ecclesiastes—and if the meaning I have put upon his words seems foolish or extravagant, childishly simple or banal, mine alone or not different from what ten million other men have thought, I have only set it down here as I saw it, felt it, found it for myself, and have tried to add, subtract, and alter nothing.

And now I know that though the way and meaning of Christ's life is a far, far better way and meaning than my own, yet I can never make it mine; and I think that this is true of all the other lonely men that I have seen or known about—the nameless, voiceless, faceless atoms of this earth as well as Job and Everyman and Swift. And Christ himself, who preached the life of love, was yet as lonely as any man that ever lived. Yet I could not say that he was mistaken because he preached the life of love and fellowship, and lived and died in loneliness; nor would I dare assert his way was wrong because a billion men have since professed his way and never followed it.

I can only say that I could not make his way my own. For I have found the constant, everlasting weather of man's life to be, not love, but loneliness. Love itself is not the weather of our lives. It is the rare, the precious flower. Sometimes it is the flower that gives us life, that breaches the dark walls of all our loneliness and restores us to the fellowship of life, the family of the earth, the brotherhood of man. But sometimes love is the flower that brings us death; and from it we get pain and darkness; and the mutilations of the soul, the maddening of the brain, may be in it.

How or why or in what way the flower of love will

come to us, whether with life or death, triumph or defeat, joy or madness, no man on this earth can say. But I know that at the end, forever at the end for us— the houseless, homeless, doorless, driven wanderers of life, the lonely men—there waits forever the dark visage of our comrade, Loneliness.

But the old refusals drop away, the old avowals stand—and we who were dead have risen, we who were lost are found again, and we who sold the talent, the passion, and belief of youth into the keeping of the fleshless dead, until our hearts were corrupted, our talent wasted, and our hope gone, have won our lives back bloodily, in solitude and darkness; and we know that things will be for us as they have been, and we see again, as we saw once, the image of the shining city. Far flung, and blazing into tiers of jeweled light, it burns forever in our vision as we walk the Bridge, and strong tides are bound round it, and the great ships call. And we walk the Bridge, always we walk the Bridge alone with you, stern friend, the one to whom we speak, who never failed us. Hear:

"Loneliness forever and the earth again! Dark brother and stern friend, immortal face of darkness and of night, with whom the half part of my life was spent, and with whom I shall abide now till my death forever—what is there for me to fear as long as you are with me? Heroic friend, blood-brother of my life, dark face—have we not gone together down a million ways, have we not coursed together the great and furious avenues of night, have we not crossed the stormy seas alone, and known strange lands, and come again to walk the continent of night and listen to the silence of the earth? Have we not been brave and glorious when we were together, friend? Have we not known triumph, joy, and glory on this earth—and will it not be again with me as it was then, if you come back to me? Come to me, brother, in the watches of the night. Come to me in the secret and most silent heart of darkness. Come to me as you always came, bringing to me again the old invincible strength, the deathless hope, the triumphant joy and confidence that will storm the earth again."

A Note

on

Thomas Wolfe

[This essay was written by Thomas Wolfe's editor at Harper & Brothers for the first publication of this group of short stories. At that time a short novel, *The Hills Beyond*, was published with them. It is now available in a separate volume from Perennial Library—THE PUBLISHERS.]

Thomas Wolfe was thirty-seven years old when he died on September 15, 1938. Nine years before, in 1929, he had published his first book and had been widely acclaimed as one of the most promising writers of his generation. J. B. Priestley has said that he thinks Wolfe must have known his time was short and that that is why he lived and worked so furiously. However this may be, nine years were all he had in which to realize his promise, and during those years he performed creative labors that would have taxed the full life span of most authors.

With the appearance of *The Hills Beyond*, his works stand completed. During his lifetime he published two long novels, *Look Homeward, Angel* (1929) and *Of Time and the River* (1935); a book of more or less unrelated shorter pieces, *From Death to Morning* (1935); and a very revealing little volume about his methods as a writer, *The Story of a Novel* (1936). At his death he left a mountain of unpublished manuscript, conservatively estimated at more than a million words—the equivalent in length of ten or twelve ordinary novels. From this manuscript three posthumous books have been edited, and up to a point they round out the same pattern, volume for volume, as his previous work. There are the two long novels, *The Web and the Rock* (1939) and *You Can't Go Home Again* (1940); and here, in *The Hills Beyond*, is another book of his shorter writings. Nothing is lacking to make the parallel perfect except a further revealing glimpse of his methods as a writer. He surely would have laid bare his literary secrets if he had lived, because he was the most open and unsecretive person in the world; since he died before he could do it, this Note is designed, insofar as it can, to fill the gap.

Illuminating as is *The Story of a Novel*, much still remains to be said about Thomas Wolfe's unusual techniques. No one, I think, ever went about the job of writing as he did. His strengths and his weaknesses, his brilliant achievements in probing to the roots of human character and in evoking the sights, sounds, smells, and very feel of his America, as well as his constant preoccupation with the elusive mysteries of communication and of form—all were implicit in his methods. He often said that he never learned anything except by experience, by trial and error, by finding out for himself. This was true. He had to do everything the hard way. And it was as true of his writing habits as of anything else. He had read many books and articles in which other writers told how they did it—and he found no help in them for himself. He would talk interminably with his fellow authors, and would even listen patiently, with a faint half-hope, when a certain pulp writer he knew would stop by at his rooms in the old Chelsea Hotel and boast about how he turned out ten stories and got good money for them while Tom was struggling to produce one. Afterwards Tom would shake his head sadly, a little wistfully. It would be wonderful if he had the pulp writer's ability to bat them out and yet could write *his* kind of thing instead of the other fellow's pulp. But even while he let himself be momentarily tormented by visions of this impossible fulfillment, he would shrug and laugh and go back to work. He had long since learned that there was nothing even the best of writers could tell him that was of the slightest use to him. He had to go his own way. In the end he always came back to that. So he borrowed nothing from others. First and last, his methods were his very own. He invented them—because he had to.

"I've got too much material," said George Webber in *You Can't Go Home Again* (p. 386). "It keeps backing up on me until sometimes I wonder what in the name of God

I'm going to do with it all—how I'm going to find a frame
for it, a pattern, a channel, a way to make it flow! . . .
The thing I've got to find out is the way!" George Webber
had just published his first book when he uttered this de-
spairing cry, and was about to plunge into the jungle
depths of Brooklyn to live and work alone until he had
found "the way" out of his dilemma. It is hardly necessary
to say that the quotation reflected Tom's own state of mind
after *Look Homeward, Angel* came out.

Till the day he died he was always as honest in speaking of his uncertainties and self-doubts as he was in affirm-
ing what he knew. So it happened that I, his last editor,
became the most convenient receptacle during the final
year of his life for his long and earnest confidences about
the work he had done and was doing, and how he was
doing it. Throughout that year I probably saw him more
frequently than anyone, and what I have to say here is
based in large measure upon the things he told me. Beyond that it became my duty after his death to edit his
unpublished manuscript, which, when stacked in one pile,
stood breast high from the floor. The better part of three
years went into studying and editing it. This was a rare
experience, which shed a great deal of new light on
Thomas Wolfe's methods. So, although I cannot speak
with first-hand knowledge of how he wrote his first three
creative books, I think I have a fairly clear idea of how he
wrote his last three.

In certain important particulars his point of view had
changed as he had grown older and more sure of himself.
Before that he had been experimenting and feeling his way
along. Right up to the end he was still experimenting, and
very importantly I think, but also his previous apprenticeship had taught him many things, leading him to modify
some of the practices that had once come most natural to
him. This was true even in superficial details. For example, those famous ledgers in which he wrote the first draft
of *Look Homeward, Angel,* and which are so often mentioned in stories about him, had long since been abandoned
for everyday use. I never saw him write on anything but
ordinary manuscript paper. True, he carried a ledger on

his last trip across the country and after his death it was found in his baggage half full of notes and jottings.* But toward the end of his life he wrote in ledgers only when he was traveling, and then merely because they were easy to carry around and keep track of. That is probably why he had adopted them in the first place. They belonged chiefly to his years of youthful wandering and were put aside when his life became more settled.

Again, Tom joked about having written *Of Time and the River* standing up, using the top of a refrigerator as a work table. If this was true, and I do not doubt it, the habit of standing while he wrote is another that he abandoned with his youth. His invariable practice when I knew him was to pace the floor with head thrown back, running his fingers nervously through his disheveled hair as he pondered some scene or character, but the moment he got it straight and the whole thing incandescent within him, he would rush to his table and sit down to capture it on paper.

Such changes in superficial habits may perhaps be regarded as outward symbols of much more important inner changes in his whole approach to his problems as a writer, and it is of these that I wish to speak. This Note is not intended as a critical appraisal of Thomas Wolfe, but as an interpretative statement containing information that may be helpful to those who are better qualified than I to determine his ultimate place in American literature. It should be borne in mind that what I have to say refers almost entirely to his last years. They may have been his most important years. At any rate they represent his final phase, the period of his greatest maturity as an artist.

Many critics have observed that the literary style of his posthumous books is often quite different from that of his earlier books. Much of the writing is more objective in tone, its lyricism more restrained. This was first noticeable

---

* These notes were published under the title, "A Western Journey," in the *Virginia Quarterly Review*, summer issue of 1939.

in the opening half of *The Web and the Rock,* but not in the latter half (for reasons to be explained later). His objectivity was still more apparent in *You Can't Go Home Again* as a whole. It is most striking of all in the title piece of the present volume. What is the explanation of this change? What lay behind it? What does it indicate about Wolfe's growth as an artist?

These questions can best be answered by telling what I know of his purposes and of the techniques he used to achieve them. Of course there is nothing mysterious about the ends which his writing was meant to serve. The motives which drove him to write, and which lent such singular integrity to everything he wrote, can be read clearly enough in his books. But his techniques are more obscure, and often cannot be derived from the evidence that is visible in his printed pages. His methods were certainly unusual, if not unique in literature. Very few people know anything about them. Perhaps that is one reason why there are so many misconceptions about Thomas Wolfe.

For example, some of his readers seem to think that when Tom was in the throes of composition, all he had to do was to open the sluice gates and the words tumbled forth in an irresistible torrent like the surge of pent-up waters suddenly released. True, he wrote like one possessed. His first drafts were always done in longhand with a pencil, and when he had a secretary, as he did throughout his last year, one of her chores was to keep a dozen pencils sharpened and ready for his need. With amazing speed he would fill innumerable sheets of paper with his vigorous scrawl, and toss them aside to fall on the floor for his secretary to pick up, put in order, and transcribe. He never hesitated for a word: the words came too fast for him, and in his effort to keep up with them he would often form only the first letter and the last with a wriggle between, so that only the initiated could decode his sentences.

But the analogy by which this process has been compared to the opening of sluice gates becomes very misleading if left without qualification. To understand what was happening with Tom when he was writing, one needs to remember all the years through which his experience and observation had slowly accumulated. One also needs to be reminded of his acute self-tortures of thought and feeling about everything he had experienced and observed. He could not put anything that had happened to him out of his consciousness until he had rehearsed it in memory a thousand times, going back over it again and again in every detail until he had got at the core of it and had extracted the last shred of meaning out of it on every level. One needs to be told, too, of his ingenious experiments with different ways of saying what he wanted to say, sometimes only worked out in his head, sometimes roughly sketched on paper. All of this preceded the moment of spate-writing and made it possible.

Beyond this, one needs to know—and the fact may come as a surprise—that Tom had become a tireless reviser and rewriter. Whether this was true of him in his younger days I cannot say, but it was certainly true of him later. Much as he had told me and shown me of what he had been doing in those last years, I was not quite prepared to discover, when I came to deal with the whole manuscript, how vitally essential rewriting had become to his whole method. Far more often than not I found that there would be at least two different versions of the same episode, and sometimes there were as many as four or five versions. There would be a first draft hastily sketched out, then later drafts that filled in the details, and it was fascinating to see how the thing had changed and grown under his hand. When he was dissatisfied with a scene or character he would not, as a rule, simply revise his draft and get it recopied: he would put it aside and rewrite it some different way from start to finish. He would pace the floor over it, and he might dictate the revision straight to the typewriter—then his secretary would have an exhausting day trying to keep up. In editing the manuscript it was very puzzling to come upon these variant versions because they were not marked (the pages were frequently out of order and were not even numbered), and only a careful comparison of the internal evidence could determine which was the last draft and the most complete realization of his intentions.

Other misconceptions about Thomas Wolfe lie back of the often repeated observation that he was an "autobiographical writer." This comment never failed to infuriate him. As he said, there are so many different ways to be autobiographical that the phrase doesn't mean much. He *was* an "autobiographical writer." Of course. But that is not to say, as the term might imply, that he was only a sort of glorified newspaper reporter endowed with total recall who therefore set down the complete factual record of everything that had happened to him from the day of his birth. Such a notion overlooks the role which imagination played in everything he wrote. It is true that he drew upon life as he had known it for the substance of his books. But so, too, has every other author worthy of the name. "A writer, like everybody else," as Tom said,* "must use what he has to use. He can't use something that he hasn't got." When Tom used what he had, he passed it through the fire of his creative imagination, and what came out in his books was something quite different from any mere record, however straight and complete, of his own life.

But didn't he use autobiography more literally than most writers? Undoubtedly he did; but that is not the whole story either. The most literally autobiographical of his books is *Look Homeward, Angel*. There he wrote of the life he had known "in a manner of naked directness and reality that was rather rare in books." † I doubt if there was a character in it who was not drawn from someone he had known. Certainly the natives of Asheville recognized the portraits easily enough, and Tom has told the story of the storm that burst upon him. He learned a lot from that experience. Among other things he said he learned that it was all right to write about a horse thief if one wanted to, but that it wasn't necessary to give his street address and telephone number. But that was the kind of book his first one was, and because it was, his readers have probably assumed that the later books were of exactly the same kind. No doubt parts of them were, but not all. After a while there began to be a difference. Tom lived by a peculiar

* *You Can't Go Home Again*, p. 326.
† *Ibid.*

time sense of his own and it took him longer than most of us require to get around an experience and over it. Moving in the ponderous cycles of Wolfean time, he slowly worked out the lessons he had learned, and began to get away from his more literal interpretations of his experience. And the surprising truth is that in the end he got so far from it that in some notable instances his use of autobiography differed in no degree from what is commonly called pure creation.

One of the most satisfyingly real characters in that whole vital and full-blooded world of Wolfe is Nebraska Crane, the Cherokee boy who grew up with George Webber and later became a big-league baseball player. If Tom never wrote anything but naked autobiography, one would have to assume that Nebraska is a counterpart of someone Tom knew as a boy. But not at all. I have asked the members of Tom's family about this and their answers are clear and conclusive. His mother, his sister, Mrs. Ralph Wheaton, and his brother Fred—all have exceptional memories for people who have ever, in even the remotest way, touched their own lives or family. If anybody like Nebraska Crane had been Tom's best friend when he was a boy, they would certainly know it. But each of them has told me that there was no one among Tom's childhood acquaintances who could have sat for the portrait of Nebraska.

Where, then, did this memorable character come from? The answer is that Tom created him. And how did he create him? What was the process? It was the same process that creative writers of a less "autobiographical" turn than Tom have always used—the process of observing a great many people of a certain type to find out what makes them tick as they do, and then of drawing upon these observations to build a character who is true to the type and yet is not an image of any person who ever lived. Tom loved baseball and baseball players. For years he was always an honored guest at the annual baseball dinner which the big-league players hold in New York after the season is over. After he died his mother found in his coat pocket a ticket to that year's baseball dinner. Tom knew most of the players, liked to be around them, and loved their talk. Out of his intimate knowledge of them—the "feel" of what it is like to be a ball player—he created Nebraska Crane. He wrote first the chapters in *You Can't Go Home Again* which describe the home-run king who is past his prime but still hoping to stay in the game another season or two. Afterwards he went back and wrote the earlier chapters in *The Web and the Rock,* building up out of his imagination the kind of childhood which might have produced Nebraska, and then making him George Webber's best friend—precisely because that was the kind of friend the youthful Tom Wolfe always wanted and never had.

Nebraska Crane is a perfect example of free invention —the kind that many critics had urged Tom to turn his talents to. And Nebraska is not an isolated instance. In the last books there are other characters which illustrate the same line of development toward a more imaginative use of experience or autobiography. One of them is Randy Shepperton, George Webber's Mercutio, who stood by him after his book came out when everybody else turned against him. Though certain external facts of his career were undoubtedly borrowed from real life, I am convinced that in his essential character Randy represents another imaginative projection of the close contemporary—sympathetic, understanding, loyal—whom Tom needed desperately during that trying period of his life but did not have. He did have such a friend in his first editor, but *he* belonged to an older generation, which made it different.

Another example of free creation is Judge Rumford Bland, the evil old blind man who owned that incredible junk shop and used it to exact a pitiless usury from defenseless Negroes. I have satisfied myself that Judge Rumford Bland, real and terrifying as he is, never existed in the flesh. Tom conjured him up out of his knowledge of many people, and out of his shame and deep feeling about one of the South's most flagrant evils. But where and how did Tom get the initial impetus to create him, as well as the detailed knowledge of the tricks such a man would employ in his usury? Fred Wolfe, Tom's brother, has given me the answer. Their father, at one time in his life, quite innocently and unsuspectingly, bought a small furniture store that turned out to be not at all what it seemed to be; when he discovered what went on there he was outraged and promptly got rid of it. For the rest, it is hardly necessary to point out—at least not to those who have read *Look Homeward, Angel*—that the lineaments of Tom's father are not to be discovered lurking behind the mask of Judge Rumford Bland. Tom built up that sinister character to depict the kind of man who would and could consent to draw his livelihood from such a "business."

Tom had given intense thought to the problems of being an "autobiographical writer," and he knew how many and varied are the uses of autobiography. In a letter to me, written many months before he died, he confirmed the fact that his development was taking the direction which these examples indicate. He called the letter "a statement of purpose," and it was very long. He spoke of the work he had most recently been doing, and referred throughout to "the book," by which he meant the whole manuscript from which the three posthumous volumes were later taken. He wrote:

Here is what the author has in mind:

He intends to use his own experience absolutely—to pour it in, to squeeze it, to get everything out of it that it is worth. He intends for this to be the most objective book that he has ever written, and he also intends, by the same token, for it to be the most autobiographical. . . . Out of his experience he has derived some new characters who are now compacted not so much from specific recollection as from the whole amalgam and consonance of seeing, feeling, thinking, living, and knowing many people. . . .

As the author has told his editor, this book marks not only a turning away from the books he has written in the past, but a genuine spiritual and artistic change. In other words, he feels that he is done with lyrical and identifiable personal autobiography; he is also seeking, and hopes now to obtain, through free creation, a release of his inventive power which the more shackling limitations of identifiable autobiography do not permit.*

* This letter illustrates an amusing characteristic of Southern

This statement of his purpose did not mean that he had applied the new method to the whole of the manuscript. Not at all. By far the greater part of the manuscript was written before he had thought his way through to this conclusion—some of it years before, as I shall show. What he meant was that he had written certain new portions in this freer vein—to see if he could do it, as he later told me—that he was pleased with the experiment, and that henceforth that was the kind of thing he wanted to do.

It is important to remember this in any evaluation of him, because it shows that before he died he had reached a new stage of growth.

One of the commonest misconceptions about Thomas Wolfe is that his work lacked form. In the main this notion has been fostered by "academic" people. (Not all professors have academic minds; neither are all people with academic minds professors.) Their reasoning runs something like this:

Wolfe is supposed to have written novels. A novel is such and such, the definition being derived from a study of literary history. That is to say, Fielding, Dickens, Thackeray, Willa Cather wrote novels; there is a certain common denominator to be found in all their books—a story, with a beginning, a middle, and an end; that then, or something like it, is a novel. Wolfe's books are not like that. Ergo, they are not novels. So what in the name of God are they?

Tom had very little to say to those who believe they can understand a work of art by tying it up in a neat little packet, pasting a label on it, and tucking it away in a pigeonhole. He did not write for them and was totally uninterested in them except as bizarre specimens of the human race, fascinating to study but unprofitable to listen

---

manners. Tom and I, being both from the South, began our close relationship on a plane of very correct formality, Mistering each other about a month before we felt we were well enough acquainted to use first names with propriety. It was during this time that he wrote the letter: hence the odd formality of its third person singular.

to. He did not know whether anything he had written was a novel, or whether it was something else the name of which had not yet been invented. If pressed for an answer he might have said that the second designation fitted rather better than the first. But really he didn't care. The question just didn't interest him. It seemed irrelevant. Questions that did interest him—and he was passionately concerned about them—were whether his writing was good, honest, straight, and true; whether it said what he wanted it to say; whether his readers would understand it as he meant it; and whether they would be moved by it and finish it saying to themselves: "Yes, that is the way life is." He did not know what more could be asked of any book.

Occasionally he might refer to his books as novels, as in *The Story of a Novel,* but it was unusual for him to do so. More often he spoke of them simply as books. So too, he never, as far as I can recall, spoke of himself as a "novelist." In his account in *Who's Who* he said he was an "author." That, or "writer," was the word he always used. The point may seem unimportant, but it touches the whole problem of form in Thomas Wolfe. For if one tries to judge his work by the conventional standards of the novel as we have always known it, defined however it may be, one is licked at the start. Not only will one not find that kind of form in most of his books, but in searching for it one may fail to see the special kinds of form which his writing does have.

His books have none of the usual artificialities of plot. His characters are never manipulated and molded to his own wishes. They do not live happily forever afterwards, neither do they fall into wells or otherwise conveniently dispose of themselves when he is done with them. They have a way of just living on from book to book, going about their daily affairs as usual, or else of dying very much as they lived or dropping out of sight and being forgotten. That is exactly how things happen in real life, but academic minds insist that an artist should improve on life. They like an author to bring his threads together in the end and tie them up in a neat knot, thus giving answers to the problems he has raised. Thomas Wolfe had no specious solutions to offer. He had the curious notion, shared by James Joyce and many another great writer, that it wasn't his responsibility to provide pat answers which life itself has not provided.

He was deeply involved with life, and that fact is what gave the true shape to his writing. For it has a natural form, an elemental form, the vital form of which all other forms are but variations on a theme—the form of life itself. Tom believed with all his soul that the most that could be expected of a writer, or of any artist for that matter, was that he observe life closely and see it as it really is—not just the surface, but the inner reality as well—and then that he depict it in all its lights and shadows just as he sees it, and do it so faithfully, in such exact colors, that even those of us who go from cradle to grave half-blind (which means most of us) cannot fail to see it also.

Perhaps some may think that this creed has as much of the scientist as of the artist in it, but such verbal distinctions lose their meaning when we are confronted with greatness. The true scientist of human nature *is* the artist. He is the only one whose vision takes in the whole man.

Thomas Wolfe was both scientist and artist. Like a scientist he was forever making notes to record his observations. "A Western Journey," previously mentioned, was just such a series of more or less factual notes. Like a painter, he also kept a sketchbook, combining and recombining his observations again and again in order to test out his powers of realizing "the exactitudes" of his vision. Just as a painter might sketch a dozen arms in order to catch the precise curve of an elbow, so Tom might write a dozen descriptions of the rusty elevated structure on Third Avenue before he got the "feel" of it just right. He described the process thus:

In his effort to explore his experience, to extract the whole, essential truth of it, and to find a way to write about it, he sought to recapture every particle of the life he knew down to its minutest details. He spent weeks and months trying to put down on paper the exactitudes of countless fragments—what he called, "the dry, caked colors of America"—how the entrance to a subway looked, the design and webbing of the elevated structure, the look and feel of an iron rail, the particular shade of rusty green with which so many things are painted in America. Then he tried to pin down the foggy color of the brick of which so much of London is constructed, the look of an English doorway, of a French window, of the roofs and chimney pots of Paris, of a whole street in Munich—and each of these foreign things he then examined in contrast to its American equivalent.*

Those are not the words of a man who was indifferent to form. They are the words of one who was so intensely concerned about it that he labored to achieve it with the most studied and exacting patience. No wonder that his writing captured so much of life.

That, then, is one kind of form he had. But there are other kinds as well.

His inner eye was fixed upon the form of every line he wrote. If you wish to test this statement, try the experiment of cutting one of his sentences. Pick, if you like, some long-winded sentence that is repetitive and full of adjectives. Strike out everything you think redundant and superfluous, and then read aloud what you have left, which represents your improvement on Wolfe. If you have an ear for music, ten to one it will set your teeth on edge. By just a little injudicious tampering, those sonorous sentences which have the majestic swing and roll of mighty music can be reduced to limping dissonance.

But what about his repetitions and his verbosity? He often used the same word a dozen times in one paragraph and strung ten adjectives together where anybody else would have been content with three. Tom was well aware of these faults and was trying hard to control the thing in himself which made him commit them. And he *was* getting it under better control in his last books. When these faults persisted, it was not because he had no sense of form. Rather, it was because his sense of form was too acute and he let it get the better of him. Being a Southerner, with a

* *You Can't Go Home Again*, p. 412.

Southerner's innate love of rhetoric, he would often be swept away by the cadence of his own words. Sometimes, more especially in his younger writing, he attached so much importance to the measured flow of his sentences that he might sacrifice his meaning to his music. Usually one will find that when he repeated a word or phrase, or let himself be hypnotized by the resounding march of his adjectives, he did it for the sake of rhythm.

That is why mere cutting was no solution of the problem. But this is not to say that Wolfe couldn't be cut. His books *were* cut, each one of them, and drastically. Whole chunks and reams of them came out, and they were the better for it. I am only saying that small cutting was often impossible because it would have ruined his style. For the most part he had to be cut as he wrote—in the large.

And it is only when Thomas Wolfe's work is viewed in the large that one can begin to see still another kind of form which it possesses. The academic people who scrutinized his individual books for traces of classical form may find something that resembles it if they will consider all the books together. Taken as one unit, they tell a single story—the story of Eugene Gant who, midway along, changes to George Webber. (Tom thought he had good reasons for this shift, and I shall later tell what they were.) In its main outline this story has a beginning, a middle, and an end. Indeed, if one is a stickler for pure form, it can be thought of as describing a circle, swinging round from *Look Homeward, Angel* with which it begins, to *You Can't Go Home Again* with which it ends. These are the two hemispheres of his world.

This cohesive unity which binds together the whole of Thomas Wolfe becomes clearer now that *The Hills Beyond* completes the picture. Anyone who reads all the books will see that they are not separate entities, not "books" in the usual sense. Tom really wrote only one book, and that runs to some 4,000 printed pages comprising the total of his works. The individual titles that bear his name are only so many numbered volumes of this master book. The parts should be thought of as having been brought out separately merely for convenience.

The unity of his rich tapestry of life is one of the most

extraordinary literary achievements I know of. It is like Joyce in that, with the advantage of being easily understandable. And his achievement appears the more remarkable when one considers the amount of experimentation that went into Wolfe's writing, the changes his point of view underwent from time to time, and the seemingly haphazard plan he followed as he carried his work along.

It is strange but true that not one of his creative books was written as the volume it ultimately turned out to be. *Look Homeward, Angel* came closest to it. Tom said that that book "almost wrote itself," by which he meant that its line of movement was clear to him from the start, and that he wrote it fairly easily, without even being aware of many of the problems that were to arise to plague him in the preparation of the later books. Even so, however, Maxwell E. Perkins of Scribner's, Tom's first editor, tells me that a large section at the beginning of the manuscript of *Look Homeward, Angel* was cut out, since it covered at length the early life of old Gant, and lacked the feeling of instant warmth and reality which came into Tom's writing as soon as the story moved on to Eugene and his immediate family background. The later books did not "write themselves" in any sense of the word, and were not planned as individual books. *The Story of a Novel* confirms this fact about *Of Time and the River*, and the same thing holds for the posthumous books. Tom always spoke of the whole mass of manuscript from which those later volumes were taken simply as "the book." He did not know whether in the end it would make one book or a dozen, and he didn't much care. That seemed to him the publisher's problem, and he was right about it. What went into each volume was largely a matter of convenience and practicability.

This may seem to contradict what I have said about form in Wolfe's writing, but there is no real contradiction. For, although Tom did not plan the various parts of his story as the published books which we know, he did plan the parts in themselves, and planned each part in relation to all the other parts. What is more, he planned the whole from first to last, and the whole was complete within him before he ever began to write. Not that he could at that time have given anyone an exact blueprint of the books that were to come. His knowledge was more fundamental than that, much more central to his purpose. He knew what kind of books he was going to write, he knew what they were to be about, and he knew precisely what effect he wanted them to have on his readers.

These statements demand proof, and I am fortunate to be able to give it in a form that will be much more convincing than any report I might make of conversations with Tom or any deductions I might offer from my study of the manuscript. In April 1923 Tom wrote a letter to his mother. At that time he was only twenty-two years old and still a student in college. He was at Harvard, studying under Professor Baker in the 47 Workshop. That was the period during which he thought he wanted to be a playwright, so he conceived of the work he had set himself to do in terms of plays. Except for this miscalculation about the medium he would use, his letter was such an exact prophecy of his later achievement that it must take rank among the great documents of literary history. He had just been visiting Professor Baker at his country place in New Hampshire, and he spoke of the visit and told of Professor Baker's faith in him. Then he went on:

I know this now: I am inevitable, I sincerely believe. The only thing that can stop me now is insanity, disease, or death.

The plays I am going to write may not be suited to the tender bellies of old maids, sweet young girls, or Baptist ministers, but they will be true and honest and courageous, and the rest doesn't matter. If my play goes on I want you to be prepared for execrations upon my head. I have stepped on toes right and left—I spared Boston with its nigger-sentimentalists no more than the South, which I love, but which I nevertheless pounded. I am not interested in writing what our pot-bellied members of the Rotary and Kiwanis call a "good show." I want to know life and understand it and interpret it without fear or favor. This, I feel, is a man's work and worthy of a man's dignity. For life is not made up of sugary, sticky, sickening Edgar A. Guest sentimentality; it is not made up of dishonest optimism. God is *not* always in His Heaven, all is *not* always right with the world. It is not all bad, but it is not all good; it is not all ugly, but it is not all beautiful; it is life, life, life—the only thing that matters. It is savage, cruel, kind, noble, passionate, generous, stupid, ugly, beautiful, painful, joyous—it is all these and more—and it's all these I want to know, and BY GOD I shall, though they crucify me for it. I will go to the end of the earth to find it, to understand it. I will know this country when I am through as I know the palm of my hand, and I will put it on paper and make it true and beautiful.

I will step on toes. I will not hesitate to say what I think of those people who shout "Progress, Progress, Progress"—when what they mean is more Ford automobiles, more Rotary Clubs, more Baptist Ladies Social Unions. I shall say that "Greater Asheville" does not necessarily mean "100,000 by 1930," that we are not necessarily four times as civilized as our grandfathers because we go four times as fast in automobiles, because our buildings are four times as tall. What I shall try to get into their dusty, little pint-measure minds is that a full belly, a good automobile, paved streets, and more, does not make them one whit better or finer—that there is beauty in this world—beauty even in this wilderness of ugliness and provincialism that is at present our country, beauty and spirit which will make us men instead of cheap Board of Trade Boosters and blatant pamphleteers.

I shall try to impress upon their little craniums that one does not have to be a "highbrow" or "queer" or "impractical" to know these things, to love them, and to realize they are our common heritage—there for us all to possess and make a part of us. In the name of God, let us learn to be men, not monkeys.

When I speak of beauty I do not mean a movie close-up where Susie and Johnny meet at the end and clinch and all the gum-chewing ladies go home thinking husband is not so good a lover as Valentino. That's cheap and vulgar! I mean everything which is lovely, and noble, and true. It does not have to be sweet, it may be bitter; it does not have to be joyous, it may be sad.

When spring comes I think of a cool, narrow back yard in North Carolina, with green, damp earth, and cherry trees in blossom. I think of a skinny little boy at the top of one of those trees, with the fragrant blooms about him, with the tang of the sap in his nose, looking out on a world of back yards, and building his castles in Spain. That's beauty!—that's romance. I think of an old man in the grip of a terrible disease, who thought he was afraid to die, but who died like a warrior in an epic poem. That's beauty. I think of a boy of twenty-six years heaving his life away, and gasping to regain it, I think of the frightened glare in his eyes and the way he seizes my hands, and cries, "What have you come home for?"—I think of the lie that trembles in my throat, I think of a woman who sits with a face as white and set as if cut from marble, and whose fingers cannot be unclasped from his hand.

And the boy of eighteen sees and knows for the first time that more than a son is dying, that part of a mother is being buried before her—life in death—that something which she nursed and loved, something out of her blood, out of her life, is taken away. It's terrible but it's beautiful.

I think of the devotion of a woman of frail physique to a father, I think of the daisy meadows on the way to Craggy Mountain, of the birch forests of New Hampshire, of the Mississippi River at Memphis—of all of which I have been a part—and I know there is nothing so commonplace, so dull, that is not touched with nobility and dignity.

And I intend to wreak out my soul on people and express it all. This is what my life means to me: I am at the mercy of this thing and I will do it or die.

I never forget: I have never forgotten, I have tried to make myself conscious of the whole of my life since first the baby in the basket became conscious of the warm sunlight on the porch, and saw his sister go up the hill to the girls' school on the corner (the first thing I remember).

Slowly out of the world of infant darkness things take shape: the big terrifying faces become familiar—I recognize my father by his bristly moustache. Then the animal books, which I memorize before I can read, and recite for the benefit of admiring neighbors, every night, holding my book upside-down. I become conscious of Santa Claus and send scrawls up the chimney. Then St. Louis. A flight of stairs at the Cincinnati railroad station—which must be gone up—the World's Fair, the Ferris Wheel, Grover at the Inside Inn, the Delmar Gardens where you let me taste beer which I spit out, a ride on a busautomobile over the Fair Grounds with Effie—it is raining, raining—the Cascades in the rain—a ride in the scenic railway

—scared at the darkness and the hideous faces—eating a peach in the back yard (St. Louis)—I swallowed a fly and am sick— and one of my brothers laughs at me—two little boys who ride tricycles up and down the street—they dress in white and look alike—their father injured or killed in elevator accident (wasn't he?)—I commit a nuisance on the narrow steps of side yard and the policeman sees me and reports me—the smell of tea at the East India House—I'll never forget it—Grover's sickness and death—I am awakened at midnight by Mabel and she says, "Grover's on the cooling board." I don't know what a cooling board is but am anxious to see.

I don't know what death is but have a vague, terrified sensa- tion that something awful has happened—then she takes me in her arms and up the hall—disappointed at the cooling board— it's only a table—the brown mole on his neck—the trip home— visitors in the parlor with condolences—Norah Israel was there —then it gets fairly plain thereafter and I can trace it step by step.

This is why I think I am going to be an artist. The things that really mattered sank in and left their mark—sometimes a peculiar smile—sometimes death—sometimes the smell of dan- delions in spring—Once Love.

I will go everywhere and see everything. I will meet all the people I can. I will think all the thoughts, feel all the emotions I am able, and I will write, write, write. . . .

This was six years before *Look Homeward, Angel*. From then on he did write, write, write—and somehow he got it all down. And it is of one piece, for he had the whole thing secure within him.

How, exactly, did he do it? What were his methods?

I have said that they were his very own, borrowed from nowhere. If I had known what they were without also knowing what they produced, I would not have believed it possible that anyone could write the way he did and achieve anything but hopeless confusion. They *seemed* so utterly without purpose or direction. But they were not. The purpose was clear in his head right along, and that is why his methods worked.

Studying the mass of his manuscript was something like excavating the site of ancient Troy. One came upon evidences of entire civilizations buried and forgotten at different levels. Some parts of the manuscript had been written as recently as four months before he died; other parts dated back to *Look Homeward, Angel,* and had, in fact, been cut from that book; still other parts had been written in each of the intervening years. The manuscript contained everything that is in the three posthumous volumes and much else besides. There were all the variant versions. There were mere notes and sketches, some of them left unfinished, the writing sometimes broken off in the middle of a sentence. There were fragments that had been cut out of each of the earlier books. There was a long fragment with whole blocks of pages missing from the beginning and middle of it which represented all that was left of the second book Tom wrote—a book called "K 19" which was never published. This was a book about a train. The action began in a Pullman car on an overnight ride between Altamont and New York, with flashbacks that covered the lives of the occupants up to the moment of their meeting. Mr. Perkins and Tom agreed that the book was not good enough to follow *Look Homeward, Angel,* so Tom abandoned it. But he did not throw the manuscript away. He never threw anything away, never lost anything. If he could not use it in one form, he would try to use it in some other, and very often he succeeded. Parts of "K 19," for example, were taken out, condensed, and made into the opening section of *Of Time and the River.* Still other parts were recast and woven into later sections of the same book. But what was left of it was in the mass of manuscript that Tom delivered to me. None of it fitted into the pattern of the posthumous books, so it still remains an unpublished fragment. But an interesting instance of the way in which Tom turned even his seeming failures to account is the fact that he introduced a Pullman car called K 19 in *You Can't Go Home Again* and made it the meeting place of certain characters whose past histories were related. There was no further similarity, but here was the basic idea of the abandoned novel—worked out afresh,

and altogether successfully, with wholly different characters.*

As if all this did not make the manuscript complex and
confused enough, Tom had changed his point of view a
number of times in the writing of different portions of it,
and had signified these changes by also changing the
names of his characters. When he dropped Eugene Gant
he hesitated for months before he finally settled on George
Webber. Why did he abandon the Gants and the Pentlands
in favor of the Webbers and the Joyners? There were several reasons. First, as he said, he had unwittingly caused
his family embarrassment and pain by identifying them
too closely with the Gants, and he did not want to subject
them to further embarrassment of the same kind. Second,
there were many important things about his childhood that
he had forgotten to say in *Look Homeward, Angel*, and
the only way to say them was in terms of a new character.
Finally, he had gradually evolved a more objective attitude toward himself and his work: as he put it, he had
stopped being Eugene Gant. He came, as he said, to hate
the very name, Eugene, and he wanted a new name to
hang out like a flag, proclaiming his emancipation from his
former self. In the letter to me previously mentioned, Tom
wrote:

The protagonist—the central character . . . —is important
now because the author hopes he will be, or illustrate in his
own experience, every one of us. . . . The value of the Eugene
Gant type of character is his personal and romantic uniqueness,
causing conflict with the world around him: in this sense, the

* There is another interesting and poignant sidelight on this.
I was in Baltimore during the final week of Tom's illness and
remained there after his death to help his family in making the
funeral arrangements. I went to the station with them and saw
them off when they left for Asheville. Down at the far end of
the platform the long cypress box was loaded into the baggage
car. I said good-bye to the family as they took their places in
the Asheville Pullman. The train started. As the windows slid
slowly past my eyes, I noticed the card in the washroom window.
It was K 19.

Eugene Gant type of character becomes a kind of romantic self-justification, and the greatest weakness of the Eugene Gant type of character lies in this fact. Therefore, it is first of all vitally important to the success of this book that there be no trace of Eugene Gant-iness in the character of the protagonist; and since there is no longer a trace of Eugene Gant-iness in the mind and spirit of the creator, the problem should be a technical one rather than a spiritual or emotional one. This is a book . . . of discovery, hence of union with life; not a book of personal revolt, hence of separation from life. The protagonist becomes significant not as the tragic victim of circumstances, the romantic hero in conflict and revolt against his environment, but as a kind of polar instrument round which the events of life are grouped, by means of which they are touched, explained, and apprehended, by means of which they are seen and ordered.

So Eugene Gant was out. For a while Tom called his new character Joe Doaks. Then he called him George Spangler. Later he gave him the family name of Joyner, only to drop that for Webber when his mind began toying with the symbolism of "The Web and the Rock" as a title, but he retained Joyner as the family name of George Webber's mother. Since the manuscript had been written over a span of years, all these names appeared in it. Eugene Gant was even there in sections that had been written earlier, and the *very* earliest sections in point of writing were in the first person singular, as the whole of *Look Homeward, Angel* originally was.

Confusing as all this seems, the wonderful thing about the manuscript—the really incredible thing—was that once the extraneous matter was removed, once the unfinished fragments and great chunks of stuff that did not belong in the books were taken out, the parts that remained fell into place and fitted together like the pieces of a jigsaw puzzle. It was simply amazing, but there it was. I discovered, too, that many of the consecutive chapters in *The Web and the Rock* and *You Can't Go Home Again* were not written consecutively. Some of them were written weeks, months, or even years apart. And yet when they were put together, they fitted.

How is this mystery to be explained? The answer lay in Tom's strange plan of writing, the unique system he was forced to invent to meet his unique need.

Since he had the whole conception of his work clear in his mind, he did not have to follow his nose in order to find out where he was going. In the main his chronology was fixed by the order of his experience, so he knew where the parts joined and did not have to write chapters six and seven before he could tackle eight and nine. This left him free to write each day whatever scene he most felt like writing that day. Yesterday he might have been working on something out of the Brooklyn period of his life, but if in the night his mind happened to go back thirty years to some remembered episode of his childhood, he would get up today to work on that, and the Brooklyn material would be laid aside until he felt like returning to it. In this way he might cover within a month various unrelated events and characters widely scattered throughout the time cycle of his story. In this way, too, while writing the individual parts he was also working on the whole thing all the time.

When one entered the front room of his three-room suite at the Chelsea the first thing that met the eye was the incongruous sight of two huge wooden packing cases which always stood in the middle of the floor. These were his bank, his repository for manuscript. When he finished writing anything and had got it typed out, he would salt it away in these boxes. Everything he had was in them, the sketch he had done yesterday together with all the unpublished material that dated back through the years to the very beginning—crisp white sheets fresh from the typewriter mixed in with old manuscript yellowed with the deposits of time and torn and dog-eared by much handling. It looked like a grab-bag, hopeless to disentangle, but he knew what was there and could quickly lay his hands on anything he wanted.

From time to time he would stop his writing for several days and go through the packing cases, taking out certain portions of manuscript and putting them together. If some fragment written six years before belonged with something he had just recently done he would weave them into a

single piece, rewriting when necessary. Thus small fragments became integral parts of larger fragments. Then
they were salted away again to await the day when they
would again be dug out and fitted into still larger con-
tinuities. The process was, I imagine, something like that
by which mosaics are constructed: first each individual
bead or jewel was fashioned; then, when there were
enough of them to work with, they were sorted out and
put together to form a part of the pattern for which they
had been designed.

The mountain of manuscript which Tom turned over to
me the day he left New York was not just the ordered parts
which he had worked into his pattern. It was the whole
mass and accumulation of his writing—everything he had
done that was still unpublished. It was the entire work-
able contents of the packing cases—minus only the earlier
notebooks and the carbon copies which he usually had
made of everything, and which he retained—minus, too,
the non-literary rubbish which he also kept in those boxes
and which included pots and pans, old shoes, stacks of letters and receipted bills, discarded hats, useless knickknacks
people had given him, a flat iron, in short everything which
he had no place for and should have thrown away but for
some reason could not bear to part with. Tom gave me the
whole manuscript, not because he thought it all belonged
in what he called "the book," but because he wanted me
to become familiar with every detail of it so that between
us we could decide what really did belong in "the book."
The rest of it would go back in the packing cases to serve
as the nest egg for books that would come later. And once
the contents of the next book or books had been agreed
upon, Tom figured that it might take him a year to put
that portion of the manuscript into final shape for the
printer.

The next book, of course, was *The Web and the Rock*.
After all the extraneous matter was removed it stood in the
form in which the reader knows it. But Tom wanted another year to rewrite the second half of it—the love story
—and it is a great pity that he was not able to do it. In
some respects that is the most disappointing of his major
books. It falls into two separate halves which do not join.

Also the halves are written in different styles. The reason is that the two sections were written years apart. The first half, down to the point where the love story begins, is much more objective and restrained. It represents Wolfe's later writing, after his attitudes had changed. Having abandoned Eugene Gant, he went back and re-created a new childhood for George Webber, working in the things he had forgotten when he wrote *Look Homeward, Angel,* as well as a few of the things that had been cut from that book. For example, the chapter called "The Butcher" was originally in *Look Homeward, Angel.* When it was cut out Tom kept it and recast it. The second half of *The Web and the Rock,* the love story, dates back to the period of *Of Time and the River.* Most of it existed in manuscript before that book was published. It was then intended as the book to follow *Of Time and the River* and was so announced, under the title of "The October Fair." When Eugene Gant was dropped, this plan had to be changed. Tom had never been satisfied with the love story anyhow and had long intended to rewrite it. He kept putting it off though, so in the end it was never redone. Tom did go through it and make certain changes in it, and some small portions of it were rewritten. Both versions of these passages were there, and a comparison of them proved very interesting. What had originally been a complete defense of Eugene Gant in that tempestuous love affair, Tom altered in such a way that George Webber was less tenderly dealt with than Eugene Gant had been, and in fact took quite a beating from the author. No doubt this was part of what Tom meant when he said there was "no longer a trace of Eugene Gant-iness" left in his mind and spirit.

Following his plan of writing more or less simultaneously over the full spread of his chronicle, Tom had thought and worked his way along to the end of *You Can't Go Home Again.* Whether he saw that as a separate volume I cannot say. He really thought of the entire George Webber story as "The Web and the Rock," with the different parts of it carrying their own subheadings. The first subheading was "The Hills Beyond," another repeated the general title, the last was "You Can't Go Home Again." How the manuscript would have to be divided for publishing convenience and necessity he did not know, nor greatly care. Each volume in the series would turn out to be whatever it had to be, and after it had been blocked out he would knit all the parts of each volume together, fill in the gaps, return to the packing cases whatever did not belong, and the job would be done.

That was the idea, but death intervened. What existed in publishable form had to be brought out as it was or not at all. The love story could not be rewritten by another hand and had to stand as Tom had left it. There were also large gaps here and there in the continuity of the text of both *The Web and the Rock* and *You Can't Go Home Again*. Some of the material that was meant to fill in these gaps had been partially written but left incomplete and unusable. Some of the gaps were bridged by sketchy notes. Others were not bridged at all and were just blanks. Tom had told me what was to go in most of these blanks. He had intended, for example, to write a great deal more about the publishing house of James Rodney & Co., but he wrote very little of it beyond what appears in *You Can't Go Home Again*, and that little was not connected with George Webber's story and was mostly very fragmentary. On the whole, *You Can't Go Home Again* was a more satisfying book than its predecessor. It was much more complete, more nearly finished. It contained more of his latest writing, and even those parts of it that had been written earlier had in many instances been revised and recast in his more objective style. But in both books the gaps remained and somehow had to be filled to provide continuity. So I wrote a few paragraphs as best I could to serve this purpose, drawing upon Tom's own words whenever they were available, and these passages were printed in italics and set on pages by themselves in order to distinguish them from Tom's own text.

Of one thing we can be sure. If he had lived, his final books would have turned out to be somewhat different from what they are. Many sections of the manuscript which had to be altogether eliminated because they were left unfinished would have been completed and put in their proper place. The gaps would have been filled as he had meant to fill them. The love story would have been recast, along with the other material that had been written earlier. And in the end there might have grown out of the manuscript, not three books, but perhaps four, five, or even six.

The present volume represents a very careful selection made from all the manuscript which still remained unpublished after *The Web and the Rock* and *You Can't Go Home Again* were extracted from the mountainous mass Tom gave me. This volume does not by any means include the whole of what was left after those two major operations. That would have been impossible. The object was to select the best, and that only. Mr. Perkins, who as literary executor gave his full cooperation to the undertaking from first to last, agreed with me that that was the thing to do. To regard every word Tom wrote as sacred and to try to publish the entire manuscript, even if that were practicable, would only be a disservice to his memory. Much of it, as I have said, was fragmentary. Some of it represented first-draft material which Tom never meant for publication. Other sections were written so long ago that Tom would not have consented to their preservation in book form without drastic revision. Still other parts were examples of experimental writing that didn't quite come off. These things were all excluded. I can best indicate the selective nature of this volume by saying that if what still remains unpublished *were* brought out, there is enough of it to fill at least three other books as large as this one.

What is left beyond this book will probably go eventually to some college library, and the scholars and Ph.D. chasers will have a picnic with it. One can already foresee the endless stream of theses that will come out of it.

The material presented in this volume has never before appeared in book form. It is published because it deserves to stand beside the other books of Thomas Wolfe. Some of his finest short stories are here. Some of the pieces also have considerable biographical interest. All of them fit somewhere into the single unified pattern of his work. In the notes below I shall try to indicate where each of these selections belongs in Wolfe's scheme of things, shall tell as well as I can when each was written, and shall add any other interesting information that I happen to possess.

"The Lost Boy." Written early in 1937, it was published in a magazine the same year. Tom used to say that he wrote a book in order to forget what it was about. *Look Homeward, Angel* contains a brief account of Grover's death. Tom felt later that he had not dealt adequately with that tragedy, which had occurred when he was still a mere infant. So he kept thinking about it, and the result was this fine and moving story. One of its interesting points is that it illustrates Tom's desire to extract the whole substance of an experience by getting at it on four levels at once. Grover, incidentally, and Ben, who reappears briefly in two later stories in this volume, were the real names of Tom's twin brothers who died.

"No Cure for It." From the look of the manuscript, all yellowed and torn, my guess is that this may have been written as early as 1929, perhaps soon after *Look Homeward, Angel* was published. Certainly it belongs to that book.

It is included here because it is amusing in itself and because it suggests an interesting literary speculation. Several people have asked me why Tom gave George Webber a somewhat misshapen body. The reason is that Tom wanted George to have a certain spiritual affinity with himself without being exactly like him in physical characteristics. Tom was a six-foot-six man in a five-foot-eight world, and he always said that this fact not only created obvious difficulties of adjustment for him but also gave him a sharpened perception for viewing the so-called normal standards of the average man. He wanted to endow George Webber with the same qualities. Eugene Gant had been six feet six, so George had to be different. Tom therefore gave him a slightly misshapen body, just enough off scale to remove him from the normal and average without making him grotesque. In the same letter to me that I have previously quoted Tom said of his new central character: "The really important thing—the *truly* autobiographical thing—was the fact of physical variation: to create a figure who would illustrate that variation and all the great human experiences that attend it." But what should this variation be? I suspect that the episode related in this story about Eugene's youth, with the boy at that gangling stage where his arms and legs seemed to be growing at a great rate while the rest of him stood still, may have suggested the solution which Tom hit upon. He simply reversed everything about the gangling young Eugene, giving George a torso that was too large, with legs too short in proportion.

"Gentlemen of the Press." Probably written in 1930 or 1931. It belongs to Wolfe's experimental period, the Brooklyn period as he described it in *You Can't Go Home Again*. That was the time when, after having published his first book, he was testing out new methods of writing and trying everything. For a while he had the idea of writing a book about nighttime in America, and he was going to call it "The Hound of Darkness." Nothing came of it except that Tom later used that title as a subheading in *The Web and the Rock*. The idea itself gradually merged with his other plans and was worked out in various things he wrote in later books. But while he was thinking of it as a separate book in itself he planned to write an entire series of episodes about what goes on in America at night. He believed that Americans are a nighttime people, that there is something in the chemistry of our blood that makes us come more alive at night than in the daytime. He wanted to find out what it was, so he started writing the series and did twelve or thirteen episodes. "Gentlemen of the Press" is one of them, the best of the lot, and the only one represented here.

"A Kinsman of His Blood." Written in 1934 or 1935. It fits, obviously, into *Of Time and the River*. It was either cut from that manuscript or is an example of something Tom had to go back and write when he realized too late that he had left it out of the book in which it belonged.

"Chickamauga." One of the best stories Tom ever wrote, it belongs somewhere in the Pentland background of Eugene Gant, although it was not written until 1937, when the Gants and Pentlands were no more. Tom had gone home to Asheville that spring and he stayed all summer. While he was there he went back into the mountains and met some of his mother's family whom he had never seen before. One of them was an old but very hale and hearty great-uncle—John Pentland of the story. Tom spoke warmly of him afterwards and said that the old man told his story in almost exactly the words in which it appears here.

"Chickamauga" had an amusing publishing history. Shortly before it was written, Tom sold a story to the *Saturday Evening Post*. It was "The Child by Tiger" which later made a chapter in *The Web and the Rock*. The editors of the *Post* had never taken anything of his before, and he was surprised and delighted by the size of their check. He decided that if they wanted his kind of stuff he would not deprive them of it, and that he would rather have their kind of money than only a fourth or a fifth as much from the magazines in which he had been appearing. So with visions of sudden wealth looming pleasantly ahead he had "Chickamauga" dispatched to Philadelphia. He said it came bouncing back in no time at all. He then tried other magazines of large circulation and high pay, with the same result. Afterwards he sent it to his old stand-bys, but they didn't want it either. He went right down the line with it, his visions of wealth shrinking step by step until, as he said, he was at last reduced to taking in his belt another notch each time the manuscript came back. The answer everywhere was the same: the Civil War wasn't timely—we were done with wars! In the end he sent it in desperation to the *Yale Review*, which accepted it at once and paid him one hundred and twenty-five dollars, their standard rate but much less than he usually got elsewhere. He never sold anything else to the *Post*. That one acceptance proved to be just a fluke—a delusion and a snare. With his proceeds from "Chickamauga" he bought himself a good overcoat, which he badly needed, and he always spoke of it fondly as his "*Yale Review* overcoat."

"The Return of the Prodigal." The two parts of this were written at different times—"The Thing Imagined" around 1934, "The Real Thing" in 1937. One interesting point about the two pieces is the contrast they afford between pure imagination and an almost straight factual record. Another is that they contain the germ of *You Can't Go Home Again* on its most literal level. Incidentally, Tom was an eyewitness of the murder which he describes in the second part, and was called to testify at the trial. That whole experience had a profound effect on him. He had been thinking about the law and lawyers for a long time, and now he decided that he wanted some day to write a book about lawyers. He was most amusing when he talked about his various encounters with the legal mind. If he had lived to write that book he would have made the fur fly.

"On Leprechauns." Though this belongs to the George Webber chronicle, it was written in its earliest form around 1931 or 1932 and later revised. As a piece of writing it comes out of Tom's Brooklyn period.

"Portrait of a Literary Critic." The date when this was written is uncertain, but it was sometime after 1935. It belongs to the time span of *You Can't Go Home Again*, that part of it which has to do with the disillusionments of fame.

"The Lion at Morning." Written about 1936, I should judge. In mood and feeling it fits into the pre-depression parts of *You Can't Go Home Again*. It is a superb analysis of character, and illustrates Tom's belief that you can tell best what a person is like by watching him get up in the morning and prepare to go about his day's work. In *You Can't Go Home Again* he applied this same technique in his descriptions of Mr. Jack, of Esther Jack, and of Fox-hall Edwards.

"God's Lonely Man." There were several drafts of this. The first, written probably as early as 1930, was entitled "On Loneliness at Twenty-three." Later versions dropped that title, no doubt because Tom realized by then that loneliness was not a phenomenon confined to youth. The essay does not belong to any one period of his career or writing, but rather to his whole life. Written in the first person, it is straight autobiography.

It is a very beautiful and tragic essay, and proves, I think, if further proof is needed beyond his books themselves, that Tom was a deeply religious man in the unconventional and truest sense of the word. Of his profound loneliness, none who knew him well can be in any doubt. But it was at the end a wise and friendly sort of loneliness, a self-contained loneliness, a loneliness that had long since accepted loneliness as the inescapable condition of his life.

During the final period preceding his death these qualities in him were unmistakable. He was working very hard that last year, harder probably than he had ever worked before, harder certainly than I had ever seen anyone else work. In a way I think his work had become a refuge from his loneliness. He rarely went out to see people any more. I doubt if there were more than half a dozen whom he saw with any frequency during that entire year. He saw me once or twice each week because we were working together. He saw regularly Miss Elizabeth Nowell, his agent, for the same reason, and because they were old friends. Beyond that, three or four people now and then—no more, except for casual encounters. He had his work to do, and his time was running out.

His enemy was Time. Or perhaps it was his friend. One never knows for sure.*

He would get up in the morning around eleven o'clock, dress, have breakfast, and be at his writing by noon when his secretary came in. From then on he would work steadily for eight, nine, or ten hours. His secretary would do her regular stint and go home, but he would keep on working. Then suddenly, around nine or ten at night, he would realize he was hungry and had had nothing to eat since breakfast, and he would go down Twenty-third Street to Cavanagh's and order a couple of thick steaks. He had a special table at Cavanagh's, at the rear, where he could sit with his back to the wall and watch all the other diners

* *You Can't Go Home Again,* p. 388.

and the waiters. Afterwards he might take a walk, or go back to the Chelsea and stop in at the bar for a talk with the bartender while he had a few beers, or sit there in one of the stalls and listen to the girl with the accordion, calling out to her to play his favorites—some of the popular songs of the vintage of 1912. Later he might drift back into the lobby of the Chelsea and talk a while with the man behind the desk or with the elevator boys or with some of the people who lived in the hotel. When he returned to his rooms he might work some more. By three or four in the morning he would be ready for bed, then seven or eight hours' sleep and up again to repeat the round.

That was the kind of life he lived that year. He stuck closely to his work and let nothing interfere with it. Sometimes I could persuade him to visit me in the country for a week-end, and we would have people in to meet him. He seemed to enjoy the change, but he also seemed to be looking forward to Monday when he could return to town and work again. At such times I would occasionally observe a kind of withdrawn quality about him, as though even when he was having fun some part of his mind was still grinding away at his work. And always, whether he was working or relaxed, alone or the center of a group, the deep and abiding sense of loneliness within him somehow made itself felt. It was most apparent, curiously, when he had other people around him and was holding them in animated talk. As one occasionally finds it in country people, there was something in the quality of his friendliness that suggested the solitude in which he lived—something in the readiness with which he gave himself without reserve; something in his spontaneity, his utter lack of guile, and his willingness to believe that others were as guileless as himself; something in the instant way he could establish a rapport with strangers. I cannot say exactly what it was, yet I believe that loneliness was really at the bottom of it. It was because he was so lonely, and knew others were lonely too, that he wanted to reach out and reassure them, as if to say: "Yes, I know just how it is. We are both suffering from the same complaint."

There had been a time back in his youth when he was

not, by many accounts, a particularly friendly sort of person. Because of his size, he had felt that he was peculiar, different from other men, and that people were always making fun of him. He said he went around with a chip on his shoulder, looking for trouble. But he had gotten over that. He had accepted himself, his body, and his world. He had found himself, and thus had realized that he was not different, not set apart or precious in any way. He knew at last that nothing he had ever suffered was unique, outside the common experience of other men. "The whole conviction of my life," as he says in this essay, "now rests upon the belief that loneliness, far from being a rare and curious phenomenon, peculiar to myself and to a few other solitary men, is the central and inevitable fact of human existence."

That conviction, coming to him as it did out of the profoundest depths of his experience, had a lot to do, I believe, with bringing about the great change in him. As a man, it changed him from a suspicious, stand-offish, and unfriendly person to one who was warm, friendly, full of instant sympathy and understanding. As an artist, it changed him, as he said, from a romantic rebel in revolt against life to the brother of all men living and a seeker after more perfect union with life.

"The Hills Beyond." In some respects the title piece of this volume is one of the most interesting things he ever wrote. It is without a doubt his most objective work. In some parts of it the style is lean and bare beyond anything one would have expected to find in Wolfe. There is both a gain and a loss in this—a gain of compactness along with objectivity; a loss of the lyrical and poetic intensity of his earlier writing. (Tom said it was good for a young man to sing, and also good for an older man to want something else so much that he would stop singing.) Moreover, "The Hills Beyond" is a work of almost pure imagination, with only a few traces here and there of factual identity with the history of his own family. Most of it represents the very last work he did. One chapter, "The Bell Strikes Three," was written as early as 1936 and was published in a magazine that year, but the rest of it came later, and was, as I happen to know, the section of manuscript which he had been writing and rewriting just before he died.

The story of how and why he wrote it is particularly interesting.

The fact has been previously mentioned that a large introductory section in the original manuscript of *Look Homeward, Angel* was cut out of that book, and that this cut section covered old Gant's early life before he met and married Eliza. Tom kept these pages, as he kept everything, and at some later time he decided that he would use them in a book that he wanted to write about the Gant and Pentland ancestors. His mother had told him innumerable stories about her family, and if he wrote them all down and combined them in some way with the early Gant material, he would certainly have enough to make a complete book. From time to time he worked at this idea, writing down his mother's stories—stories of the Pentlands—and putting them away for safekeeping in his packing cases. He even thought up the title for the book: he would call it "The Hills Beyond Pentland."

Meanwhile *Look Homeward, Angel* came out and the violent repercussions of its reception unsettled him for some months. When he was able to get back to work the thing he was most interested in doing was to carry forward the story of Eugene Gant. He tried to do that in the abortive "K 19," and put it aside. Then he wrote *Of Time and the River*, and the love story that was intended as its sequel, "The October Fair." "The Hills Beyond Pentland" was announced as the book to be published after that.

But it was at just this juncture that Tom changed his course and threw the Gants and Pentlands overboard. The many problems of working out what he wanted to do in terms of the Webbers and Joyners engaged all his energies for several years, during which he wrote *The Web and the Rock* and *You Can't Go Home Again*. Gradually "The Hills Beyond Pentland" had slipped into the background and was lost sight of as a book.

But the sections of manuscript he had written for that book were not lost. They had never been lost. They had, in fact, been in pretty constant use. A characteristic thing had happened. At one time or another Tom's packing cases contained all the Pentland stories and all the early Gant material that had been cut from *Look Homeward, Angel,* together with everything else that he wrote as he went along—and all of it was there to be used as he needed it. And he found that he did need the ancestors quite a bit. Eliza Gant, and later Aunt Maw, were always delving back into the past, bringing up some forgotten bit of family history. There seemed to be no end to what those two could remember. Before Tom was quite aware of what was happening, they had managed between them to remember pretty much all of what he had once planned as "The Hills Beyond Pentland." He had scattered it through all the other books.

But Tom did not let go of an idea easily once he had got it fixed in his mind. For years he had meant to do a book about the ancestors, and by God he still would! As soon as *You Can't Go Home Again* was finished, he turned back to the task in earnest. It was not till then, he told me, that he realized how completely he had nibbled away all the Pentlands and Gants. That was too bad, but just the same George Webber, like Eugene, had to have ancestors. There was nothing left to do but invent them. So he did. He started from scratch and wrote "The Hills Beyond." The chapters which are here published under that title bear no resemblance, except in a few unimportant details, to anything Tom ever wrote or intended for "The Hills Beyond Pentland."

I have asked Mrs. Wolfe about the new characters who appear in these pages for the first time. With the exception of old Bill Joyner and perhaps Miss Hattie she can't place them in her family tree. Old Bill belongs there all right, but his sons—Zachariah, Rufus, Theodore, and Robert, and Robert's son Edward—were hatched from cuckoo's eggs. There is some basis in family history, too, she says, for the schism between the Presbyterian and Baptist branches, but the fact was the reverse of the way Tom has it in the story: *his* ancestors were the Presbyterians, while George Webber is represented as coming from the Baptist side. Beyond these similarities, which touch only a small portion of the story, Tom made up the rest of it.

Tom's account of the early Joyners is complete within its own terms, yet it remains unfinished. He was working on it right up to the last, but there was still a lot more he was going to add to it. George Webber's grandfather was Lafayette Joyner, son of old Bill by his second marriage. Lafayette is mentioned in the story, but that is all. How he came to town, how his daughter Amelia met and married John Webber, how the story would have gone on to develop the relationship between the town Joyners and the country Joyners, are questions that remain unanswered. Tom would have answered them if he had lived to complete it. He also intended to make a good deal more of Rufus Joyner and Miss Hattie, both of whom are merely sketched in.

As it stands, "The Hills Beyond" brings the story of the ancestors down to about 1880. *The Web and the Rock* begins with George Webber's birth in 1900. Tom was going to fill this gap of twenty years and make "The Hills Beyond" a complete book in itself. It would then have ended where *The Web and the Rock* begins, thus rounding out the Webber-Joyner cycle.

And time passing . . . passing like a leaf . . . time passing, fading like a flower . . . time passing like a river flowing . . . time passing . . . and remembered suddenly, like the forgotten hoof and wheel . . .

Time passing as men pass who never will come back again . . . and leaving us, Great God, with only this . . . knowing that this earth, this time, this life, are stranger than a dream.

With these closing words of "The Hills Beyond" the eloquent tongue of Thomas Wolfe is stilled. His books are ended.

They are joyful and hopeful books, and at the same time deeply tragic. And as he pointed out in the essay on "God's Lonely Man," there is no contradiction between those emotions. As one finishes the pages so teeming with the full red blood of life, so pregnant also with awareness of the death that lies in wait for every man, one suddenly remembers with something of the shock of its first impact the three-year-old fact that Thomas Wolfe is dead.

That is the real tragedy—for us. He had just come into the fullness of his powers when he died. What he might yet have written had he lived is now lost to us forever.

EDWARD C. ASWELL

August 1941